Mardi Gras and Mayhem

Jann Franklin

Rougarou Press

CONTENTS

Also By Me

Find my books at jannfranklin.com and your favorite online retailers

Please help a girl out and leave a review after you've finished a book—either at the online store you purchased it, or a book lover's site such as Good Reads or Book Bub—or all of them! This author sure appreciates it

:)

Small Town Girl Series

Jen's life isn't perfect, but it's beautiful. A beautiful mess.

J en was living her best big city life, until her husband Mike uproots them to small town Louisiana. Life throws you curveballs, but you've got to keep swinging. This heartwarming series resonates with joyful, almost nostalgic feelings of encouragement. Readers living in big cities will feel the quaint, small-town Southern charm leaping off the pages, and experience a yearning to visit their very own Graisseville. And readers from small towns will see versions of themselves and their own community in these characters, nodding and laughing along with Jen and her family. There is something for everyone to relate to and thoughtfully consider.□

Trading Bright Lights for Lightning Bugs
Shining Stars and Mason Jars
Cheese Grits and Hissy Fits

Small Town Girl Mystery Series

Why is murder so much fun?

Evangeline Delafose found Graisseville, Louisiana just as she remembered—boring and uneventful. Until she solved a murder. Now she's hooked. Follow Ev as she takes on each mystery, with her frustrating but loveable private investigator by her side. And, of course, a bit of insider info from the quirky residents of her small town. You'll laugh, cry and roll your eyes at the antics of this charming small-town Southern sleuth and her exasperating private investigator.

Muffalettas and Murder
Boudin and Bloodshed
Fruitcake and Fraud
Mardi Gras and Mayhem
Sweet Tea and Suspects

How Did I Get Here?

H ow did it happen? How did I end up back in my hometown of 298 people? My kids played a major role, urging me to move closer to family. Not closer to them, of course.

"Mom, that would be weird. Our mother living in the same town? No, you should live closer to Uncle Nate and Aunt Bonnie. Grandpa too. You need to make some changes."

I'd been in Graisseville for three months when my brother Nate found something to occupy my empty social calendar.

"Ev, I'm working on a case that's officially inactive. The sheriff has read your books and he's a fan. Would you look at the case through fresh eyes? Hopefully find something we missed."

I'd written a series of crime fiction novels featuring New Orleans police detective Lou Bergeron. With my husband Doug gone, I had no desire to visit Lou down at the police station, to flesh out his cases and celebrate his successes. I wasn't sure I would ever write again. But after three years of surviving without my husband, someone found me useful.

The Michael Cook case became my reason to stop surviving and start living.

Before I'd realized it, I'd also gained a private investigator. Shorty Cormier had come back from the Gulf War with a purple heart and a prosthetic leg. Our fathers had been the best of friends, spending many afternoons at the Cormier farm. The man drove me crazy, but I counted him as one of my oldest and dearest friends.

When Shorty discovered my new project, he jumped in and used his private investigator skills, not to mention his license, to help me solve the case. We even impressed my brother. A Gulf War veteran with a prosthetic leg and a woman who wrote mystery novels cracked the case! A case that had stumped the entire sheriff's department.

A few months later, we solved the murder of Remy Robichaux and collected a reward from the victim's family. Just last month we'd solved our third and fourth cases, although the murderer slipped through our fingers. But it still counted.

Speaking of my PI, let's not forget my nickname. Shorty had called me *Doc* ever since my graduation from LSU with a PhD in English Literature. My parents bragged to everyone, including the entire village of Graisseville. Their daughter was a doctor! The word spread, a normal occurrence in small towns, and soon the story transformed. Skeeter and Muriel Bergeron's daughter Evangeline graduated from LSU medical school! My husband, Doug and I visited my parents after graduation, and puzzled over people greeting me as *Doc*. My parents corrected no one, but eventually people figured it out. Shorty's family continued calling me *Doc*. They enjoyed having a doctor in their adopted family, even if it was a doctor of books. Why no one called my father, the veterinarian, *Doc*, was still a mystery.

Sheriff McDreamy, as my best friend Elizabeth called him, took me out on New Year's Eve, our first official date, and we'd had a couple of dates since. I hadn't broken the news to my brother that I was dating his boss, but it was on my task list, just after cleaning out my junk drawer.

As we headed into Mardi Gras season, I geared up for my winter classes at LSU, and Shorty continued his private investigation business in the supply closet at the Graisseville Gas n' More. The rent was cheap and the traffic flow was high. Shorty and Annabelle were engaged, but we had no wedding date yet. Everyone was happy, and it had only been a month, maybe more, since our last case. But Shorty and I couldn't wait for the next one.

THROUGH THE VICTIM'S EYES

W hy couldn't someone host an interesting Mardi Gras party for once? Oh, wait! I was that someone. When Beau was alive, we were New Orleans' power couple. Our parties were front page news, with a who's who guest list. If only my husband could have stuck to what he did best: looking good and looking the other way.

I thought being a widow would be, well, the perfect marital status. I'd have the best of both worlds: power and admiration. The most wealthy and powerful men would admire my ability to run the Romero empire, even offer to broker a business deal or two. They'd be quick to take me out on the town too—at thirty-six, I still turned heads.

And I'd finally be in control of everything in my life. The South insisted on bowing to the 1950's, when men smoked cigars as they wielded their influence, and women wore cocktail dresses and poured the martinis. But this woman? No, I inherited all of our business ventures—the legal ones and the ones off the books—and I had the brains to make them more successful than Beau could have ever done. That man was long on looks but short on business savvy.

The life of a widow hadn't worked out as planned, not by a longshot. Instead of seeing me as their equal to be admired and befriended, the men feared me and the women despised me. I only answered to myself, but I had no friends. Beau was the only one I could trust...until I couldn't. Maybe this party would be different...but then again, who was I kidding?

And once again, Jacqueline had invited the biggest losers in the city to her party. What did she do, drive down Bourbon Street, slow down, and open the door? No one in the room had anything to offer me. At least the food was good. Say what you will about Jacqueline, she *did* know how to feed the masses.

And she didn't skimp on the seafood, bless her heart. Crab dip with those fancy crackers I adored, petite lobster tarts, and seared Ahi tuna croquettes. Although, po'boy sandwiches, really? Yes, it screamed Louisiana cuisine, but so did Creole bouillabaisse, and that dish had a lot less carbs. You could take the girl out of the Louisiana swamps, but you couldn't take the swamps out of...

Well, look who showed his face! Some people wouldn't take a hint, even if I'd wrapped it in a bouquet and hand delivered it. What, *her* too? Did Jacqueline invite all the people I couldn't stand? The list measured about half a page, possibly three-quarters—no wonder every nook and cranny of this dumpy venue featured an angry business associate, jealous wife, or jilted lover! But why was my sister-in-law here? Of course she had to find me and waste ten minutes talking about her stupid job! Thank goodness the Bouviers showed up to save me from my idiotic sister-in-law. Where did she go? Ah, she probably headed to the open bar. And since when did Bea and Jacqueline kiss and make up? Ugh, if Sheriff Ray walked through the door, it would be official: every single person I detested would be roaming this flea-infested room. Yeah, time to finish this calorie-laden po'boy and head for the door.

"Chantilly, you're looking flushed. Are you feeling alright? Do you want some water? Oh, no, something's wrong—she's throwing up! Someone call an ambulance!"

Hmmm, that was interesting. Out of all the ways I thought I might die, this one never made my top five...

CHAPTER 1

"Dang it, Doc? Why'd ya' go an' tell Elizabeth I'd load her stuff too? It's bad enough ya'll gotta go on a dadgum girls' trip tuh New Orleans! But now I gotta gallivant all over town an' cram all ya'll's stuff into yore Bronco?"

"I'm sorry, Shorty, but Cliff's over at Cal's helping him put up a new swing set. So neither one of them can load Elizabeth's bags into my car. Besides, Annabelle says you're a genius at taking a bunch of suitcases and getting them all settled into a small space. Why, she told me it's downright artistic how you stack and place everything just perfectly."

Okay, that last part was pretty much a lie. Annabelle had never told me Shorty was good at loading a car. To my knowledge, they'd never taken a trip together. Although he often helped Annabelle load her car for trips to Georgia to visit her sister. She'd mentioned Shorty kept his cool, stacking and shuffling until her two-door Prius almost burst at the seams. So maybe it wasn't *technically* lying.

And it worked. Shorty's chest puffed out a couple of inches and he stopped complaining. Thank goodness! His steady stream of bellyaching slowed to just a few drops of grumbling. "Yeah, well, I *am* pretty good at takin' a situation and findin' the best solution. Ya' see, it's like stackin' bales o'hog feed. Ya' gotta look at the space, ya' know, an' get a good feel for how much room ya' got…"

But honestly, was this situation an improvement? Yes, I didn't have to hear Shorty complain, and that was a definite blessing. But listening to him explain his process step by step? Maybe the whining had been better. *Sorry, Lord, for my ingratitude. You took away the complaining, and I thank You for that. Please grant me patience during this time. Help me see it as an opportunity to learn how to correctly load a car. And stack hog feed.*

"Islands in the Stream" by Kenny and Dolly solved my dilemma. Not one of their best ones, in my book, but Shorty had claimed it as Annabelle's ringtone.

"Hey Baby Cakes, how's yore day goin'? I'm jus' about t'head over tuh Elizabeth's an' load her bags for yore girls' trip. Now, Dumplin', I jus' can't tell ya' how excited I am that yer gettin' away tuh the bright lights o' New Orleans. I hope ya'll have a real good time, Sugar Drop."

Oh, yeah, this was definitely the worst of all three situations. I'd much prefer Shorty's dissertation of loading suitcases or his steady stream of complaints over this grocery list of pet names. My stomach tightened at the nauseousness of the syrupy nicknames, yet it gurgled in happiness over the visions of sugary goodness floating in my head. The two diverse reactions created an oddly cozy, yet sickly, sensation that lingered for hours.

"Oh no, Cupcake, I don't mind a single bit! Ya' know I jus' love helpin' yore friends. Anythin' else I can do t'help ya'll get ready?"

And not a single bit of sarcasm...yeah, the man was completely in love. Annabelle felt the same way, which was why she said yes.

"Ev, I couldn't ask for a more loyal and devoted man! Did you know Shorty joined my church last Sunday? We're attending a couples' Bible study, and we pray together over the phone every morning. My kids adore him, and my mom thinks he's easy on the eyes. Ev, she giggles whenever Shorty calls her *ma'am*. Giggles! And don't get me wrong, I'm committed to being Mrs. Cleophas Alphonse Cormier, until death do us part. But I want just one more adventure, with my girlfriends. You know what I mean? Then I can settle down and share my life."

I did know what she meant, but Shorty wouldn't. He'd never understand why Annabelle needed one last hurrah with her buddies. So I'd volunteered to be the bad guy, and Shorty still hadn't forgiven me.

"That was Annabelle, in case ya' couldn't figure that out. Doc, I still don't understand why she's gotta go all the way tuh New Orleans t'find a weddin' dress! I bet Baton Rouge has fancy dresses for gettin' hitched. But no! Ya' gotta call out a favor from some high falootin' friend with some high falootin' dress shop. Well, ya'll better come back with a mighty fancy dress for our weddin' day, or I'm likely t'think ya'll are jus' takin' Annabelle down there so she can get away from me."

"Oh, no, Shorty! That's not true at all. I've been wanting to take Elizabeth and Annabelle to New Orleans and show off my old stomping grounds. It just worked out that Doug's cousin Babette owns an upscale bridal shop. Honestly, it's an offer too good to resist! Babette has excellent taste, and she's promised a wonderful deal on Annabelle's dress. And if we find bridesmaids' dresses there too, well, it's an even better deal."

The echo of my trunk slamming reflected Shorty's opinion of Babette's deals. "Well, all I gotta say is my mama never drove no ninety miles t'buy no dress. An' yore mama didn't neither. Now, yore daddy an' I think this little jaunt jus' reeks of a girls' trip. Yeah, we think ya'll are usin' my weddin' as an excuse t'hijack my bride an' take her traipsin' around Bourbon Street, while she's still single."

I didn't need my Ph.D. to read between the lines. All I had to do was count the number of fancy words Shorty had strung together in our conversation. We had *high falooting*, *jaunt*, *reeks*, and *traipsing*. Oh, and we couldn't forget *gallivant* from his earlier tirade. When my friend introduced these kinds of words into a conversation, he'd worked himself up about something. I had a separate list for *mighty fancy*, *getting hitched*, and *hijack*. They weren't the same caliber as the others, but they pointed me to the same conclusion: Shorty didn't like me taking his fiancée out of town for any length of time, especially to New Orleans during its most unpredictable season. And I wasn't talking about hurricane season.

"An' why does it have t'be durin' Mardi Gras, Doc? Why, that town's more dangerous than gettin' between an alligator an' his supper. An' it's even worse during Mardi Gras, what with all those crazy Yankees comin' tuh town, drinkin' those fancy hurricane drinks, an' passin' out in the streets. Let the good times roll, my Aunt Fanny! Those no-good tourists can jus' roll on back home."

A famous Mardi Gras expression, *laissez les bon temps rouler*, or *let the good times roll*, comes from the Cajun French in Southwest Louisiana. It's the official mantra during Mardi Gras season, and people take it to heart. The words "Mardi Gras" are French for "Fat Tuesday," representing the last night to celebrate all one's vices before giving them up for Lent. Leave it to Louisiana to extend it into forty-seven nights of celebration, where the fun never ends and the tourists flood the streets to spend their money and trash the downtown. Doug and I had always steered clear of the more popular areas of New Orleans, opting to host our own Mardi Gras party, usually a murder mystery. Our friends would dress up as the suspects, Doug would a brisket, and we'd all end the night clear headed and in our own beds.

"Shorty, you know me! I never partied on Bourbon Street when I lived in New Orleans, and I'm not about to start now. Besides, we're staying in Babette's bed and breakfast, over in the Gentilly District. Google says it's safer than 78% of other Louisiana cities."

Ah, we couldn't have this kind of conversation without the horse snort. "Doc, that don't make me feel a whole lot better. 78%? Why, if Gentilly was in school, that'd be a C+. My Annabelle deserves more than a C+! The woman never made less than a B in school."

How did we head down this road? I definitely missed a turn somewhere. And could I get us back on track? No, the train had left the station, destination unknown.

"But ya' know what would make me feel better? If ya'd take Diane with ya'. I tried t'talk Annabelle into takin' her, but she won't do it. I'm beggin' ya', Doc! Yer comfortable around guns, ya' even have a couple. Please tell me yer takin' one on this trip."

Diane was Shorty's .38 Special who occupied residence in his truck. She'd spent most of her life locked in Shorty's glove compartment, only coming out for target practice. Since Shorty had dusted off his private investigator license, Diane had stepped out a couple of times. She reminded me of Zydeco, always ready and willing to defend.

"If it'll make you feel better, how about I take my SIG Sauer? I do my target practice with that gun, so I'd feel more comfortable with it. Just remember, New Orleans has strict gun regulations. I can't take my gun to most places in the city. But I can have it in the car and inside the bed and breakfast. Would that make you feel better?"

"Yeah, it would. But do me a favor, will ya'? If anybody asks, it was *yore* idea t'bring the gun."

"All right, ladies! Let's get this girls' vacation started! Uh, I mean, let's get this essential trip to find my wedding dress started."

We let Annabelle ride shotgun, since she was the reason we'd planned our extended weekend. Elizabeth was busy rooting around the backseat, rearranging Shorty's carefully contrived stacking.

"Well, I've got to hand it to your fiancé, Annabelle. He sure knows how to pack a car. Trouble is, there's no room for me *and* my stack of bridal magazines. I thought we were going to talk wedding details on the trip, leaving our time in New Orleans strictly for fun and frolic? How can we achieve this essential task if I have to stack everything on my lap?"

She shoved the suitcases with both hands, but nothing budged. "And why do we have so much stuff? Ladies, this is a four-day weekend, not a vacation spanning five continents! Ev, I blame you and your constant overthinking. Why you need a suitcase just for shoes constantly baffles me." For emphasis, my bestie smacked both hands on the luggage called into question.

"We've gone over this a million times, El. But for Annabelle's benefit I'll go through my list again. First, I have walking shoes that are just that: walking shoes. They're not very cute, but they keep my feet cocooned in cushiness. Then I have my *cute* walking shoes. This pair is when we have to park a good distance from our destination, so my feet can remain blister free but I still look trendy and chic. Next is my..."

"Okay, okay, I get it, Ev! You've brought a lot of shoes. It's all good. Elizabeth, your feet are so tiny, you can probably fit a dozen pairs into a makeup bag. Now hand me a magazine, and we'll start looking for my dress!"

"Annabelle, I'm going to ask a personal question, one that Elizabeth and I have been pondering. And if you want to tell me to mind my business, then that's fine. But why are we shopping for a wedding dress when you don't have a wedding date? Shouldn't we know what month you're saying I *do*, so we can choose the right dress?"

My shotgun passenger continued to flip through her magazine. "First, it's the South. I could get married in December and still wear a sleeveless dress and sandals. The temperature's going to range from sixty to eighty-five degrees—and anywhere in between! No, I'm not going to match my dress to the weather. I'm going to find the perfect dress, with perfectly accessorized shoes and veil. Once I have those major life choices completed, then I'll match the temperature to my wedding attire."

Annabelle paused, her eyes skimming a cream, A-line, chiffon and sequin gown. "But I'm not getting married in July or August! No amount of air conditioning is going to cool down the church during those months. Elizabeth, what do you think of this one? Ev, keep your eyes on the road—I'll let you weigh in once we stop for our mandatory bathroom break."

Elizabeth marked her place with an index finger while she studied Annabelle's choice. "It's elegant, I'll give you that. But the neckline plunges a little too much for my taste. As my grandmother always said, 'When you've got a blockbuster movie, you shouldn't put any spoilers in the ads. Keep the trailers short and don't reveal too much.'" The sound of silence forced her to look up. "You know, don't show off too much of your figure to the public. Save it for your husband behind closed doors. Did I mention my grandmother worked in a movie theater for years until she married my grandfather?"

Laughter filled my Bronco as we clued into the meaning of El's words. "Yeah, my grandmother used a lot of movie references to get her point across." She handed the magazine back to Annabelle.

"No, you're right. I'll keep looking. But I do like the cap sleeves. At fifty-four, my arms aren't what they used to be."

Elizabeth turned back to her magazine. "Got it—no sleeve-less gowns. Ooh! How about this asymmetrical dress? It's an A-line with sequins, like the last one. And it keeps the spoilers in the movie theater, where they belong."

The miles flew by and soon we'd reached our destination: Sweet Magnolia Manor, just off Mirabeau Street in the Gentil-ly District. Doug and Babette's mothers were sisters. They'd lived next door to each other after they got married, and Doug had grown up with his cousin. She was more like my sister-in-law than a cousin to me.

Babette and her husband Marcel purchased a shotgun house near downtown New Orleans and remodeled it as a bed and breakfast. Shotgun homes get their name from the theory that if a person opened the front and back doors and fired a gun through one of them, the bullet could exit out the other door and hit nothing in the house. Babette and Marcel had painted the wood exterior white, and the doors and shutters teal, and added a front porch swing and wicker furniture to create coziness in the front of the house.

Babette Bouvier flew out the door to greet us. "Oh, ma chère cousin, I'm so glad to see you! It's been far too long. How was the traffic? Horrible, I'm sure—it is Mardi Gras, you know!" Babette pulled me toward her, encircling my shoulders in a hug. She stepped back and placed one manicured hand on each of my arms. "Oh, you are looking well, my love, healthy and happy. And these are your friends, yes? Marcel, come outside! Our guests are here, and they need help with their luggage!"

Marcel appeared, the yin to Babette's yang. It's true, many times opposites do attract. In the Bouvier's case, their physical diversity suited them well. Marcel's six foot four-inch lanky frame complimented Babette's five foot two-inch pleasantly plump stature. As Mr. Bouvier's skin darkened while toiling in his beloved garden, Mrs. Bouvier remained in the house, avoiding sunlight like a vampire as she created savory dishes from her husband's bounty. Babette's translucent skin bared just a handful of freckles, right across the bridge of her petite nose. Yet, as different as the couple looked, their personalities had woven together during their marriage. Marcel and Babette were one of those rare couples that could practically read each other's minds.

"Oh! How did you sneak up behind me, mon cher? Never mind, I need you to...oh, I see you've almost got the car unloaded. Bon, bon! I'll go on ahead and get out the...let me guess, you've already pulled out the glasses for iced tea. And the serving tray too? But did you remember...oh, of course you did. Je t'aime, cher, je t'aime!"

Our girls' weekend was off to a fabulous start as we gathered in the dining room to feast upon Babette's culinary delights. In true New Orleans fashion, Babette had decorated every room in green, purple, and gold. Festive masks and beads hung from a six foot evergreen. In Louisiana we slid straight from Christmas into Mardi Gras. A simple change out of decorations and the tree radiated the new holiday.

"Now, you are our first guests at Sweet Magnolia Manor, and we've been working nonstop! That didn't leave much time for cooking, so these treats are just a little something I whipped up. They're called Pecan Praline King Cake Cookies, isn't that the most divine name? My friend Aimee Broussard used this recipe to win a national dessert contest, and she passed it on to me. She's such a dear!"

Poor Annabelle almost choked on her cookie. "Aimee Broussard? You mean *the* Aimee Broussard, the food blogger and cookbook author? She's my hero!"

Babette handed over a glass of mint iced tea. "Oh, yes, well, she does all that, too. But she's so wonderful, just the picture of Southern hospitality. I'll see if she can stop by so you can meet her. She always enjoys meeting new people. But ladies, I'm afraid Marcel and I will be out of pocket this evening and most of the day tomorrow. I'm sorry to say we have a visitation and a funeral to attend."

How did one express the proper amount of sympathy with half a Pecan Praline King Cake Cookie in one's mouth? Perhaps with a sip (or two) of mint iced tea?

"Oh, Babette, I'm so sorry! Who passed?"

Babette's robin's egg eyes filled with tears as she struggled to answer.

Marcel cupped her hand. "Oh, ma chère, why don't you go lay down for a while, before the visitation?"

A couple of sniffles and my cousin found her smile. "It's all right, cher. Evangeline, it was Chantilly Romero. Do you remember her? She's...she was a local businesswoman who owned the Ami Fidéle whiskey distillery, among other business ventures."

My fifty-something brain rattled my cage of memories, and one cried out. "Yes! That name rings a bell. I saw her in the papers a lot when I lived here. As I remember, she was a prominent member of the New Orleans movers and shakers."

Marcel's hand tightened around his wife's pudgy fingers, and his shoulders stiffened. "On the surface, yes. But there has been talk that she ran a high-stakes poker game out the back of Ami Fidéle. Some say the weekly poker games made more money than the whiskey. She didn't have a gambling license, but New Orleans' most influential people paraded in and out of the distillery every Friday night. So she never got shut down. In fact, many people speculate Clifford Benoit has broken his fair share of bones, to make sure the house always got its cut."

Babette squeezed Marcel's bicep. "Hush now! All you're doing is spreading gossip. Why, if even a fourth of those rumors were true, Chantilly would have been in prison."

I couldn't help it, it really wasn't my fault. But it had been a solid month since Shorty and I'd solved the Sid Hebert case. "Who's Clifford Benoit? He sounds like some sort of enforcer to me."

Despite Babette's glare, Marcel continued his rumor fest. "Yes, well maybe. Chantilly called Clifford her bodyguard, and the guy never left her side. Some people think he may have helped Beau Romero to the pearly gates. Or at least helped *Chantilly* help her husband to his final destination."

Babette let out a gust of air, punctuated by a French word I didn't recognize. But Marcel loved telling stories, and he had a captive audience. "Yes, the coroner's report stated Chantilly's husband Beau died of natural causes. But many people, people who knew the couple well, think Chantilly had a hand in Beau's death. But that's all it was, just speculation. The police could never prove a thing. In fact, just this morning at the bakery, people were talking. There's a consensus that someone took matters into their own hands."

"Oh, Marcel, enough! These ladies came for *les bon temps*, not to discuss dead bodies and murderers."

Elizabeth nearly choked on her cookie. "Uh, Babette, you must not have heard. Your cousin Ev has solved *four* crimes, with the help of Annabelle's fiancé. She'd love to hear all about this latest murder!"

CHAPTER 2

"Elizabeth! That makes me sound so morbid! Look, we're here to find Annabelle a wedding dress and to have fun while we accomplish our official task. Let's leave the crime solving to the police."

My traveling companions locked eyes, coming to some sort of agreement with a single glance. Somehow Annabelle won the election for spokesperson.

"C'mon, Ev! Why should the police have all the fun? Let us help you solve the murder. Please? I've got mad research skills, and I have contacts at all the libraries here in town. And Elizabeth, don't you have some essential resources you can contribute?"

In her excitement, my bestie clutched my elbow like a vise. "Yes! Cliff attended LSU vet school, and several of his classmates set up practice here in New Orleans. I've gotten to know their wives, and they're on the boards of a bunch of charities and other organizations. I bet I could talk to them and get some great intel on this Chantilly Romero. And you can talk to Ethan, right? He'll take care of all the internet goings on. We can do this, Ev! We can be your private investigators!"

"Look, guys, I appreciate your enthusiasm. But no one has asked us to solve this mystery. We can't insert ourselves into an active investigation without being asked. Anyway, none of us have a private investigator's license. Even if we're hired, we'd be extremely limited. And that brings me back to my first point: no one has asked us to step in. And I'm pretty sure no one will."

Babette's tears had dried, leaving her eyes shiny and clear. " I'm asking, Evangeline. Marcel and I, that is...oui, chéri?"

My cousin-in-law fixed his eyes upon me, like a scientist studying an animal with multiple heads.

"Evangeline, is this true? You've solved four crimes? Babette, how could we not know this? Of course, yes, please! I spoke ill of Chantilly earlier by spilling gossip. But she was a shrewd businesswoman, and she took us under her wing when Babette opened her shop. She navigated us through permits and zoning regulations—the woman helped us more than we could ever expect. And once again, she answered our exasperating questions and remained patient through lack of business knowledge when we purchased Sweet Magnolia Manor. While we didn't agree with all her business advice, we appreciated all she did for us. Yes, ma chère, you're right! Evangeline, we'd like you to look into Chantilly's murder while you're here. In exchange we'd cover your meals and place to stay."

The Bouviers patted themselves on the backs for their decision, but I wasn't convinced. "I appreciate your confidence, but I'm out of my element here. Shorty's the one who makes sure we're following all the rules of private investigating—I don't even *know* the rules!"

My bestie flashed a set of pearly whites that would make any dentist proud. "But you don't have your private investigator license, Ev. So why would you need to follow the rules? You're a regular Miss Jane Marple! Why, she never needed a license to snoop, and neither do you."

Before I could refute Elizabeth's argument, my newly minted associate chimed in. "Oh! If Evangeline's going to be Jane Marple, then we want to be Nick and Nora Charles! We're the only married couple in this merry band, so it makes sense. Chérie, do you agree? Would you be Mrs. Nora Charles? You've always reminded me of Myrna Loy."

Marcel and Babette were fourteen inches apart in height—how did two people kiss when their lips were so far away? Yet somehow, through much practice, of course, they succeeded. "Chère, those are the most romantic words you've ever spoken! Of course I'll be the Nora to your Nick."

Marcel clapped his hands, and I cleared the floor by a good two inches. Okay, maybe just one. For such thin hands, the man created quite a noise. "Bon, bon! All right, ladies, two more detectives to cast. Let me take a look at you, Elizabeth." My friend stood motionless as our host and hostess measured her up and down. "Mmm, what do you think, Chérie? In my mind, she's clearly..."

"Kinsey Millhone, from Sue Grafton's Alphabet Mysteries! Oui, I see it too. Tell me, Elizabeth...do you enjoy peanut butter and pickle sandwiches? No?"

Babette needed no words to answer her question—El's puckered lips and scowl told it all. "No matter! Bon, let's move on to Annabelle. Which amateur sleuth will you be?"

"You don't need to analyze me, gang. I already know! You may expect my answer to be someone from a literary classic, since I'm a librarian and all. But I want to be my all-time favorite heroine. She's featured in a series of books that ignited my love of reading, a series that eventually led me to become a librarian and share my passion for books. Okay, please don't laugh."

I touched Annabelle's arm. "Honey, we won't laugh. We promise, there is no amateur sleuth too...amateurish for our team. We don't discriminate—we're an equal opportunity sleuthing company. Now tell us!"

Our fifth sleuth hesitated. "It's Nancy Drew. And you promised not to laugh."

As if on cue, the women squealed. "Oh, I love Nancy Drew! Why didn't I think of her?"

Our token male nodded his approval. "I'm a Hardy Boys fan myself. But you made an excellent choice. I call to order our team, the...? What shall we call our merry band of sleuths? How about The Gumshoe Krewe?"

"Uh, love that name, but we're getting too far ahead of ourselves. I'm not sure this is such a great idea. And if Shorty figures it all out, that I got his fiancée involved in a murder investigation, well, he'll have my hide. And I like my hide."

Wait, what was that? A snort? Either Shorty or his horse had hitched a ride to New Orleans. Or, more likely, Annabelle had developed her fiancé's annoying habit. Or was it endearing? I'd learned to tolerate, even embrace, Shorty's reaction to irritating situations. But could I handle a pair of horses? *God, please double my normal order of daily patience.*

"What Shorty doesn't know won't hurt him, Ev. We can't tell him!" Annabelle's chocolate eyes were pleading. "He's been looking for an excuse to fly down here and rescue me from marauding Mardi Gras hoodlums. If he hears I'm anywhere *near* a murder investigation, he'll be on our doorstep so fast it'll make your head spin. Can't we leave him out of this? Please, Ev?"

"Um, that would be a big fat no. I've got to tell him what's going on. We've never had secrets and I'm not going to start now. That's the only way I'll agree to investigate this murder. Now, I will *try* to convince him to keep his happy self within the Graisseville village limits. That's all I can do."

"What? Ya'll got a real live murder in yore backyard? How'd ya' get all the luck, Doc? It ain't fair! All I got over here is a little vandalism. Somebody toilet papered Ruby Bergeron's house last night, an' let me tell ya'! That's a list o'suspects longer than my Aunt Myrtle's size 13 feet."

Hmmm, I'd been away from Shorty less than twenty-four hours and I kind of missed the guy. What was that saying...? Oh yeah, *absence makes the heart grow fonder.*

"I'd better tell Ruby t'figure it out herself, cuz I got a murder case needin' my detectin' skills. We both know I'm the one who solves all our cases."

Or was it *out of sight, out of mind*? Yes, those were the words that best described our relationship. "Hey! That's not true. Okay, it's not completely true. Well, it's kind of...oh, never mind! Anyway, I'm not calling for your help. I'm just filling you in on the turn of events. The Bouviers have asked me to solve the murder, and Annabelle wants to help. But I told her we had to make you aware of the situation, because I know you worry about her."

"Well, that's mighty nice o'you, Doc. I'm guessin' Elizabeth wants in on yore little murder case, too."

"Uh, well yes, she does." Where was he going with this?

"So tell me, did ya' call Cliff too, an' tell him all about the murder an' ask *his* permission t'let his wife play detective?"

"Um, well no. I didn't. Do you think I should?"

And there it was...the missing pairing to Annabelle's snort from earlier. "How should I know, Doc? I ain't a marriage counselor. Now that ya' mention it, I don't know why *yer* callin' me about this whole thing! Shouldn't my future wife be the one doin' the callin' an' the talkin'? If she thinks it's somethin' I need t'know, I reckon she'll tell me herself. We don't need no go-between gettin' all up in our marital business."

The subconscious part of my brain took over, carrying me to a parish courtroom in the near future. Or would that be state jurisdiction? Federal maybe? Anyway, there I stood, dressed in the most unflattering orange jumper with silver cuffs around my wrists and ankles. The judge beckons me forward.

"*Before I pass sentence, Mrs. Delafose, I'd like to hear from you. What exactly compelled you to drive from New Orleans to Graisseville, quite a long stretch of road I might add, and shove your cell phone down the throat of the deceased, one...*" The judge squints at the document in front of him. "*...Mr. Cleophas Alphonse Cormier? Take your time, please. I'm sure there's a reasonable explanation that your attorney neglected to mention during the trial.*"

"...but if ya' think Annabelle an' I can't carry on a conversation without ya', then I'm sure glad ya' spoke up now! Mebbe we shouldn't get married, if ya' feel that way."

"Now hold on! I never said that. You and Annabelle are perfect for each other. Don't ever let anyone tell you different. Just because..."

"Awww, I'm just messin' with ya', Doc. Annabelle already texted me, said she's gonna do some research for yore case. She's loves doin' that kind uh thing, so I don't see no problem with her helpin'."

That vision I had of the future was looking more and more possible. "But, hey! Are ya'll sure ya'll don't need me t'come over there an' help out some? I mean, it's a murder case, Doc! We've had three o'them murders, an' I solved every single one o'them. Ya'll need t'let me lend a hand."

"Well, if you were here, that would make it much easier to shove my cell phone down your throat. But I'm going to resist the urge and tell you to stay in Graisseville."

"Huh? Why ya' gonna stick yore phone in my throat? Hello? Hey, Doc!"

"All right, Gumshoe Krewe, we've all spoken with our respective loved ones, so we can move forward with the investigation."

Elizabeth settled into the couch. "By the way, Cliff says *hi* to all, and he's not surprised Ev's started a murder investigation while on vacation. In fact, he's surprised it took her an hour and a half to find one. And he promised not to tell anyone, especially Mitch."

Babette glanced at Marcel, then at me. "And who is this...Mitch?"

"Oh, you mean Sheriff McDreamy! He's our local sheriff, and he looks amazing on a fifty-foot billboard. They've been on...how many dates now, Ev? Four? Five?"

"Thanks, Elizabeth. And it's four dates. Well, five if you count our business meal. But officially four. Babette, I'm so sorry I haven't mentioned Mitch before. But please understand, I haven't even told anyone in my family—not the kids, or Nate, or even my father. Right now I don't really know where this relationship is going, and..."

The Bouviers moved toward me, gliding together as if dancing a...well, dancing some sort of dance where two people walk side by side. What was that...line dancing, maybe? No, too fast...

Anyway, the couple halted on either side of me, Marcel behind me and Babette in front. Marcel spoke, but I knew his words came from both of them. "Evangeline, ma chère, you have many years left to love and to love again. We all knew our cousin's job brought him close to many dangerous people, and a day might come where he would give his life to the job he held dear. But Douglas would not want you to be alone. We've never told you this, but one evening he came to visit us. As the three of us sat on our porch and drank Babette's mint iced tea, and we spoke of his job and the darkness he faced every day. We prayed together that God would keep him safe. But if that was not according to His will, that our Father would provide for you and the children if Douglas couldn't be there to take care of you. And God has answered our prayers and more! But, Evangeline..."

Between Marcel and Babette's grip, I could hardly breathe. "...Sweet cousin, we also prayed that if God parted Douglas from you, that He would bring you someone to walk with you and hold your hand for the rest of your days. It's not that you aren't strong enough! Through Christ, you can walk through fire. But we realize how much of a helpmate you are, so giving and so loving. Your time as a wife isn't over, Evangeline. Mark these words...you will love again, and someone will cover you in a love so thick that no evil can penetrate it. That is our prayer for you. And God answers prayers."

I couldn't catch my breath for fear of bursting into tears. Or gasps, more likely, since the Bouviers had me in a Christian death grip. Well, okay, that seemed harsh. They covered me in prayer for the next few minutes, which was lovely, but I struggled to breathe. What was the proper etiquette to ask people to please relax their hold, especially in a time of closeness and intimacy? And what if the same people were praying? Did I interrupt a conversation with the Almighty to request more breathing space? Oh, Muriel Bergeron, why didn't you cover this in the many lessons of good manners you shoved into my education those eighteen years before I left Graisseville? Or even during the weeks I came home between semesters?

C'mon, Muriel! Surely the etiquette of requests during prayers could have taken a front seat? I mean, did I really need to know which fork I should place on the napkin beside the plate versus the fork that I should place in front of the dinner plate? Oh, the questions I had for my mother when

I reached the pearly gates! *"Mother! Why didn't you prepare me..."*

"Amen! Evangeline, we approve of this McDreamy person. Although, I question his mother's state of mind when she named him."

Our Father, Who art in Heaven, hallowed be Thy Name. Thy Will be done, of course! But could You please order a double dose of patience? Much like the order I request when hanging out with Shorty all day? In Your Name always, Amen.

"Okay, let's get down to business! Tell me everything you know or have heard about Chantilly Romero."

Oh, that name! To have a name that conjured up visions of delicate lace, cake, and cream... Yes, Evangeline was a beautiful name, but still...Chantilly Romero! I couldn't help it...my subconscious...oh, who were we kidding? It was my total, full-blown conscious self that imagined the scenarios.

"Oh, Miss Chantilly Romero? Yes, ma'am, party of twenty."

Yes, Romero was her married name, so the Miss didn't apply. But still...a party of ten times two? Even if I offered free jambalaya, I couldn't wrangle twenty people to any gathering I hosted. But Miss Chantilly Romero could.

"Mrs. Chantilly Romero? Yes, of course! You want to host a party of five hundred guests? Yes, ma'am, of course! What would you like to offer as the appetizers?"

Five hundred? Well, of course that could happen! Five hundred lobsters and crabs and...

Doug's cousin interrupted my...well, unsupervised daydreams...and began our investigation. "Let's start with the way Chantilly was murdered. She swallowed a poisoned shrimp po'boy! And at a Mardi Gras party? That's just bad Southern manners! In fact, I'd say it was an act of Northern aggression. Those Yankees who come down here every season..."

Babette was on to something, blaming the tourists. Well, she might be. Honestly, I had no idea what she was talking about. But my sweet relative by marriage was on a tear, and I knew what *that* looked like.

"Well there is the party hostess, Jacqueline Dubois. The poor girl is only twenty-eight. With those wavy lengths of sunshine blonde hair, and a five foot seven figure, she does turn heads! And those sparkling emerald green eyes...most warm-blooded men fall in love with one look in her direction."

Marcel's eyebrows dipped as he put on a frown. "Chérie, that woman's far too wrapped up in herself. She's a bowl full of eye candy for any influential man in our town! And she takes advantage of it."

"Hush, Marcel. She and Chantilly are dear friends. Or were, that is. She and Beau were the best of friends as well. Jacqueline went to culinary school and she made the po'boys herself, I think. But did she?"

"Did she what, Babette?" Honestly, I was so confused. Was everyone else?

"Evangeline, did Jacqueline make the po'boys herself? And did she even go to culinary school? Or graduate?'

Oh boy, we had a mess of confusion! This mystery was stumbling and staggering, primarily because New Orleans was a huge city, not a small town. Was there a group in the know, or even a network of people to give us the scoop? Who had the scoop on the Romeros? Maybe Elizabeth's connections? Hopefully Marcel and Babette had some reliable contacts too.

"Oh Marcel, we can't forget Jean Breaux! Remember him, Chér? Mmmm, how he adored Chantilly. Why, he worshiped the ground she danced upon! But she was already engaged to Beau Romero. What happened then? Mon chèr, help me remember!"

Marcel took up the story. "Oui, Chérie, your memory is correct. Jean's love for Chantilly was pure, much like ours. But alas, she didn't return his affections. She strung him along, as silly young girls do with their suitors' hearts. She used him to make her fiancé jealous. Jean realized her actions weren't real, and he lost interest. Thank goodness he respected the marriage and didn't try to change her mind."

"Oh? Marcel, are you certain Jean and Chantilly were never a couple? I don't know them, but maybe that's what they want everyone to think. Maybe they were just cooling their jets."

Marcel turned toward me, with question marks. "Cooling their jets? Evangeline, what does this mean...cool jets? Neither one of them owns an airplane."

"Uh, did Jean pretend to lose interest so he could throw off suspicion? Maybe he was biding his time, hoping Chantilly would walk away from Beau and their marriage. Then he could swoop in and be the hero. You know, save her from all her sorrow."

Marcel shook his head, emphasizing my error. "No, cousin, no, that couldn't be true. Chantilly loved Beau with all her heart. When she met him, she only had eyes for Beau. Jean Breaux was just a...how do you say?"

Babette whispered in his ear, and Marcel nodded. "Yes, Jean was *rien*...nothing. Chantilly saw him as a toy, someone to occupy her evenings. He was simply a blip along the path of romance. No, Beau has always been Chantilly's one true love. Yes, they had their difficulties. What do you say? Their ups and downs. All couples do."

Should I? Yes, I definitely should. Ugh, even though Marcel had gone on and on about true love and romance, I still had to ask. "Marcel, Babette. To your knowledge, did Jean know anything about poisons? Could he have played any part in killing Chantilly?"

The couple never exchanged a glance—they knew exactly what the other one believed. Babette answered for both of them. "No, Evangeline. Jean doesn't know anything about poison. He couldn't have killed Chantilly. She means nothing to him anymore."

CHAPTER 3

"Before I forget, does anyone have some paper and a pen? I didn't bring my sleuthing notebook, and I need to take notes." Did Jessica Fletcher take her detective tools on vacation? I'd never seen her use any tools, not even a magnifying glass. Should I buy a magnifying glass?

"Cousin, did you hear me? There's a dollar store just down the street. Marcel can go get you a notebook and pen. Highlighters, yes? Maybe some of those cute little sticky notes?"

Her question hung in the air, competing with the sound of Marcel's car driving away. Wow, those two were so in sync it frightened us mere mortals. "Those supplies all sound wonderful. But Shorty and I mainly use an erasable white board. Will there be anyone else in the house this weekend? If not, we could set up a strategizing area in the living room."

Babette nodded, her baby blues squinting in concentration. "Mmm, oui. Our next guests don't arrive until Wednesday. But where would we get a white board?"

The strains from "La Vie en Rose" floated through the air. Babette put her husband on speaker. "Chérie, shall I get a white board and some markers? I can stop at our office supply store—I'm sure Eric has one we can purchase. Hmm? What do you think?"

Sometimes those two were downright scary. Or maybe Babette's phone had some sort of listening device on it? "Yes, my love, that would be perfect! Why don't you get a notebook for each of us, and some pens? Oh, and those sticky notes and some highlighters."

"They're all on my list. Anything else? Maybe some snacks and drinks to, um, assist our sleuthing skills? Oh, wait a minute! You've already thought of that, haven't you?"

On second thought, Marcel and Babette were downright handy to have around. Maybe they'd come to Graisseville on a regular basis, supplying Shorty and me with snacks and sticky notes? "Of course, Cher, of course. I'm going to the kitchen to brew some more tea and prepare a charcuterie board. While discussing suspects and their motives, I think savory snacks are the best. Yes?"

"Oui, absolutely! I'll be back soon. Je t'aime. Goodbye, ladies!"

Babette refused to discuss the case until Marcel returned. "Nora Charles never worked on an investigation without her beloved Nick, and neither will I. But I'm so excited, Evangeline! Marcel and I have been looking for a hobby to spice up our date nights. Perhaps solving mysteries just like you will be our new date night fun, yes?"

Had I created a monster, maybe even two? One glance at Annabelle's eager eyes and Elizabeth's grin that wouldn't quit told me I'd created exactly four monsters. Why did humans find crime so fascinating? Most people didn't want to commit the crimes, and we certainly didn't celebrate the ones who did. One thing I'd learned from my sleuthing was that people enjoy puzzles. Oh sure, crosswords and jumbles. Maybe a basic jigsaw or three dimensional puzzle if we felt especially bold. But the puzzles that required us to delve into the inner workings of human behavior and emotions? Oh, those mysteries were the best!

"Uh, well I never thought of solving crimes as a date night activity. But that's probably because I solve the cases with Shorty, and we're not dating. But now that you mention it, why not? Sleuthing could be something interesting to do on a date. Remember though, solving a crime doesn't happen in one evening, at least none of the cases I've ever solved. And it can be a little, well, dangerous."

Should I bring up my first case, where the killer held me at gunpoint in my home? Honestly, that was the worst of Southern etiquette, planning my living room for my death. My second case wasn't dangerous at all. No one threatened my life. Oh, well, there was that dead rat, and Shorty's busted windshield. Okay, but my third case definitely had no danger, being a simple fruitcake theft and all. And my last case? Hmm, I wasn't ever in any real danger. I mean, yes, a murderer did grill me a ribeye steak, then zip tie me and leave me in his guest room. But he told me that he wasn't planning to kill me, and that was reassuring. And Shorty did show up six hours later and rescued me. Then we got to eat Chocolate Ganache, and it was to die for! Okay, poor choice of words. But it was worth going off my diet, anyway. Oh, and then we had vanilla ice cream with chocolate chip cookies. Not as good as the ganache, but definitely a treat.

"Dangerous? Just how dangerous? Evangeline, have you risked your life to solve these crimes?" Babette's eyes darkened a shade to reflect her concern, and her tiny nose crinkled.

"Uh, no, well, yes. Maybe, I guess. But I got an almost new car from a grateful client, and money to buy a washing machine. And, my last case, after Shorty cut my zip ties, we had the most amazing Chocolate Ganache, and…"

Nope, Babette's eyes told me that even the ganache wasn't worth risking my life. According to her, anyway.

"Babette, don't worry. Ev hasn't really been in much danger, not really. She solves the case, and law enforcement takes over after that. I mean, there was the first case, when the killer broke into Ev's house and held her at gunpoint. But her brother saved her, and Annabelle's fiancé showed up right after that. So she wasn't really ever in…"

Elizabeth's explanation didn't help. Her words added fuel to the fire. Just as Babette opened her mouth to resume the inquisition, Marcel appeared with arms loaded. "Here are our supplies! Wait, from the looks on your faces, you started the investigation without me. Catch me up, mes amies—what did I miss?"

Would Babette spill the beans on the dangers of going after a murderer? No, the sparkle in her eyes ensured her silence. The woman didn't want to give up the excitement of solving a mystery. "Chéri, you've missed nothing. But do you remember where we put that revolver your grandfather left you?"

Marcel leaned in the required fourteen inches and planted a kiss on his wife's cherry lips. "What a strange question, my love. It's on the top shelf of the closet in our bedroom, beside a box of bullets. But why do you ask?"

Babette grabbed the plastic sacks, making a show out of examining the contents. "Oh, no reason. Why, these notebooks are darling! Merci, my love. You purchased exactly what we needed, as always. Not only are you handsome, but your intelligence is beyond measure."

Okay, that last remark straddled the border between sweet and nauseating. Hmmm, were those two going to make my stomach churn as much as Shorty's list of pet names? Honestly, I'd only been around the couple for short periods of time—family gatherings, maybe out to supper once or twice with Doug. After his death, they'd brought me some food and sent a few texts, but we hadn't seen each other in quite a long time. But if I could handle Shorty calling Annabelle every item in a bakery display window, I should be able to handle Marcel and Babette. And was it any worse than Sheriff McDreamy, or Sheriff McSmoochy? Although, it was only Elizabeth who used those pet names, thank goodness!

"All right, let's get the white board set up! Marcel, did the board come with a stand? No? That's okay, we can prop it on a chair. It won't be eye level, but it'll be fine. Babette, would you hand out the pens and notebooks? I'd love the teal colored one, if you don't mind. Oh, Marcel, great job on the markers! Let's start our elements chart."

As I drew the grid, I explained my strategy. "Okay, Krewe, along the left side of the board, top to bottom, we'll list the suspects. Across the top from left to right we'll add the three elements. The first one is Motive, which is the reason the suspect killed Chantilly. Then we have Means, the proof that suspect had the knowledge to kill our victim. And our last element is Opportunity, which is how the suspect had the chance to kill. When we get to this element, we'll be proving out alibis and..."

Yeah, my team looked about as lost as last year's Easter egg. "Okay, let's forget about opportunities and alibis. We'll focus on motive first. Who had a reason to kill Chantilly Romero?"

Yes, little lights popping on! Heads nodding too. "Team, let's start with Jacqueline Dubois. Based on the Bouviers' information, she's a suspect. Babette, you two mentioned Jacqueline was a friend of Chantilly's. Is that true? How close were they? Because Jacqueline had lots of opportunity to poison the po'boy, since it was her party."

"Oui, they were good friends, dear friends! They've known each forever, and spent many hours together chairing committees and serving on boards. No, Jacqueline couldn't have possibly killed her. Non, impossible!" Babette's voice took on a frantic tone, and Marcel took her hand.

"Cousin, I get it. You can't imagine Jacqueline killing her dear friend. But Babette, would you consider us dear friends?"

My cousin-in-law leaned forward in her chair, rubbing her fingertips down her thighs. "Oh, yes, cousin! Of course I do. You are one of my favorite people, a joy to be around. Marcel and I have been looking forward to this weekend, and spending time together. Ma chère, it's been so long..."

More lights popping. Babette recognized the path I'd been leading her toward. "Oh! I understand. I consider us close, but we haven't seen each other for several years. Oh, that makes my heart sad. I've not been a good friend, have I, cousin?"

Okay, maybe Babette hadn't gone far enough down the path. Maybe she'd missed the path entirely? "No, no, it's all right. I consider you a close friend as well. What I'm trying to say is, you are a kind hearted and loving person. You think the best of everyone. But perhaps you are thinking too highly of Jacqueline and her relationship with Chantilly. How well do you really know those two? You could be right about their friendship, but you could also be mistaken. That's all I'm saying."

Marcel cupped his wife's hand. "Evangeline's correct, Chérie. You always seek the best in everyone, even if there's nothing to find. I think we should leave Jacqueline on the grid, until we do some investigating." He patted Babette's hand to confirm his decision.

"Oh, all right. But I just can't imagine anyone who cooks as well as Jacqueline might be a murderer. Only bad chefs should be killers."

Our resident librarian offered her two cents. "Actually, Dorothea Puente, also known as the Death House Landlady, wrote a cookbook while serving a life sentence in Chowchilla. They accused her of drugging and killing nine of her boarding house residents, and burying their bodies in the backyard."

We couldn't have been more shocked at Annabelle's speech, if she'd announced that she'd helped Dorothea with the murders. "The jury only convicted her of three murders though, and she died while serving a life sentence. I'll tell you one thing...her prison tamale recipe is superb. Shorty can't get enough of that dish."

Marcel scooted his chair a couple inches towards his wife. Or was it a couple inches away from Annabelle? Elizabeth studied our librarian, her eyes registering admiration. What kind of friends did I have? No doubt the Bouviers were pondering the same question.

Annabelle continued. "Anyway, I think Marcel's right. Let's leave Jacqueline on the board. And what about Jean Breaux? The prisons are full of people who have killed for unrequited love."

Babette opened her mouth, then snapped it shut. But Marcel nodded in agreement. "Oui, yes, keep him on the board. Who really gets over their first love? Evangeline, add to the list Clifford Benoit, Chantilly's bodyguard. He's worked for the Romero family for years and years, which means he has a lot of...how do you say...?" He looked to Babette. "Chérie?"

"Dirt. Clifford has a lot of dirt on the family. He knows where they've hidden the skeletons."

Marcel grinned, his lips setting off his teeth with a wide brown frame. "Oui, dirt! Skeletons! And dead bodies, too."

Whew! These people found too much fun in murder cases. Well, Doug enjoyed his career in law enforcement, and bringing criminals to justice. Maybe it ran in the family? "Good, that's good. Who else? Babette? Marcel? C'mon guys, you're going to have to fill in the grid with the names. Elizabeth and Annabelle have never lived here, and I didn't run with those circles of people. It's all on you two."

"Hmmm, what about Sheriff Doug Ray? Marcel and I don't know anything that directly makes him suspicious. But we've heard things, rumors really, that he's been looking the other way for the Romeros and their shady activities. He's coming up for reelection, and there's talk that he's going to have a hard time winning. Seems people are tired of their sheriff being more crooked than the folks he's putting away. Maybe Chantilly told the sheriff she had proof he'd allowed criminal activity to continue in the parish. So he killed her."

"Oui, oui, you're right, Chérie. Yes, the sheriff is someone we should investigate. Also, Jacqueline hosted her party just outside the city limits, so the sheriff would be the lawman, not New Orleans police. She and Sheriff Ray enjoy a long friendship, and she knew he'd make sure the party wasn't disturbed."

My wrist cramped from the writing, and my brain cramped from the spelling. With Louisiana's French heritage, the names were long to write and even harder to spell. "Whew! Thank goodness Doug Ray is so short and I can figure out the spelling! Okay, let me take a break and enjoy Babette's mint tea. You two think some more on our suspect list."

"Beatrice Romero, Beau's baby sister. Yes, she should be on the list—would you agree, Chérie?"

Nope, no chance to drink that tea. And yet another long name, although it should be easy to spell. "Wonderful, fabulous! Anyone else? Going once, going twice...okay, let's start with these five. We can add more, or hopefully cross some off the chart. Now let me get that tea."

As we sipped tea and worked on the charcuterie board, I reflected on my new mystery. When would I ever feel completely comfortable working a case? Maybe I wouldn't, because every case was so different. This puzzle could be my most difficult, simply because I was out of my comfort zone. Yes, I'd lived in New Orleans for many years, but I'd never met Chantilly Romero and her circle of associates. Doug and I kept company with cops and their families, or my fellow professors at Tulane. No, New Orleans didn't consider police officers and university professors movers and shakers in The Big Easy. The ethical ones, anyway.

"Evangeline, we must apologize! Marcel and I have never had to think this way about our friends. We always assume the best of people, especially the people we know. This, this new way of thinking is difficult, for me especially. My mother taught me that a proper Southern lady assumes the best of everyone, no matter their stature or upbringing. God made us all in His image, and none of us are any better than anyone else. But for Chantilly's sake, I must put aside my mother's teachings, and question the motives and words of these people."

"Babette, there's no need to apologize. But you're exactly right. If you want to find out who killed your friend, you've got to be more suspicious of people. And you'll have to listen to gossip, no matter how sordid and ugly the rumors. If there's one thing I've learned in this business, it's that where there's smoke, there's fire."

Babette nodded her head, but her husband's eyes registered exclamation marks. "Oh, I'm so excited, Evangeline! As you know, I was born and raised in France. I didn't move to New Orleans until I was twenty, to attend university. Most of your delightful analogies escape my understanding. But this one, I know!"

He leaned forward. "In French we say something similar. I'm assuming you aren't talking about an actual fire. Or are you?"

His wife's giggles made me smile. Marcel spoke perfect English, but still hadn't mastered the complicated world of

American idioms. In Babette's eyes, that made him even more charming and attractive. Love rarely makes sense.

"You're right, I'm not. When we see in the air, we can expect that 90% of the time there is a fire. The same holds true for gossip, stories, etc. The entire tale may not be true, but parts of it probably are. And yes, we're not supposed to gossip. But for the investigation, we need to pay attention to anything mentioned in your circles about Chantilly or the suspects. We don't get to rely on fingerprints or DNA samples, or even phone records or surveillance tapes from cameras. The sheriff isn't going to share those records with us. We've got to take the information we gather and sift through it, separating the clues from the red herrings."

Marcel threw his hands up in the air—did people really do that? "You've lost me again, Evangeline! Why are we talking about fish? I thought we were talking about clues."

Babette nodded, her eyes wide like our dessert plates resting on the coffee table. "I'm lost too, cousin, and I was born and raised here. What is a red herring?"

Maybe I knew more than I thought. "We're going to learn a lot about our victims and our suspects. Some things will be relevant to our case and some things won't. The parts that aren't relevant are called red herrings, or information that distracts us from solving the case. We just have to keep digging and gathering more information, so we can determine which pieces point us to the killer, and which pieces are distractions."

Nods punctuated by murmurs of understanding greeted me like dear friends. Dear friends, ready to solve the case. "Great! Okay, so Babette and Marcel, you're up. What do you know about these five suspects?"

The Bouviers stared at each other for a good five seconds, the longest I'd ever experienced. "Uh, not much really. Beatrice is...was great friends with her sister-in-law. We've never heard of any problems between them. She's a gemologist, so I don't think she'd have a reason to know about poison."

Babette paused to access her memories from a week ago. "We were at the Mardi Gras party last Friday, and we spoke to both Chantilly and Beatrice. They were standing together, near the kitchen, talking quietly. Marcel and I walked over to greet them, chatted a bit, then Bea said she was going to get a drink—she asked if we wanted anything but we said no. Then Marcel saw a business associate and we parted ways. It wasn't long after that when people started screaming that someone poisoned Chantilly's shrimp po'boy."

Marcel clicked his tongue, making a *tsking* sound. Wasn't that an American habit? Or did the French also tsk-tsk? I grabbed my notebook and penned a note to research my all-important question. Oops! My notebook page glared at me, its starkness almost blinding. I couldn't have just that one question! What would Babette and Marcel think of me? Ugh, think, Ev! What else could I write? But the only words popping in my brain were that Zy needed more dog food. Nope, couldn't write that tidbit of news in my notebook, although it was a step up from researching *tsk-tsk*.

"Well, there was that couple at the party...remember them, Marcel? They kept standing outside the kitchen, even though Jacqueline and the staff asked them to move. We'd never seen them before."

I wrote, *Mysterious kitchen couple* on the board. "Okay, so we have seven suspects, then. Marcel, Babette, could you make some phone calls? See if you can get interviews with the suspects. When we meet with Jacqueline, we can ask her about this mysterious couple. If we get a name then we can interview them too. Elizabeth..."

My bestie sat at attention, awaiting orders. "Yes, Miss Marple! What can I do?"

"For starters, you can stop being such a smart aleck. Then you can dig into your contact list, try to get some interviews going. I need you to put together a group of people that rivals your Aunt Lila's gossipy book club!"

"She's Cliff's aunt, but yes I'm on it!" Elizabeth disappeared, snatching one last cube of cheese on her way to the bedroom.

"What about me, Jane? Uh, Miss Marple? What can I do?"

Ah, our resident librarian, who'd better stay safe during the case, or her fiancé would never forgive me. "What do you need to start your deep dive? I'm thinking we'll use your mad research skills, to dig up all you can on our victim and suspects. You might uncover some more potential killers too. Do you need to go to the library?"

Annabelle stood up, saluting me. "No, ma'am! I've got my laptop—all I need is the wi-fi login and password. I saw it on a sign in the foyer, so I'll get started right away!"

"Wonderful! Everyone has their marching orders." A furrowed brow on Marcel's face caused me to restate my words. "I mean, everyone knows what their tasks are. Let's spend an hour completing our assignments and meet back here. I'll take that time to collect my thoughts."

My team exited the room, which left me and my empty notebook. And the charcuterie board. As I munched on cheese and crackers, I added my thoughts on the suspects to my notebook. Oh, and I looked up whether the French *tsk-tsk* just like the Americans. My thirty seconds of research confirmed the sound was definitely an American thing. At least I'd solved one mystery.

CHAPTER 4

One mystery solved and just one left. Well, maybe the tsk-tsk mystery wasn't that big, but still...

"Bon, mes amies! Babette and I have made great progress. Ma chère is busy in the kitchen, preparing our lunch. She's creating her famous cranberry pecan chicken salad on sourdough bread, with strawberry salad on the side and Louisiana crunch cake for dessert. All this crime solving has made a large appetite for Babette and me. You all as well, I hope."

One glance at the charcuterie board reminded me I'd been eating nonstop for the last hour. Oh, and don't forget the...King Pecan Pralines? Praline Pecan King Cookies? Whatever they were, they'd filled up a good part of my stomach too.

My traveling companions wandered into the strategy room. Elizabeth's eyes had brightened at the mention of food. "Did I hear something about chicken salad on sourdough? With pecans and cranberries? Sign me up, please! Annabelle, what about you?"

Our friend rubbed her eyes. "Oh, that sounds divine. And Shorty says *hey ya'll*, and can he please crash our girls' weekend to work on the case? I said no way! Why does he get to have all the fun?"

Annabelle slid a hand to her mouth, barely covering a yawn. I couldn't resist teasing her. "Girl, did you carve out time to take a nap? We've got a killer to catch, we don't have time for sleep. Did you accomplish anything, other than catching forty winks and talking to your pookie bear?"

The sleepy look bowed out, replaced by a flushed face. "Uh, well Shorty called *me*. And wait a minute! Ev...how'd you know what I call him?"

Such a perfect opportunity for a horse snort, but I'd let my PI corner the market on that noise. Instead, I crossed my arms and squared off against my friend. "Really, Annabelle? I've solved four cases that stumped our local law enforcement, yet you can't believe I know Shorty's nickname?"

Okay, only three of them stumped law enforcement—no one really cared who stole Miss Pearlie's fruitcakes. In fact, the thief still wasn't speaking to me, and I honestly believed he charged me more than the regular price for my new tires. Next time I'd send in my father to negotiate the price—no one would overcharge an eighty-five year old retired veterinarian and beloved member of the community.

"Well? Ev, are you listening? If you're such a master sleuth, how did you know?"

"Huh? Oh, I went with Shorty to the Gas n' More. He filled his tank and went inside for some Crawtators. I got bored, so I looked for something to do. He always locks the glove compartment and the console, so I had no luck there. But I poked around the seat cushions and struck gold. I found

$1.87 in change, an unused lottery ticket, and a note that said, *Stay safe, Pookie Bear. Love, your Anna Dumpling.* That lottery ticket won me five dollars, but I gave it to Shorty. Since he'd paid for it." Wow, I didn't know anyone's face could turn that red.

"But, hey, that's a great nickname for the love of your life, Annabelle! It's cute and sweet, and it doesn't make me nauseous. Well, not much anyway."

If Annabelle's face turned any brighter, she could walk out on Mirabeau Street and stop traffic. Was that shade of red from embarrassment or anger? Maybe I crossed the line.

"Hey, look, if it makes you feel any better, I used to call Doug my sweet little mango. See, he used to bring me mangos when they were in season, and one day..."

Thank goodness for Babette! My rescuer appeared with a tray full of sandwiches and more tea. "Annabelle, you're among friends, so there's no reason to be embarrassed. When Marcel and I began dating, we called each other all sorts of pet names, and our friends teased us unmercifully. They said we were so nauseatingly sweet, we made them sick to their stomachs. But as our love matured, much like a magnolia tree, we've become less irritating with our pet names. That's why we named our bed and breakfast Sweet Magnolia Manor. Because our love has deep roots like our favorite tree, and it blossoms sweetly."

Annabelle's face returned to its original color, and she grabbed a sandwich. But I had one burning question. If Marcel and Babette's love had matured with time, causing them to be less nauseatingly sweet, how bad were they in the beginning? *Thank You, Lord that I didn't know those two at the beginning of their romance. And thank You for this infor-*

mation. It makes me realize that, compared to other people, Shorty's list of pet names really isn't so bad. Yes, it's nauseating, but it could be a lot worse, I guess. Amen.

Between munches Annabelle thanked her hostess. "Thank you, Babette, for the sandwich and the words of encouragement. Yes, that does make me feel better. But everyone, please, please! Do not tell Shorty that you know his nickname. He didn't like it at first, he said real men don't have pet names. But I told him John Wayne's wife used to call him *sweetums*. And if the Duke could have a pet name, well, then Shorty could too."

"What? John Wayne's wife called him *sweetums*? I never knew that! And Nate's such a John Wayne fan, I can't believe he never mentioned that. I can't wait to go home and share that bit of trivia with him."

It was Annabelle's turn to square off with me. "Ev, how in the world would I know what any of John Wayne's wives called him? I made it up, okay? Now can we talk about something else, other than my love life? How about this killer we're trying to catch?"

I turned my palms up, facing my friend. "Okay, hold your horses, girlfriend. We're getting back on topic. Let's start with Marcel and Babette. Cousins, how did your phone calls go? Did you get any interviews set up with our suspects? I'd really like to talk to Jacqueline, and quiz her about our mysterious kitchen couple." And start on my sandwich, of course. My stomach had already called, asking when it could expect one of Babette's culinary wonders. I couldn't be too upset—fighting crime made a person hungry.

My cousins sat side by side, fingers interlocked in a relaxed holding of hands. How did they do that, eating sandwiches with only one hand? They'd always made marriage look so easy. Several years ago, after the seventy-fifth time Doug forgot to pick up milk on the way home, I'd called Babette.

"Does your husband ever drive you crazy? Because mine drives me crazy all the time! He makes promises he can't keep, and his mother never taught him how to throw his clothes into a laundry basket, or put food back into the pantry. The man can't even make a sandwich without leaving the kitchen a wreck. Honestly, I could strangle him right now!"

My harsh words fell against a trickle of laughter through my phone. "Oh, cousin, Marcel does that too. Why, he grew up in a chalet in Lyon, with a maid and a cook! Mademoiselle Adrienne kept his room clean and tidy, and Madame Sagnier prepared all the food. Oh, my love never placed a dirty plate in the dishwasher, or a pair of socks in a basket! I'll be honest, we struggled our first few years. After climbing out of bed to keep from smothering him, I reached a conclusion. That was my last time to restrain myself from harming my spouse. From that day on, before my feet hit the floor, I reach over and touch my husband's arm. And I pray for him."

"No, that's too simple. Babette, that can't possibly work."

"Oh, but it does! Now, you must touch his arm or his shoulder, even his hand. That's most important, Evangeline.

He doesn't have to be coherent, or even conscious. As you feel the warmth of your husband beside you, thank our Lord for your marriage. Thank Him for all the things you love about Douglas, the sweet little things from when you first fell in love. His eyes, his smile, the way he holds the door open for you. Then, thank Him for the blessings He's given your marriage—your children, your home, the memories you share. You must ask God to protect Douglas every day, as he leaves the safety of your home to provide for your family. Ask for peace in your heart as you pick up his dirty clothes, as you stop by the market for the milk he forgot to purchase. Ask God to remind you of the things Douglas does for you every day. Does he help the children with their homework? Perhaps fix a sticky latch on the back door? Whatever these blessings are, ask God to help you focus on them, and remind you to thank your husband for doing them. Evangeline, I tell you. If you pray these prayers faithfully, God will bless your mar riage."

And she was right. As I prayed each morning, at first grudgingly but eventually with joy, I felt my heart change. Instead of constantly finding fault with everything my husband did, I began to find joy and love. Yes, he still missed the laundry basket by a good three feet every night. But he was home to throw his dirty clothes on the floor. Thank goodness for Babette teaching me how to find joy in my marriage instead of fault! If I'd continued to count my husband's mistakes, keeping a ledger of all his supposed sins, our marriage wouldn't have been as beautiful. And upon his death, I'd have regretted all those grudge-filled thoughts and actions. Worse, I would have had no way to make it up to him. *Thank You, Lord, for Marcel and Babette, and their demonstration of how marriage ought to be. Maybe I'll have that again someday...but please no goofy pet names. And if he could get his dirty clothes into the basket this time, that would be great. It's not a deal breaker, by any means, but it would be a bonus. Amen.*

Hmmm...where did Mitch's clothes end up every night? Beside the laundry basket or in it?

"Evangeline? Did you hear me? I said the calls went well and we have interviews scheduled with all five suspects. Don't forget...Babette and I have Chantilly's visitation tonight. But, we did manage a couple of interviews before then. Jacqueline and Jean have agreed to talk to us this afternoon. We can inquire about the mysterious kitchen couple with both of them. We've got the other three scheduled tomorrow, after the funeral."

"Wonderful! Let's all take some time and focus on questions. Let's decide what we'd like to ask each one. But I don't think every one of us should attend the interviews. Such a crowd would make it more of an interrogation than an informal meeting. Speaking of that, what did you two say when you set up the interviews?"

Babette touched Marcel's arm, a signal that she'd handle the response. "We felt honesty was the best policy. New Orleans may be a large city, but news travels fast. I called Jacqueline and explained that my cousin Evangeline is visiting. I told her that you consult with law enforcement, and have solved several murders. Marcel and I have hired you and your team of experts to simply ask some questions and do a little digging, for our own peace of mind. Jacqueline was quite willing to meet with us, and share what she's told the New Orleans Parish detectives."

"You've hired a team of experts? Wow, that sounds, well, that sounds official. And expensive. But I'm happy with our agreement of free food and lodging. We're family, Babette. And even though it's family by marriage, I'm closer to you two than many of my blood relatives."

Nodding heads around the room confirmed my decision. "But I know how you feel about stretching the truth. Maybe we can work out some sort of small payment, so you can sleep at night."

"Oh, no, Evangeline, I told the truth. We're paying you in chicken salad and charcuterie! Besides, Marcel and I have talked it over, and we hadn't planned to take your money to stay here, anyway. Now, with all your help to solve Chantilly's murder, we won't accept a dime. No, that's the end of the discussion! Ç'est fini!" Babette and Marcel crossed their arms over their chests, lips closed tight like a sealed envelope.

"All right, but we may have to buy bigger clothes after this weekend, so you'll be getting a bill for that. Now, let's decide who's going on the interviews and which one of us is taking the lead."

My team kept their eyes on me, but Elizabeth spoke their collective mind. "Ev, you've got to be at every interview. Girl, you're the only one who has any idea what you're doing!"

That last sentence was debatable. "I suppose so, El. Annabelle, I'm not fussing at you, I'm just asking. Did you find out anything about our suspects or the victim?"

Our researcher blushed just a shade but kept her composure. "Uh, not really. I started with Clifford Benoit, because he sounded the most interesting, with the most dirt. But from everything I found, he's been loyal to Beau and Chantilly. Since Beau's death, he's never left Chantilly's side. There are a lot of photos floating around the internet with our victim as the star. And right behind her, in pretty much every one of them, Clifford is standing with a scowl."

"Hey, it's a start! I guess you didn't see anything about this bodyguard knowing anything about poison?"

Our researcher shook her head. "No, not really. But I'm rested and ready to go! I'll spend the afternoon on my laptop and finish my research. Ya'll go have fun without me. Uh, Babette, could the lunch leftovers stay here with me? I'll need sustenance, I'm sure."

My cousin nodded her head. "I'll put everything away and label the contents. You will have no problems obtaining your necessary nutrients for research."

With Annabelle's food issues resolved, I turned to my bestie. "Elizabeth, how productive was your hour? Did you get in touch with your friends?"

"Uh, well, yes, and a lot of them will be at the visitation tonight. We're meeting for dinner tomorrow after the funeral. Is that all right? I'm afraid my mother didn't lecture me on the proper etiquette for conducting a murder investigation in or around a funeral. So, I did my best."

That was Elizabeth...always concerned about manners and being polite. I should ask her for some refresher lessons. "Well, I'm no Emily Post, but it sounds fine to me. Now tell me, will this group of ladies equal Lila's book club in knowledge of the down and dirty? And how willing will they be to share the dirt?"

"Oh, don't worry, Ev. These ladies are going to give Lila's club a run for its money. But I was wondering...could I come to the interviews with ya'll this afternoon? Please don't tell my husband, but I'd really like to see what you do, Ev. What do you think? I promise to be as quiet as a church mouse. You'll hardly know I'm there."

"I don't know, El...on one hand, a fresh set of eyes could be helpful. But on the other, four people could seem like an interrogation. Krewe, what do you think?"

Marcel bit his pen, staring at the ceiling for inspiration. "Mmmm...What if you three ladies meet with Jacqueline? She'd be more at ease, perhaps, if it was all women."

Babette nodded, her waves of blonde locks bobbing in agreement. "Yes, I think you're right, mon cher. Elizabeth, I mean Kinsey, why don't you join Ev, I mean, Jane...Miss Marple? Anyway, why don't you join us? Marcel, uh, Nick can make some more calls and keep, uh...what's Annabelle's name a gain?"

"Okay, everyone. Let's just forget about the code names—we have enough suspects to keep straight without trying to remember alter egos. All right? Let's have Babette, Elizabeth, and me talk to Jacqueline. Marcel, I'm thinking the reverse is true—maybe Jean would feel more comfortable if it was just you guys."

"Oui, that's true. Let's do that. But I would like a list of questions you want me to present. Please remember, Evangeline, this is my first murder investigation. I need someone to guide me along."

"Of course, of course. Let's go through that right now." My team reclaimed their seats, notebooks open and pens upright. Wow, such a feeling of déjà vu, but from where? Oh, yes! My college students. Only this group didn't yawn or pull out their phones nearly as much.

Annabelle stacked her plate and pointed it to the back. "Don't disturb me—I'll have my head in my laptop." And her mouth filled with food, no doubt.

"Okay, team, let's get started. I talk to the person I'm interviewing as if I don't really know what I'm doing, as though I have no idea who the killer is and I'm just asking questions. You know what I mean? My goal is to disarm the suspect, make the person feel at ease, which puts them at a disadvantage."

Who was I kidding? I really *didn't* know what I was doing. None of my suspects felt threatened or intimidated by my stellar sleuthing skills and thought provoking questions. They'd all felt at ease, or gave that appearance. In fact, I always believed the suspects had the advantage, not me. Maybe that actually put them at a disadvantage? Hmmm...

"Ev, did you hear me? What questions can we ask the suspects, to make them more comfortable? Should I ask how the suspect killed Chantilly? Or is that too tough? Would that question be too soon in the first interview?"

Oh boy...the words *the blind leading the blind* flashed into my head. And yet, I did have four solved cases under my belt. *Dear Lord, I wish I had Shorty's bravado. I could use his common sense and confidence right now. I know, I know...I whine and complain about him all the time. You're right! I'm so sorry, Lord. Please forgive me. Could You, in Your infinite and all knowing wisdom, grant me some insight into leading this case? It can be temporary, I'm totally fine with that! Please, just help me teach these people how to interview suspects. In Your Name always, Amen.*

"Hey! Is anyone here? Annabelle, where are ya'?"

Oh my goodness! Okay, yes, I had wished for Shorty's bravado, and his common sense and confidence. But still...Lord, *I didn't ask for Shorty to actually appear on the doorstep, just a good six feet from me at the time of my prayer. Yes, I know Your Will is always true. I understand that. But really? I kind of, actually hoped that I could solve this case without my private investigator.* God answers prayer all the time. But many times it's not exactly the way we'd hoped.

"Hey, ya'll!" Shorty tipped an imaginary hat, his Stetson resting in his hands. He shifted the hat to his left hand and reached for Babette's hand with his right. "How ya'll doin'? Ya' must be Miss Babette."

My PI abandoned Babette's hand for her husband's, gripping it in a firmer, more Southern male handshake. "Hello, sir. Nice t'meet ya'. Hey, my name's Shorty Cormier, Annabelle's *fee-awnce-say*! Aww, but ya'll probably already know who I am! I bet she jus' can't stop talkin' about me."

He turned to the rest of us. "How ya'll ladies doin'? Hey, Doc, *lah say lay bon tomps roo lay!*"

Laissez les bon temps rouler? And, were those Mardi Gras beads around my PI's neck? "Hello, Shorty! What are you doing here? I mean...it's so good to see you! Are you here to carry Annabelle back home?"

Focus, Ev. Having Shorty around could be a good thing. The man had played a huge part in solving our cases, and he'd done just as much work or more as I had. Oh, who were we kidding? He'd pretty much done all the crime solving. Ugh!

There was a large part of me hating this revelation. Yes, I liked the adoration and respect my friends gave me over my sleuthing skills. But I had to be honest. Shorty was the brains of our outfit.

"Dumplin'! Where are ya'? C'mon, an' give a kiss tuh yore *fee-awnce-say!*"

"Uh, she's doing some research, but I'm sure she heard you. The whole block probably heard you. And what in the world are you doing here? You can't see your bride's wedding dress!"

"Aww, don't worry about that now, Doc! I'm here t'help ya'll solve the murder. Ya' didn't think ya' were gonna get t'solve a case without me, did ya'? Now, where's my buttercream cupcake?"

Did Shorty mean Annabelle or a snack? Sometimes it was hard to tell. *Dear Heavenly Father, please hear my prayer. Lord, I try really hard to get along with Shorty. And, I think I do a pretty good job. Don't I? Lord, I'm not trying to contradict Your work. I'm really not! But a big reason I get along with Shorty is because I don't have to put up with...uh, what I mean is, I don't interact with Shorty and Annabelle together. Right now I've got my hands full with Babette and Marcel, and their telepathic communication. I'm just not sure I can handle the sugary sweetness of two couples on top of solving a murder. Oh dear, we're doing this, aren't we? Okay, then Lord, grant me a couple tons of patience, and pronto please. Amen.*

"Hey, there's my great big slice of strawberry shortcake! C'mon over here, an' give me a kiss!"

Okay, I was pretty sure he was talking about Annabelle that time.

Chapter 5

I'd studied Annabelle's face as she crossed the room to greet her fiancé. Everyone else heard her voice rise with excitement, eyes gleaming with happiness. But I observed a...what was it? It was just the barest of pauses before her greeting to Shorty. Oh, and a tightness around her eyes.

"*Sweetie*, what a surprise! I thought we agreed this was a girls-only weekend?"

Yes, there it was, a tone of irritation. Of all the things Shorty had said and done, Annabelle's voice had always resonated with joy and delight. The woman put up with all of her fiancé's quirks and habits. But crashing a girls' weekend, her last fling, was different.

"I know, I know. But I went down tuh the coffee shop this mornin', an' I got t'thinkin' how much ya'll could use muh help. So I threw some clothes in a bag, filled up my truck with gas, an' here I am!"

Elizabeth caught my eye, making sure I observed the slight darkening of my best friend's eyes as she dropped her chin just a hair. We exchanged a look confirming that Annabelle wasn't pleased.

I stepped forward to break the tension. My PI and I rarely hugged, until he rescued me from zip ties and a tawdry reputation less than a month ago. Since I'd become his best man, maybe I should make it more often? My feet scooted closer so we faced each other. Shorty squinted at me. "Hey, Doc. Whatcha need?"

As I lifted my arms I stepped forward and grabbed his middle, like the Heimlich maneuver only from the front. This gesture of warmth hadn't started well. Maybe I should add some words to my embrace, smoothing out the awkwardness a little?

"Oh, Shorty, we're so glad to see you! Did you have a good trip?"

The heat of Annabelle's glare pierced the side of my head, but I pushed through. "Have you eaten? I'm sure we can find you something to take the edge off your hunger."

Edge off your hunger? Where did that come from? Most of us knew he'd been eating Crawtators and drinking orange soda during the road trip—a short hour and a half.

"Uh, hey...uh, Ev. It's good t'see ya' too. Yeah, I could stand t'eat a little somethin'. Iffen ya' don't mind. Whatcha got?"

Dropping Annabelle's hand, Shorty hopped toward the back of Sweet Magnolia Manor, which logically housed the kitchen. Babette scurried after him, like a good Southern hostess. Soon we heard sounds of the refrigerator opening and dishes clattering. We probably had a good ten minutes, because Babette's kitchen contained lots of food options.

I clutched Annabelle's hand. "Oh, I'm so sorry! I never dreamed Shorty would drive all the way here to crash our party."

The squeeze against my palm felt weak, a gesture that wasn't quite sincere. "It's okay, Ev. I love Shorty, from the bottom of my ballet flats to the tips of my Number 7WV Nutmeg colored hair, courtesy of Hannah down at the Bristle n' Blush. But the way he goes on and on about the fun you two have solving your cases...well, I just wanted, for once, to experience it first hand."

The squeeze grew tighter, pushing my fingers closer together. It didn't hurt, but Annabelle got the point across. "As I mentioned, one of my childhood heroes was Nancy Drew. For a few moments there, I felt just like her. You know? But now that Shorty's here, you'll go off with him and catch the murderer. And I'll play the supportive fiancée and friend, cheering you on." She let go of my hand and pushed the air out of her lungs, flopping down on the couch.

"Hey there, my little rhubarb pie! Why, ya' look a little out of sorts—I know how ya' feel! Chasin' crooks makes ya' plumb wore out." He sat on the couch and took Annabelle's hand, balancing a plate stacked with food with the other. "So, catch me up on the case, everybody! What'd I miss?" He dropped her hand to concentrate on his snack.

Babette appeared in the doorway. "Uh, I've got to make a run to the store—we don't have as much food as I'd hoped...I mean, thought. Shorty has requested gumbo, and I think it's a good idea. That's a dish that will feed a large group of people—or a small group including someone with an appetite the size of Maurepas Swamp. Let's go, Marcel!"

For once Babette's husband hadn't tuned in to her psychic vibes. He'd fixed his eyes on the new guest, in awe of someone who could eat him out of house and home. "Uh, coming, chérie. It was nice to meet you, Monsieur *Shor-tee*. I hope to see you soon. Goodbye, ladies."

Marcel's astonishment flew over my PI's head. "Mmm-mmm! That Miss Babette sure is a good cook! Honey pot, we need t'get some uh her recipes, after we solve this case. Ya' ladies can go over what ya'll know, while the *Boo-vee-yays* are grocery shoppin'. Doc, ya' wanna go first?"

I didn't time myself, but I spoke for less than five minutes while Shorty frowned and nodded his head.

"Ya'll don't have much yet, but that's okay. An' ya'll found a white board—good, good." My PI deposited his empty plate on the coffee table, then gestured toward the board. "We got five suspects, plus this kitchen couple. My little bread puddin's gonna be lookin' up all these people, right Puddin'?"

We trained our eyes on Puddin'.

"Hmm? Oh, sure. I could do that, just like I always do. But what if we let Ethan take care of all that? He always finds out the good stuff, anyway. All I dig up is articles in the society pages and editorials." Shorty held her left hand loosely between them, but her right hand was free to play with the fringe on the arm of the couch. She held the tassels flat in her hand, running her thumb over them in a caressing manner.

Shorty pulled her hand to his lips, planting a loud kiss just below the knuckles. "Oh, Honeybun! But yer really good at research, an' it'd really help us out. Wouldn't it, Doc? Ethan might miss somethin', so we really need ya' t'do yore research too. Okay, Sugar Buttons?"

What the heck was a sugar button? Some sort of candy, maybe? "You know, Shorty, I think Ethan can handle the research—how about we bring Annabelle into the interview process? Let her tag along with me this afternoon while we interview Jacqueline. Babette and Elizabeth want to go too, so I think it would work well. What do you say?"

"Awww, Annabelle don't have any interest in getting' up close an' personal with a killer, do ya', my little petite praline?"

Yeah, that nickname was the absolute worst by far. And why didn't Shorty just pick one and use it all the time? Wasn't that what most couples did? My brain shifted into overdrive as it accessed my memories prior to my move back to Graisseville. Yes, Doug only had one nickname for me, *Mare*.

Originally, it had been *Marion the Librarian*. Doug and I had met in a library on the Louisiana Tech campus. After a couple months of dating he'd confessed his attraction to librarians. "I think it goes back to my sophomore year in high school. I'd been cast in the play 'The Music Man'. And no, I'm not a great singer or anything—but they needed warm male bodies for the ensemble. Anyway, I had to be at every rehearsal, so I'd seen the play more times than I could count. And I don't know what it was, Evangeline, but that librarian took my breath away. Maybe it was her green cardigan and matching plaid skirt. Maybe it was her tortoise shell cat's eye glasses. But that young lady made my heart skip a beat—I couldn't get her out of my mind!"

In college, my husband tried to pick up a couple of library aids, until security kicked him out. That was how he ended up in my library. It was the smallest of them all, and the quietest, which was why I frequented it. And it contained the only security team who hadn't banned Doug from the premises. God works in mysterious ways.

"Women who wear glasses are incredibly sexy. At least, I think so."

My junior year, the week of spring finals, and I had no time for romance. Who did this guy think he was? His voice was deep and husky, which probably meant he was pretty cute. No, I had enough going on in my life. My lips pressed into a thin line, complimenting my furrowed eyebrows. Squaring my shoulders toward the voice, I prepared to unleash the full effect of my irritation.

Oh, those eyes!

My face disobeyed the order to register annoyance. Hmmm, maybe I *did* have enough time for romance. But was this guy actually flirting with me? This guy, with the smoky gray eyes and curly hair the color of a dark moonless night? My heart skipped a beat, and my eyebrows and mouth scurried to regroup. Unfortunately, my face didn't have much experience changing looks so quickly. My eyebrows arched as my jaw dropped slightly. Nope, not the sweet, sexy look my brain had ordered up. My face resembled those teenage girls in slasher movies just before they're ...well...slashed.

"Oh, I'm sorry! I didn't mean to scare you! Hey, I'll just leave you alone."

The only man who'd ever told me glasses were sexy prepared for a hasty retreat. His eyes widened considerably, then softened. They weren't smoky, really, more like the color of my Darjeeling tea—charcoal made lighter with two teaspoons of milk.

How tall was this guy? I studied the young man, pushing up my glasses for a clearer perspective.

My would-be suitor towered over me. The look on his face reminded me of my dog, friendly but hopeful for a kind word. The guy ran his hand through the most beautiful curly waves. His nervousness relaxed me, and I felt a smile sneak onto my face. My breath slowed and my grin settled into my face like a warm blanket. Normally, new people made me nervous, and boys doubly so.

After Doug's confession for his obsession with librarians, and admitting he'd been kicked out of almost all the libraries on campus, I took another look at my boyfriend. Persistent or obsessive? A believer in romance or a stalker? Fortunately for me, Doug was the former and not the latter. And my nickname *Marion the Librarian* shortened to *Marion*, then to *Mare*. And no, I couldn't remember a time he'd ever compared me to baked goods.

"Ev, did you hear me? I said it's okay. I'm happy to do the research." Except she clearly wasn't. Shorty had dated some of the most passive aggressive women residing in East Baton Rouge Parish, but he couldn't recognize the attitude if it climbed up on his shoulder and smacked him in the back of his head. Should I say something? Maybe I should stay out of it? Who were we kidding? I couldn't keep my mouth shut.

"Shorty, I left something in the car—could you help me get it out?"

My PI couldn't keep his eyes off Annabelle—he'd missed that girl something awful. "Can't it wait, Doc? Say, when's these interviews? We need t'be gettin' ready for 'em. Hey, can one o' ya'll sweet ladies call Miss Babette, an' remind her t'get my orange soda? These *Vee-Are-Bee-Oh*'s include all the drinks an' food, right?"

Lord, please put a rush on that two ton order of patience? *On second thought, just send whatever You've got in stock.* "No, Shorty, VRBO's don't include food and drink. Marcel and Babette feeding us a payment for working the case. However, as much as you eat, we should exclude yours . They're small business owners, not big corporation CEO's. Why don't you and I go right now and get that fridge stocked with all your favorites? Let's go!"

Had I grown a second head? A quick pat down of both shoulders assured me I hadn't. And yet Shorty continued to stare at me with bug eyes and open mouth. "Doc, I jus' got here! Besides, muh punkin' bread an' me can go take care of all my snacks an' drinks. Now how many bedrooms do we got here? Ya'll know I'm a gentleman, an' I won't be takin' up no bedroom for a lady. I'll be mighty happy here on the couch." So certain was Shorty of his chivalry, he began measuring his new sleeping arrangements. He motioned Annabelle off his proposed bed and laid down. Boots on one arm and head on the other, it was a tight fit. As much as he squirmed and wriggled, he couldn't squeeze his six foot frame on a five foot eight-inch couch. Thank goodness Babette wasn't around! I'd probably learn all sorts of new French phrases if she'd witnessed my friend's Ariat boots sliding up and down her furniture.

"Shorty, there are three bedrooms, and one has twin beds. Elizabeth and I can take that one, Annabelle can have the one with the queen, and you're welcome to the third. That room is the master with its own bathroom. We three women can share the other bathroom."

There is a saying, *some things are best kept secret.* Unfortunately for me, Shorty felt the groom shouldn't have any secrets from his best man (best woman?). Some secrets were harmless, like Annabelle's middle name was Harlene. Honestly, I'd keep that a secret too. Others were rather sweet, like Shorty was nervous about becoming a stepfather. Even though Annabelle's kids, Jeb and Caroline, were in their late twenties and adored him, he had concerns.

"Doc, what if Jeb comes tuh me for advice about women? What'm I gonna say? I never was serious about any girl, 'til I met Annabelle. I'm bound t'give him all sorts o'bad advice, real bad advice. An' Caroline has kids! What if she asks muh opinions on what kinda diapers t'buy! Or what if she wants me t'tell her if she should spank her kids? Why, I don't got any kids uh my own, I don't know what t'tell her."

My distracted friend didn't notice the chuckles escaping my throat, and I turned them into coughs. "Shorty, Jeb has a pretty serious girlfriend, doesn't he? I don't think he's going to ask you for any dating advice. And I'm pretty sure Caroline's kids are in school, so she won't need any suggestions about diapers. And I'd bet she and her husband have their discipline system down, so I think you're off the hook about that. Annabelle's kids are all grown up! Just love their mother, and take good care of her. Love the grandkids you have now, and the ones you're going to get in the future. And most of all, pray for them all, every day. That's all you need to do, I p romise."

But some secrets I honestly didn't need to know. Maybe that was why, on the day Shorty decided to confess another secret, my mind couldn't wrap around what he was trying to tell me. "Doc, I jus' wanna let ya' know, Annabelle an' I are gonna wait 'til we're married."

"Uh, wait to do what?" To be fair, I was trying to open a jar of pickles, and the jar was winning. These were the times I missed Doug the most, and the memories of my husband being in the next room to solve my problems clouded my brain so it couldn't see the obvious.

"Doc, *ya' know*. We've never, uh, ya' know, all the time we're datin'. So it jus' makes sense t'keep waitin'. We talked tuh the preacher, an' it's all spelled out there in the Bible. Might as well start out our marriage doin' what the Good Book says, right?"

I'd pulled out a butter knife, tapping lightly around the edges, just like my mother taught me. Had that ever worked when she'd tried it? No, I remembered her yelling at my father, "Skeeter! Come in here and open this jar! Please!" Dad would stop whatever he was doing and answer his summons to the kitchen. Yet my mother always considered the butter knife step two of her process. Why mess with tradition?

"Never did *what* all the time you were dating?" Shorty had discussed taking Annabelle to The Angola Prison Rodeo shortly after they started going out. The event, staged at the Louisiana State Penitentiary, is the longest running prison rodeo in the United States. Its slogan is "the wildest show in the South," so Shorty thought it was right up Annabelle's alley. Several prisoner organizations sell food at the concession stands, using family recipes. There's also an arts and crafts festival during the rodeo, where prisoners make handmade items to sell. I'd convinced Shorty to hold off on the rodeo, until they'd known each other a while. They'd never gone to the big event while they were dating—maybe they'd decided to wait until they were married? And why wouldn't the pickle lid budge?

"Doc, ya' ain't makin' this easy! We ain't gonna get *up close an' personal* until our weddin' night!"

The pickle jar might have won the battle, but I was determined to win the war...with my secret weapon of course. "Here! Open this jar! Please!" Goodness, I even sounded like Mother.

With a *pop!* Shorty had the jar open in a flat three seconds. "Here ya' go." He handed me the jar and lid, then crossed his arms and waited for my brain to catch up to the conversation.

We stood facing each other, my heart slowing down as my frustration melted into the air. Shorty's words replayed in my head, and my brain processed his meaning, now that I'd solved the problem of the stubborn pickle jar. The burning began on the tips of my ears, moving towards my mouth to plaster my face with one giant red blanket of embarrassment.

"Oh! Well, uh, good for you. Yes, good for you, then. Uh, care for a pickle?"

All that to say the entire room already knew Shorty and Annabelle wouldn't share a bedroom. Yes, all of us, because of course I'd confessed my secret to Elizabeth. What are best friends for?

"Really, Ev? Well, good for them! Especially in this day and age. But, oh, honey! What an embarrassing conversation! How red did you turn?"

"I couldn't really tell, but it felt like someone had turned up the thermostat a good ten degrees. But I had to tell you, of course. You need to share in my discomfort."

After finalizing the sleeping arrangements, I'd convinced Shorty to drive my car around the block with me. "It started making a funny sound, right as we drove through Metairie, and I'm not sure what it is." Why hadn't I started with a problem that only my friend could fix? A lesson learned for next time.

Shorty braked at the stop sign. "I'm not hearin' anythin' strange soundin', Doc. Are ya' sure ya' heard a funny sound? Mebbe it was the music ya' were listenin' to—those crazy rock an' rollers make some weird music."

I chose to ignore a potential discussion on whether Lily Rose qualified as a *rock an' roller*. "There's nothing wrong with my car. I need to talk to you about Annabelle. She wants to be more involved in our cases, take on tasks other than doing research."

Shorty turned right and pulled into the Big E-Z Gas Station. "Doc, she's muh *fee-awnce-say*! I think I'd know if she wanted t'be workin' on our cases." His words spoke confidence, but it hadn't traveled to his eyes.

"Well, I think she's been trying to tell you that for a while, and earlier she mentioned something about letting Ethan take the research, but you shot her down. I say let's have her come along to the interview this afternoon, okay?"

The storm in his eyes told me Shorty didn't love the idea of his fiancée rubbing elbows with a potential killer. Maybe try a different approach?

"Look at it this way. Babette is friends with this Jacqueline Dubois. And it was her party! I can't imagine she's the killer. And it will make Annabelle feel included. You know her child-hood hero is Nancy Drew, right?"

The storm remained, but I got a small nod. "Of course I knew that, Doc. 'Member I got her that buncha old Nancy Drew books for our anniversary?"

"Okay, then! Let her play detective, under our watchful eye. If things get too serious, then we'll take her out of the game. Okay?"

Clouds passed, leaving a tiny ray of light in Shorty's eyes. "That sounds all right. Anything else, while ya' got me all tuh yoreself?"

Actually, there was. "Since I took on this case with Eliza-beth and Annabelle, I'd like to be the lead on it, instead of us being equals. And I think Annabelle would feel more at ease if her friend was in charge, not her fiancé. In fact, I'd like you to remain in the background, more as a consultant. After all, this is a girls' weekend, not a Shorty and Ev weekend."

My Bronco lurched forward as it fell into drive. I'd shown my PI the back seat—how would he react? Would he try to make the best of it, or sulk?

"Yeah, sure, sure, Doc. Iffen that's what ya'll want, I'll do it. An' I think it'll be fun t'see ya'll ladies be detectives an' all, tryin' t'solve the case. Tell ya' what! I'll be yore *pro-fess-orr*, how's that? Yeah, I'll hang back, observe ya'll, an' iffen ya'll need my help I'll be right there. Yeah, this is gonna be lots o'fun!"

Something told me this case would be anything but that. I chose to keep my opinions to myself, for once. We pulled into the driveway and Shorty headed for the door. As I caught up with my nimble PI I knew he'd decided to make the best of the situation.

"Good news, everyone! Ev's gonna take the lead on this case, an' Imma jus' gonna be a *pro-fess-orr*. Ya' know, a teacher. Yeah, all of ya'll are gonna work the case. I'll jus' sit back, keep my trap shut, an' iffen ya'll need me I'll be right here. My sweet honey lemon cake, Imma gonna go back out an' get my suitcase. Then ya' can show me tuh my room."

As my PI hopped back outside Annabelle grabbed my arm. "Ev, I don't know how you managed that, but thank you. And while you're on a roll, could you convince Shorty to stop comparing me to confections and pastries?"

CHAPTER 6

Changing Shorty's nicknaming habit would have to wait—we had an interview in an hour with Jacqueline Dubois. Despite my urging, The Bouviers returned with enough food to feed an army—or four women, one man, and one man with the appetite of an army.

As the leader, I did my best to, well, lead. And Shorty did his best to, well, keep his mouth shut. Where should I begin? I started with simple instructions. "How about all of you sit round the kitchen table and make a list of questions to ask both Jacqueline and Jean? Shorty and I will go in the living room and get Ethan started on the internet search."

Ethan hadn't gone back to LSU yet, so he should have time to help us. He was about to begin his last semester in college, which meant interviewing for a job and completing his senior portfolio. This might be our last chance to have his help in solving a case, at least until he graduated in May.

"Hey, Ev, hey Mr. Shorty! Don't mind the noise—I'm in Colorado skiing with my fraternity buddies. We're in the lodge having some uh...um...some uh, *hot chocolate*."

What my cousin was or wasn't drinking while on vacation wasn't my concern, so I skipped over his obvious lie. "Sorry to bother you, Ethan, but we just picked up another case. Do you have time to do some research on your vacation?"

Most twenty-something men skiing with their friends would say *no ma'am*, but Ethan and I shared two Bergeron family traits: a desire to help others, and a love of puzzles. Crime solving checked both boxes. "Definitely, Ev! But I'd better wait a while until, uh, I've finished this, um, *hot chocolate.*"

Shorty's laughter filled Sweet Magnolia Manor. "Son, have one o' those *hot chaw-kuh-lets* for me, will ya'? Miss Ev'll send ya' what ya' need. Ya'll have fun now!"

My PI couldn't stop chuckling. "Oh, Doc! T'be young an' carefree again. I'll tell ya', those were the days. Not a care in the world! Aw, well, back tuh bizness. Yer gonna get that tuh Ethan, right?" Shorty leaned into the back of the couch, arms behind his head, obviously thinking about his younger days. He still couldn't stop chuckling.

"Yes, I'm doing that right now, instead of reminiscing about my youth. We've got Jacqueline the party host, Jean the ex-boyfriend, Clifford the bodyguard, the sheriff, and Beatrice the sister-in-law. How about I see if Ethan can scare up a guest list for the Mardi Gras party?"

My PI had stopped giggling, but his eyes remained fixed on his youth, hazy, as they replayed the past. "Yeah, sure." He settled back into the couch, headed back down Memory Lane.

"Oh, and I'll ask for a staff list, if he can find that too." I kicked an Ariat. "Hey! You're not playing professor right now.

I need you in the game. Is there anything else Ethan should get?"

A grunt from the couch signaled a return to Reality Road. "See if he can find anything out there on the *inner-net* 'bout any stories talkin' up the murder. Ya' know, people who came tuh the party, got a supper *an'* a show, an' put their stories out there for the world t'see. Who knows? We might even get lucky with some photos, or even some video."

When Shorty focused, he was pretty handy to have around. "Yes, I think Ethan looks for that, anyway. But I'll remind him, because I'm pretty sure we won't get any help from the sheriff or his people. You know, since it's an active investigation."

Another round of chuckles, only they headed toward me. "Yeah, Doc. The last time we worked an active case, that sheriff was sweet on ya'. We ain't gonna have that luck this time. Unless..." He sat up, his shoulder blades actually leaving the comfort of the couch. "Hmmm, ya' know, with some lipstick an' a slinky dress..." Shorty stood up and circled me, studying every aspect. "Yeah, yeah, ya' know, I haven't paid attention lately, cuz I'm taken an' all, but yer lookin' pretty good nowadays. Yer payin' more attention tuh yore clothes, an' ya' got a haircut, didn't ya'?" He stopped in front of me, left arm crossed over his chest and the right propping his hand under his chin. "Look, it's Mardi Gras—people go all kinds o' crazy. Besides, Doc, how serious are ya' about Sheriff Dupre? I mean, iffen ya' flirted a bit with this Sheriff Ray, would the other sheriff be upset? Cuz I don't wanna mess up what we got right now, with him sendin' us cases an' all cuz he's sweet on ya'."

"Shorty, I really don't feel comfortable flirting with one of our suspects, just to gain access to the case records. And yes,

I think Mitch would be upset. I mean, I would be, if he flirted with some suspect to get something he wanted."

My PI flopped back down on the couch. "Aw, he'd never do that, Doc! That's against their rules—they can't flirt with suspects. Not until they're done with the case, anyway."

"Oh good, that makes me feel so much better. I'm so glad to know Mitch isn't flirting with any suspects on *active cases*—just the ones he's already solved."

Thunk! Those Ariat boots landed on the Williams Sonoma acacia wood coffee table, retail value: more than a month of Shorty's military pension. I cast a frown in his direction and he dropped his boots to the hand tufted chevron rug. I grimaced, but he ignored me. Both items were probably cast offs from Babette's home, but that didn't make them any less pricey.

"By the way, Shorty, this plan of yours that has me flirting with a suspect, it just might be the worst idea you've ever had."

Shorty checked his phone. "Nah, that ain't true, Doc. I've had plenty o'bad ideas. Jus' ask Annabelle."

My team peeked into the living room. "It's okay, guys—we can join them. Shorty and Ev act like this all the time. Really, it's okay." Was that Annabelle or Elizabeth who reassured everyone? Honestly, it could have been either.

Annabelle took the lead. "We did our best, Ev, we really did. But we honestly have no idea what we're doing." She paused as her fiancé sat up. He settled back into the contours of the couch, remembering his promises of silence. He even closed his eyes, pretending disinterest.

"Uh, we did our best. And this is what we've got, with Jacqueline. We thought we'd start out by asking her who she thinks poisoned Chantilly. Then we'll ask where she was when the murder, um, when the victim..." Annabelle took a breath. "We'll ask where she was when Chantilly expired."

Shorty's eyes creased, desperate to stay shut. His eyes succeeded, but his mouth failed—a horse snort escaped. We waited, certain he couldn't help himself, but he stayed strong. Just a wave of his hand, signaling his fiancée could continue. "Uh, we also want to question Jacqueline about her knowledge of poison. You know, see if she has any experience in, well, *poisoning*." Annabelle spoke this last remark in a whisper, betraying her lack of confidence.

Before the professor could comment, I jumped in. "Good! That's really good, everyone. I'm so proud of you, of *all* of you! These are wonderful questions, and we want to know the answers to every single one of them. But I'd like to make a suggestion." I had to catch my breath—my gushing took most of the air in my lungs, and the living room had started to spin.

Shorty's left eye slid open. "Yeah, all those questions are pretty good n' all. But *I* got a question: how're ya'll gonna ask this lady about how many people she's poisoned? I mean, she's not gonna be real keen on tellin' ya'll much." To my relief, the eye fluttered shut. "In all my experience as an *in-ves-tuh-gate-tor*, I've never had no one confess tuh crimes nobody's accused 'em of. But mebbe that's jus' me. Mebbe ya'll have better luck."

Annabelle slammed her notebook against her thigh. "Oh, he's right! I'm a horrible private investigator! Ev, just put me back on research. That's what I'm best at."

Her sniffles woke up both Shorty's eyes. "Butter Cream, don't cry! Yer doin' real good. I didn't mean nothin' by that, honest!" His eyes jumped toward me. "Doc, tell her!"

Nope, this wasn't going to be a fun case. "Annabelle, Shorty's right. These are all great questions. You're definitely on the right track. How about this? We'll all go back in the kitchen and take another go at them, just the questions for Jacqueline. Shorty, you stay in here and work out the questions for your interview with Jean."

Shorty stood up, moving his boots toward the kitchen. "Yeah, okay, that's good. But can I work in the kitchen? It's closer to the food."

In a perfect world we'd have nailed down all the strategies and questions for both suspects before the interviews. But we weren't living in a perfect world. In the world I lived in, we had less than forty minutes.

Our preparation wasn't on the level of Jane Marple, but honestly it never was. Shorty would eat tofu before he'd write up a list of questions for an interview, including the one with Jean Breaux. No, he'd fly by the seat of his pants, like he always did. Poor Marcel! He would expect an investigator extraordinaire, by French standards. Or by New Orleans' standards, anyway. At least he'd have an entertaining experience.

The theme from *Blue Bloods* interrupted my thoughts. "Hey, Ev! I heard you got a case. Wow, that's fantastic!"

How in the world did Mitch know about my new murder investigation? My heart beat more quickly at his ring tone...was it the thought of Mitch, or Tom Selleck? Yes, I thought he was pretty great, well both were pretty great. But I was excited he was calling me. Mitch, not Tom. When Mitch started our conversation with the words, *I heard you got a case*, my first thought was...*do you want in?* Do you want to take over my case, and keep me from spreading my wings?

"Thanks, I appreciate that. But how in the world...?"

"Oh, well, Nate stopped by the coffee shop in Graisseville, on his way to work. I think it was the barista...maybe a customer? Anyway, someone named *Maggie* mentioned your case to him, and he passed it on to the receptionist at the Zachary substation, who is friends with Rebecca, my assistant. And, well, she knows we've had a few meals together. I hope that's okay, but she mentioned it to me. So I wanted to call. Plus, I missed your voice."

Of course it was okay. I mean, I guess it was okay. How did my secret get out? Great! Now my brother knew? Oh boy, that would cause a whole other string of telephone calls.

"Well yes, Mitch, it's fine. I'm just surprised to hear your voice. Because last time we spoke, we weren't going to talk again until I got back to Graisseville."

Yes, I really needed to know the answer to my next question. "And, how did you leave this with Nate? Was he angry or happy I had a case in New Orleans? Does he know we've been going out? How does he feel about it? Is he upset I haven't told him yet?"

I really needed to tell Nate about my *quite a few* dates with Mitch. *Happy Mardi Gras, brother! And one more thing...I'm dating your boss. Have some King Cake!* Yeah, that wasn't a conversation I'd made room for in my life.

"Ev, is it okay that I know about the case? I really don't want to intrude on your girls' weekend. I just wanted to call and tell you...well, that I'm thinking about you. And I'm sorry about Nate getting involved—I really don't think he knows we're...uh, whatever we're doing. Are we dating? I'm never really sure with you."

Was it the small town vibe? Or was I having cold feet? I decided it was the small town thing. I'd never liked people in my business. "No, it's fine. I should have told Nate what's going on with us. You know, that we're dating. I'm so sorry, Mitch. Honestly, I just didn't want to get into all that family drama." Mitch's father had passed, so he only had his mother and his twin brother, Mike. To my knowledge, he'd never endured an interrogation disguised as a meal. He found the weekly examinations of my life choices charming. Of course he'd only met my brother, who worked for him.

No, he just had Mama Dupre, who called the newspaper and notified the deacons at Lafayette First Baptist when either of her boys came to visit. Or, heaven forbid, both the boys came home at the same time. God bless her, other than the alert a Dupre boy had returned home, she made sure there was no drama hitting the gossip grapevine.

Nope, it was just my family, with all their protectiveness and their public drama. Yep, just my father and my brother trying to take care of me, and making sure the entire village applauded their sacrifice. I could hear their words.

First my brother. "Seriously, Ev? You've got my boss interested in you? Yeah, he's an actual normal guy, but still..."

He'd shake his head side to side, mostly for effect. "Let's review your recent dating history since Doug passed. The first three years you swore off all men. That was a good decision."

Good? Really, Nate? Thanks to my kid brother and his stories of Doug's sainthood, men had sworn off me initially.

But that was okay, because I had two kids to mother. And yet, his version irritated the fire out of me.

"But then, suddenly, you became interested in, what? A drug dealer? What were you thinking, Sis?"

What was I thinking? The police hadn't accused Josh Fairchild of anything. He was nice, polite, actually a pretty cute guy. And yet, maybe a drug dealer. Well, accused of being a drug dealer. Yes, okay, the jury eventually convicted him of dealing drugs. Oh, and possibly laundering money, but the police could never prove that. Okay, well maybe they did—I hadn't kept up with Josh. All right, never mind—forget Josh Fairchild! I should focus on Bachelor #2—Cayenne Cormier.

Nate had never known about him, because Cay was never serious. I'd hoped he might be...or maybe I didn't? That didn't matter, because he loved his restaurant more than he loved...I mean, liked me. And, according to Shorty, he'd found someone else. Wow! That stung my pride. Which brought me to Bachelor #3: Mitchell Dupre.

"Ev? Did you hear me? I just want to help. If you need anything, please let me know. Have a wonderful girls' weekend, okay? Uh, well, I'll let you go."

Yep, definitely the best of the bunch.

"Thanks, Mitch. I appreciate that. Seriously, I will let you know if I need you. I promise." Yes, I heard it. The need, the desire, really. Men always had that same purpose. Okay, I sounded way too harsh but...well, anyway...I was just going to say it. Men want to fix things. But Mitch was my boyfriend, or my guy friend, anyway — I didn't need him to fix anything.

My bestie Elizabeth would tell me I was being way too difficult. Well, she was still married to her best friend. Cliff hadn't died and left her alone.

I could never forget the convicted felon sitting on death row because he murdered my soulmate. The police knew he'd murdered several people before Doug, but they couldn't prove it. So don't talk to me about love and losing. Oh, and by the way...Rocky Ragusa had never apologized for killing my husband and ruining my life. But I couldn't think about that. I had this other case to solve.

Thank You, Lord, for saving my hysterics until after Mitch had ended the call. He has enough to deal with in his life—he doesn't need my baggage too.

CHAPTER 7

W e made it to Jacqueline's house with five minutes to spare, despite the hordes of Fat Tuesday tourists. I'd conducted a couple of interviews without Shorty, but it was rare. And when I did, there was no one around to notice when I screwed up, or forgot something. Well, the suspect, but not my good friends and family. My heart thumped every time I reviewed that truth. What did my favorite professor say when I told him I wanted to teach? "Ev, fake it until you make it. The stronger your voice, the more authority you project. And the more authority you convey, the more respect you'll receive. Don't let your students see your fear." Did that apply to best friends and family? And what about suspects?

"Ev, honey? You all right? We have a couple of minutes—why don't we pray?"

"Elizabeth, that's a wonderful idea! Why don't you lead?" Thirty seconds later my heart slowed and my jagged breaths smoothed out. Peace filled my soul. I opened my door and my team followed me up the steps to Jacqueline's front door. Who had seventeen steps up a hill to their front door? My jagged breaths and pounding heart returned, but not from fear.

"Let's all pause for a minute or more before we ring the doorbell." Oh, Ev, why hadn't you taken some time and started an exercise program? After I solved the case, for sure!

My companions nodded their heads—they weren't in much better shape. Only Babette breathed without gasping, her temples absent of shiny beads of sweat. I leaned in for a closer look. Nope, not a drip of perspiration. Even Babette's smile radiated with health and energy. Maybe I should start a village walking group at the park?

"Everyone have their breath back? Good. We're going in." I stepped forward and pressed the doorbell to the right of the dark green door, almost taking out the plaster of Paris duck in the corner. I glanced at the faux concrete fowl, which sported a jester hat and purple beads. Already Jacqueline Dubois annoyed me.

"Good afternoon, Mrs. Bouvier, ladies. Please come in—Mrs. Dubois is waiting for you." The maid, complete with starched white apron and matching cap, stepped back as she widened the opening for us. Or was she the housekeeper? Aunt Eula Mae Fontenot was the richest person I'd ever visited, and she only had a cleaning lady who also cooked her supper. Elizabeth was probably the next richest, or Lila Trahan, and they only had cleaning ladies. They had to cook their own meals. A forced whisper snaked into my ear. "Ev! Stop daydreaming and get inside."

As we stepped through the door my mind made notes. Keep your eyes peeled, Ev, and try to ignore the exploded Mardi Gras store strewn about Jacqueline's home. Masks and beads and harlequins peeped out of every orifice in the home.

Back to the case, Ev. Look for a maid or butler blending into the background. And just how rich was Jacqueline? Judging from her foyer—the size of my kitchen and living room combined—I'd say spectacularly wealthy. Glancing at her double winding staircase I had to wonder...had Jacqueline slid down the banisters? I certainly would have, or at least considered it.

"Hello, Babette! It's so good to see you. I hate that it's under these circumstances. Please come in—I've got coffee and beignets on the table." The almost thirty year old glanced at the dining room table, which featured a vase of fresh flowers upon a pearl linen tablecloth. Just in front of the Baccarat crystal vase, a silver tray held a matching coffee pot and five pearl cups with saucers. Another silver tray, more rectangular than the coffee one, guarded a stack of beignets. If Shorty got wind of what he'd missed, I'd never hear the end of it. The hill of fried paradise rivaled the fire ant mound in my backyard.

Jacqueline's eyelids lowered just a hair, following the edges of her mouth as they slid toward the floor. "Mimi! I told you to purchase beignets from Café du Monde. Where'd you get these fried miseries?"

Sorrowful eyes gazed upon our group—Mimi owed the entire room an apology. In our hostess' eyes, anyway. "I'm sorry, ma'am! But as it's Mardi Gras, the line for Café du Monde was around the building. And I had to run back to the house and meet the delivery boy from the pharmacy. So I didn't have time to go back downtown and get the beignets. I also had to polish the silver and air out the curtains. As you always say, ma'am, a fresh year means a fresh house."

Who says that? My mother probably had, at some point, until she gave birth to Mad. After my sister's arrival, Mother had given up several housekeeping details, like ironing all the sheets and towels and my father's work pants and white coats. Mother could have used a Mimi, most definitely. But the veterinarian and bank teller's salaries hadn't made that possible.

If Mimi had been holding a dish towel, it would be completely dry. Her hands had reddened from all the wringing throughout her speech. "And so, Mrs. Dubois, I'm sorry to say I had to purchase the beignets from the grocery store...ma'am."

Could I help poor Mimi? It was worth a try. "Mrs. Dubois, really, it's not a problem. Babette's been feeding us so well, we shouldn't be consuming any more calories. If it's alright with you, I'll just take a cup of coffee, black. Ladies?"

My team recited their appreciation with the coffee orders, and a grateful Mimi leaped forward to fulfill their requests. I stole a look at Jacqueline. Her eyelids hadn't moved, but she'd parked her mouth in its regular spot. She was still angry with Mimi, but she'd evicted the lines on her face. No doubt her smooth unblemished skin resulted from some sort of plastic surgery, and her doctor had cautioned against frowns and glares. My instinct concluded Jacqueline Dubois had a hard time following her doctor's orders. And why would a twenty-eight year old need plastic surgery?

"All right. Mimi, remove the...*food*. I'm not going to dignify their presence by calling them beignets. Then you can finish your duties and start supper. Don't forget I have Mrs.

Romero's visitation this evening at six—I'll dine when I return."

Mimi shot me a glance of gratitude, which was all she could squeeze in as she fled the room. I didn't blame her—something told me no one wanted to be on Jacqueline Dubois' bad side.

Our hostess stirred her coffee. "I'd really hoped Mimi would work out. She has excellent references." Jacqueline raised her cup to her lips. "Good help is so hard to find. Babette, if you hear of anyone bragging about their housekeeper, please let me know. I'm going to have to steal another one."

It was official...I'd upgraded my opinion of Jacqueline DuBois from annoying to downright unpleasant. Or had I downgraded my opinion?

"Ev? Are you ready?" All eyes were on me, so I pulled out my notebook and teal pen. Each investigation took its own twists and turns, but my resources and tools stayed consistent. Thank goodness for that.

"Once again, Mrs. Dubois, thank you for taking the time to speak with us. As Babette explained on the phone, my colleague and I consult with law enforcement from time to time. We've solved a few cases, most of which have stumped the authorities. The Bouviers want us to ask a few questions and do a little digging, for their own peace of mind. Don't worry—you're not under suspicion." My smile did little to melt the frosty exterior of Jacqueline's features. If I had thawed her attitude though, would it drip down her face, like a melting snowcap?

"I can tell you what I shared with the Orleans Parish detectives." Our hostess settled into her dining room chair, a white leather high-backed piece of elegance costing more than my refrigerator. It did pair nicely with the white marble dining table. How did I know the linen tablecloth covered white marble? Why, I'd peeked, of course, during Jacqueline's rage against beignets purchased at the grocery store.

I rearranged my body on the chair, trying desperately to balance my notebook and pen. Never mind, my coffee—I was terrified of spilling it on either the tablecloth or the chair. And neither were ideal locations. "All right, let's start with the party. Did you spend any time with Chantilly? How was her demeanor? Did she seem nervous or upset?"

Jacqueline sipped her coffee—the woman had never spilled a single drop or crumb in her entire life. How could she have so much white in her home if she did? "Oh, no, I hardly saw Chantilly! In case you've forgotten, I was the hostess. I spent my time flitting from guest to guest, checking on the food. I couldn't spend much time with Chantilly."

Babette's cup remained on the table, a wisp of steam rising. "Yes, she's right, Evangeline. Jacqueline was the perfect hostess! I didn't see her though, as the guests arrived. In the past, when the emcee announced the names, Jacqueline rushed forward and greeted them. But I'm sure she was busy with the food, and it was excellent, as always. Yes, Jacqueline spent a great deal of time in the kitchen perfecting the dishes and supervising the appetizer stations in the dining area."

"Appetizer...*stations*?" My brain tugged at my arm, demanding to know why I hadn't asked about guest announcing. I reminded my brain that, according to books and television, wealthy people arrived at events in limousines and fancy cars. They lounged on a red carpet, waiting for their names to be announced so they could step into the limelight.

Most of the parties I'd attended featured potluck meals with card games afterwards. Sometimes, as Doug and I walked through the front door, someone had yelled a "hi!" or maybe an "about time!". But there had never been someone in a tuxedo announcing our entrance. Hmmm, the next time I attend a party, I should suggest a guest announcer. Or was the person called an announcer for guests? And just how much did a tuxedo cost to rent?

"Hmph! Obviously you don't attend formal affairs, Dr. Delafose. At most parties, servers stroll about the venue, offering various appetizers and hors-d'oeuvres. But at my affairs, *my* guests indulge themselves with culinary works of art! Each station has a special theme, ranging from..."

Babette reached for her friend's arm. "Jacqueline, we don't have time today for you to explain the appetizer stations. But they were marvelous! Perhaps at a later date, you and I can meet again and discuss the success of your event? Despite Chantilly's unfortunate demise, of course."

Jacqueline took another sip, the corners of her mouth tightening. Was she upset Babette had cut her short, or angry Chantilly had cast a shadow on her otherwise spectacular event? The lines disappeared as she set down her cup. Her plastic surgeon should be proud. "Yes, of course, Babette, as you wish. But it was my best gala yet, wasn't it? Oh, why did Chantilly have to choose that evening to die?"

The outburst stunned all of us, but I recovered first. "Uh, yes, why indeed? So, uh, so inconvenient, I'm sure. Now Mrs. Dubois, you spent most of the evening checking the appetizer, um, stations—is that correct?"

Our hostess nodded as she pushed away her coffee. "I'd had my heart set on beignets! Oh, why do these things happen to me?"

No, Ev, don't say it—don't mention the obvious, that at least she's alive. Unlike her friend. "Yes, it is a disappointment, I'm sure. But back to our interview, if you'd be so kind. Did you spend the entire evening in the main area supervising the stations?"

Had Mimi left the window open? Where did that gust of wind come from? Oh, wait! That was Jacqueline. "You really don't know anything about parties, do you? No, I didn't spend the entire evening supervising appetizers! After making a couple of rounds to make sure everything met my superior standards, I spent the rest of the evening in the kitchen. My favorite sous chef called in sick, and I didn't want anyone else screwing up my kitchen, on the pretense of *assisting* me. No, I toiled in the kitchen all evening, until I heard the screams."

"Screams, Mrs. Dubois?"

A smaller gust blew out of Jacqueline's mouth, fluttering the calla lilies in the vase. A vase that, if sold, could pay my credit card balance in full. "Yes, screams, Dr. Delafose! I believe it's common practice that when a person falls to the ground, throwing up like a party girl, people react strongly. You know, with screaming and gasps of astonishment. A fainting here and there. Or so I've heard."

Jacqueline's contempt upgraded her to my list of people needing prayers. As in, *Lord Jesus, please keep me from smacking this person upside the head, because I know that's a sin. But You've got to meet halfway on this.* Or was she downgraded? The jury was still out on that one.

"All right then, moving on. When you arrived at the crime scene, what did you see?"

I'd learned to read our suspect's face by observing her mouth and eyes. The woman worked hard to keep her face free of creases, which resulted in a blank canvas. She hadn't mastered the art of shooing away her emotions from those two places, thank goodness. Jacqueline's eyes relaxed, and her mouth played Follow the Leader. "Jean…Jean Breaux was leaning over Chantilly, giving her chest compressions. No one wanted to touch those putrid foamy lips."

Babette rolled her eyes at me. "So Jean was next to Chantilly when she died? We were on the other side of the room, so I have no idea."

"Yes. Well, I guess so. I mean, he was close enough to realize she was dying and tried to revive her. You know what was strange, though? Her thug of a bodyguard, Clifford Benoit, was nowhere to be found. I mean, he never left her side, but maybe he'd gone to get real help. You know, like a doctor? He used to work for the New Orleans Mafia…I bet he still does."

In May 1994, the FBI arrested seventeen people, including Anthony Carollo, for racketeering, illegal gambling, and conspiracy. At the time Carollo was the undisputed boss, commanding respect within the other criminal families throughout the United States. According to the FBI, Carollo's arrest and subsequent death in 2007 ended organized crime in Louisiana. Most people didn't agree.

"In fact, it wouldn't surprise me if the sheriff's got his paws in the mafia. He was the first one on the scene of Beau Romero's death, and both those men were up to their ears in illegal activity. Sheriff Ray could have easily played with the crime scene—made it look like a natural death." Jacqueline gained a new interest in her neglected coffee cup, and refilled it with coffee and cream.

Tea was more my speed, not coffee, but I tolerated it in the name of Southern hospitality. After the third person asked me if I'd grown up in England, I'd learned to pour as much cream as humanly possible into my bitter cup of assimilation. Then I'd go home and placate my taste buds with a cup of lavender mint. Most times, two cups. As I'd gotten older, I had to give up the cream, which made my taste buds heave wrenching sobs of sorrow. As I swallowed sip after sip, I imagined the inside of my mouth filling with tears of protest. No doubt my vivid imagination made the coffee taste even wo rse.

Maybe this was a good time to break out the Southern hospitality, to shut down this line of questioning, to get Jacqueline off the defunct mafia and back on track? "Mrs. Dubois, this is a delicious cup of coffee. Could you tell me where you buy your beans?"

Jacqueline cocked her head to one side, like an owl studying, well, the stupidest bird on the planet. "They're flown in from Maui. That's in Hawaii, in case you didn't know. They're called Kopi Luwak, and they'll run you about $160 a pound."

So much for Southern hospitality. If my mother took the time to look down from Heaven, I hoped she recognized my efforts. More than likely, she was shaking her head, telling Saint Peter, "You know I tried, I really did."

Thank goodness for Babette. "Jacqueline, my dear friend, wasn't there a rumor about Chantilly giving up a baby for adoption? Do you know anything about that?"

How long did it take to stir two spoons of sugar and a drop of cream? "Oh, yes! I'd forgotten about that indiscretion, it was so long ago. I was only twelve, but my mother told me later. Yes, when Chantilly was twenty, or so, she left New Orleans to live with an aunt for about a year. Rumors flew, of course, and many people swore she was pregnant with the baby of a prominent government official. The gossip mill said it was a judge, but not a state or federal one. Just some local circuit or appellate judge. At any rate, he was twenty years older, at least, and married. Chantilly never mentioned a baby when she returned—just went on and on about how fabulous her aunt's house is, and all the fun she'd enjoyed. So who knows?"

Oh, the kitchen couple! In my excitement, I nearly spilled my cup of bitterness. Jacqueline risked a scolding from her plastic surgeon to hand me a full on glare. *Lord, this is really horrible, but if that glare could cause just a tiny wrinkle on Jacqueline's face, I wouldn't mind. Okay, yes, that was a horrible thing to pray—sorry!*

"Mrs. Dubois, did you invite a couple to your party that no one else knew? Babette, tell us about the man and woman at the party that you and Marcel saw. You said they stood outside the kitchen, even though Jacqueline and the staff asked them to move repeatedly. You said you'd never seen them before."

Babette put down her coffee. "Oh, yes! Marcel and I noticed a couple, in their mid-forties, perhaps. She was short, about five foot four, and he wasn't much taller—maybe five foot seven. They were both dressed in black and blended in with the crowd. She had light brown hair, while he was almost bald. The staff told them several times they were blocking the door to the kitchen, and I saw you escort them out of the kitchen."

Jacqueline stood up. "You're mistaken, Babette. I didn't throw anyone out of my kitchen. Mimi! These ladies are ready to leave. Come escort them to the door. Thank you for stopping by. Babette, I'm sure I'll see you at the visitation." I'd always wondered what the phrase *in a huff* meant exactly. After witnessing Jacqueline Dubois' exit, I had my answer.

My lungs and heart rejoiced as I strolled down the seventeen steps—going down was always so much easier. My cousin's healthier heart and lungs actually permitted her to speak.

"Well, Chantilly always said, 'you can take the girl out of the Louisiana swamps, but you can't take the swamps out of the girl.' Jacqueline married high class, but she didn't bring any into the marriage, that's for certain."

Babette's comment surprised me. "But I thought you and Jacqueline were old friends."

My cousin blew out a breath, rivaling our hostess. "Hmph! Marcel told us that woman's too wrapped up in herself. I should have listened. She married a man almost forty years her senior, and he left her everything, except good manners. New Orleans is really a small town that thinks it's a big city—we've got to stay on good terms with everyone to keep our businesses going. Jacqueline showed her true colors today. She's no friend of mine."

Babette stopped halfway down the mountain. Was she crazy? "What are you doing, Babette? We're practically to the car! You can't stop now." My eyes danced as my brain played visions of an air conditioned car and a pitcher of mint iced tea waiting patiently in the refrigerator. No doubt Shorty had eaten all the food, like the swarm of locust God sent to Egypt in Exodus 10. My PI had left the iced tea, of that I was certain—he hated any drink with a garnish. According to Shorty, if God wanted leaves and twigs floating in a drink, then He would have created it that way.

"Oh, don't worry, Evangeline, I'll be quick. I've got to ask Mimi something. I'll be right back. Here." She tossed the keys. "Start the car and get the air conditioning running. I'll just be a minute."

New Orleans in January was normally cool—usually around sixty-five degrees, plus or minus. But the humidity hit seventy-five percent or more. Air conditioning was a must. We gathered in Babette's Suburban, panting like puppies waiting for our owner to drive us home.

My cousin threw open the door, scaring all of us. "I've got it! And I did it without Jacqueline knowing that I've got it."

My father would say Babette was happier than a pig out in the sunshine. Her smile strung across her face from ear to ear. Had she cracked the case?

"Oh, Henri's going to be so excited! I got Mimi's phone number. Marcel and I have a friend who's been searching and searching for an innkeeper to run his bed and breakfast. I think Mimi will be perfect!"

CHAPTER 8

O n our drive home Babette chattered into her phone, telling Marcel all about Henri's new innkeeper. But I spent the time looking ahead to our next interview. Was it safe to let Shorty and Marcel talk to a suspect by themselves? After my meeting with Jacqueline, I doubted Shorty's ability to hold his own with high society. These people weren't everyday working people, like my PI. And they weren't college educated professionals, like me. These suspects moved about within a circle I'd only witnessed from afar. Not only did those people have money, they had power and influence. And Shorty didn't respect those kinds of people.

I couldn't blame him. Based on his life experiences, people with money and influence called in a loan just before harvest, knowing the farmer couldn't hand over any money until he'd brought in his crops and sold them. They sent soldiers to war, but made sure their own children never fought in a battle. Those people made the rules but didn't follow them—they had their own set of rules.

"Annabelle, based on our experience today, how do you think Shorty's interview with Jean Breaux will work out?"

It was hard to hear over Babette's chattering, since we were in the front seat. I twisted my torso like Gumby, trying to position my ear towards the back seat. Annabelle leaned forward, and so did Elizabeth. We resembled a football huddle discussing the next play. Well, except we were in a car and my side ached from my awkward position.

"I've been thinking about that, Ev. Shorty doesn't put up with rudeness—thank goodness he wasn't there today! He'd have told off that Jacqueline Dubois, for the way she treated poor Mimi. No, if this Jean Breaux is anything like Jacqueline, I don't think Shorty needs to interview him."

Was Babette ever going to stop talking to her husband? She'd just seen the man an hour ago—what could they have to discuss? "Oh, Chéri, it was so much fun! I can't wait for you to interview Jean—you're going to have the best time! And we got thrown out of Jacqueline's house—isn't that marvelous? We should think about opening a private investigation office. I'm going to start shopping for fedoras and trench coats."

Hmmm, they did have a lot to discuss, but it wasn't about the case. Should I interrupt the lovebirds? "Babette...Babette! Excuse me, but I need to ask you about Jean Breaux. What's his background? Was he born into money, or did he earn it, like you and Marcel?"

The landmarks told me Sweet Magnolia Manor was ten minutes away, but this conversation should happen without Shorty around. Babette put Marcel on speaker and filled us in on Jean's background. "He came from a modest family, the only child of a cab driver and a housewife. He joined the Army because he wanted to serve his country, and fought in the Gulf War."

Annabelle chimed in. "Oh, just like Shorty! They'll have that in common."

"Shorty served in the war? Then yes, he and Jean will have much to discuss. Anyway, his unit came under fire and he took a bullet in the leg, which is why he limps. He received a medical discharge and worked his way through college as a waiter. He went on to law school, and has a practice downtown. But his family left him a small inheritance, which he used along with his earnings from his law firm to open an upscale restaurant in the French Quarter. Perhaps you've heard of The Blue Moon Eatery?"

My stomach executed a happy dance at the name of Jean's restaurant—the heart wasn't the only organ with memories. "Oh, yes! Doug and I went there all the time. They have the best Crawfish Monica on the planet."

The Bouviers chuckled as if on cue, and Babette continued. "Yes, I'm sure that's true. I prefer the grilled crawfish salad, while Marcel always orders the shrimp and grits. Frankly, all their food is delectable, which is why Jean caters for us exclusively. Although we have to throw Jacqueline a few jobs here and there, to keep the peace. But we prefer Jean, for his food and his temperament."

The lawyer comment concerned me. "Do you think Jean would be comfortable with Shorty interviewing him? They both served in the military, and left for medical reasons. But that's where their similarities end—would it go better than, say, our last interview?"

More chuckling in stereo—how irritating! My cousins even laughed in sync. "Yes, Evangeline, Jean remembers his roots, and he has great respect for the working class. Most of his clients are just like Shorty, in fact. Yes, I think the interview will go well. Better than ours, I'm sure."

Oh, how I regretted skipping Jean's interview. But I had to settle for Marcel's narration, which took place when Shorty and Annabelle went out to supper. According to my PI, he and Jean bonded over their military experience, and Jean invited them to his restaurant that evening. Marcel had a slightly different story, which he told once the couple had driven off.

"So, Cher, the interview went well? If Shorty received an invitation to The Blue Moon Eatery, it must have been a success."

Marcel choked on his iced tea, but recovered. "Ah, well, one might say that. Although the word *success* could be too strong of a word, Chère. But let me take a seat and relax a little before the visitation."

Babette's nose crinkled in irritation, an emotion I'd never seen expressed toward her husband. Thank goodness! The Bouviers were human after all. Marcel tried a softer approach. "Ladies, let's all sit down, have some more iced tea. Or maybe coffee? I could make us all a pot."

My cousin waved her hand, another sign of frustration. "Ugh! We don't have time for that, we've less than an hour before Chantilly's visitation. Cher, I understand you want to relax a bit before going out again, but could you relax while telling us about your interview?"

Marcel tapped his glass as he sighed. Yes, there it was! A dark cloud rolled over his face, then it was gone. If I kept a journal, I'd have to note the inaugural event. Both Marcel and Babette showed outward irritation with each other. The world made sense once more.

"All right, Chère, I can do that...for you." He stretched his legs so that his size fourteens rested on the coffee table, ankles crossed. A quiet *ahem* from his wife and he dropped them to the floor. "Our conversation began pleasantly, as Shorty began his interrogation with Jean's service in the Gulf War. I can't say for sure, but I think the point of the questions, at first, was to verify Jean's story."

No surprise there. Shorty had encountered many people claiming to be veterans, fighting great battles overseas. He prided himself on exposing their lies. "It ain't that hard, Doc. Most o'them don't even know the gear we took with us. See, all I gotta do is go on an' on about the great weapon we used in the Army—the Spitfire. Yeah, I drone on an' on about how useful it was, an' my CO even let me take it with me when I got discharged. Yes sir, the Spitfire is all a feller needs when he's fightin' for his country."

"That's wonderful, Shorty. I mean, not the droning part, but that you got to take your favorite weapon home with you." I made a mental note to call my United States Congressman. The military had no business sending home weapons with their veterans. Who was my congressman? Congresswoman? Come to think of it, who had I voted for in the last election?

Always with the horse snort. "Doc, that's the trick! The Army don't issue no weapon called the Spitfire! That's the name o'my first pocketknife I got when I was in Cub Scouts."

"Oh, thank goodness! I thought you had some weapon of mass destruction hidden out in your barn." Scratch that internet search—no need to find who to fuss at for sending home weapons with veterans. On second thought, I should probably find out who my representatives were. Yes, keep that task on the to do list.

"Yeah, I got kicked out o' the Scouts, when I accidentally set fire tuh my leader's tent. But he told me no hard feelings, not everyone's cut out for that sorta thing. He even let me keep my pocket knife, an' I still got it. Remind me t'bring it over next time I visit."

Shorty set fire to his scout leader's tent? No, Ev, don't even go down that road. But make a mental note to ask Dad about it at the Bergeron family interrogation...I mean, lunch.

"Ev? Are you listening? Honey, you're daydreaming again."

And back to Reality Road. "Sorry! Yes, Marcel, you're right—Shorty was testing Jean's story about being in the Army. Did he mention taking home his favorite weapon, the Spitfire?"

Marcel's jaw snapped toward me, his mouth gaping a good two inches. A perfect opening for catching flies—thank goodness Babette kept a clean and tidy bed and breakfast. "Evangeline, but how did you know? And is that legal? Does America let all its veterans take home...uh, souvenirs that can kill? In France, we're proud of our soldiers, but we give them medals, not weapons." His head twisted back and forth. "I'll never understand this country."

"No, Marcel, don't worry, Shorty didn't take home any weapons." I was definitely leaving out the part where my friend set fire to a tent. I'd never asked if anyone was in it—honestly, I preferred to assume there wasn't. "No, Shorty meets a lot of people who try to tell him they're veterans, once they realize he served in the military. He's devised a story with an imaginary weapon issued by the government. When the pseudo-soldier agrees that yes, the government handed out Spitfires to his unit too, Shorty reveals the truth and outs the impostor."

Marcel continued to shake his head, back and forth, as if he was watching a tennis game. "No, Chèrie, I will never understand this country." More tea sipping as he processed his next words. "Jean passed the test, I suppose. He told Shorty his unit hadn't been lucky enough to utilize the Spitfire. But he remarked how grateful he was for the chance to serve his country, and that America paid for some of his college. He attended law school at Loyola, working his way through as a waiter in the French Quarter. That's when he began to dream of owning his own restaurant someday. He met Chantilly, when she came to him for a prenuptial agreement. She and Beau were engaged, but Jean managed to fall in love with her, anyway. He and Beau became fast friends, and he always respected their marriage, although he could tell it when it was in trouble."

Marcel stopped to gather his thoughts and quench his thirst. Elizabeth voiced our thoughts. "Poor Jean! Unrequited love is the worst! Did he ever marry, Marcel?"

"No, he never did. According to Jean, even after Beau passed, he didn't pursue Chantilly. Their friendship meant the world to him, and so did the respect of Beau's memory."

We spent a few moments sipping our tea, our hearts breaking a little for Jean, except for Babette. "Oh, that man has plenty of women falling all over themselves to be on his arm! And he takes full advantage, dancing and dining with a different woman every night. But his restaurant and his law firm always come first. That's the real reason he never married."

We stared at Babette, her outburst casting a damper on our moment. "Goodness, Babette! Not everyone is as fortunate as you, to be married to your one true love. Some people have loved and lost. I, for one, have found it next to impossible to move on from my lost love."

It was my turn to receive the startled stares. "Evangeline, I'm so sorry! You're right. I'm blessed beyond measure to have Marcel by my side, every day. And I don't mean to diminish what you've gone through since losing Douglas. I'm just trying to say that Jean is a successful, handsome, charming man. He could have chosen to fall in love and get married. There's no need to feel sorry for him."

Marcel took her hand. "Ma chère, you're right. But you've counseled Jean throughout the years, and matched him with several delightful women. The heart wants what the heart wants. But let me continue." Babette squeezed his hand.

"Shorty asked about Chantilly's rumored pregnancy, and was the father really a local judge? Jean squirmed a bit, and told us there were several rumors flying about. He confirmed there was a pregnancy and a baby, but Chantilly would never disclose the father. Jean had heard the man was a famous jazz singer. When he learned she was pregnant, he denied the baby was his, and broke off all ties with Chantilly. One of Jean's friends at the time insisted it was the saxophone player from The Dirty Dozen Brass Band. But of course we'll never know."

Marcel crossed his legs, right over left, reminding me of a clown I'd seen as a child. The circus performer had wobbled around the ring on stilts, before taking a seat on a six-foot chair and crossing his legs. Marcel's legs weren't quite as long, but they seemed just as thin and skinny. "Shorty asked if Jean might be the father, since he admitted to being in love with her before. Oh, that man doesn't understand social graces, does he?"

Was that a rhetorical question? Maybe I should answer anyway. "But, Marcel, investigators have to ask the tough questions. Even if we don't get a straight answer, we like to observe the suspect's body language, to see if they're hiding something."

More head shaking. "I suppose. But it was still uncomfortable. Jean denied being the father, he said he barely knew Chantilly. She'd returned to him shortly after he prepared the prenuptial contract, sobbing. Her parents had postponed the marriage so she could live with her aunt in Georgia for a year. The poor woman confessed she was pregnant and it wasn't Beau's child. Her parents decided she must live with her aunt until the baby was born and her body recovered. Her aunt would find suitable parents for the child, and Chantilly could return and marry Beau. Being Catholic, abortion was out of the question. Jean told her he'd marry her and adopt the baby, but Chantilly refused. Babette, ma chère, could you refill my glass? Merci."

My pen scribbled furiously as I filled Jean's page. Maybe he really was the father of Chantilly's child, and he'd carried resentment towards her all these years? Or maybe it was much simpler—Jean's love had simmered, then cooled, until it settled into a dense brick of hatred.

"After all, revenge is a dish best served cold." Marcel picked at the buttons on his shirt. "Eugène Sue penned that famous phrase in his book, *Memoirs of Matilda*. Actually," Marcel reached out to accept his tea glass, "the translation reads 'and then revenge is very good eaten cold, as the vulgar say.' As much as I love Jean, he could have a strong motive."

Marcel gulped his tea, turning his back on his manners. "You know, Evangeline, I'm starting to think about my friends in an entirely different light. And I don't like it." His gulps slowed as he drained the glass.

"Look, Marcel, I get it. It's uncomfortable thinking about the dark side of human nature, especially your friends. Let's switch gears. Did Jean talk about the night Chantilly, uh, died?"

Marcel dropped his glass on a coaster with a *clink*. Either he was incredibly thirsty or incredibly uncomfortable. He'd drained an eight-ounce glass in less than twenty seconds. Babette scurried to refill his glass.

"Yes, we discussed how Jacqueline enjoys serving and hosting. Well, more hosting than serving, normally. But that evening the woman ignored most of her guests, choosing to spend all her time in the kitchen. Jean remembered that she paid careful attention to all her food, which is normal for a caterer. But that evening she hovered over all the food, like a helicopter, especially the sandwiches! She refused to let the staff near the ingredients for the po'boys, or the bread. Jean could hear her screaming in the kitchen, threatening anyone who came within two feet of the sandwich preparation area. Several of Jean's staff work catering jobs for Jacqueline as well, and they told Jean later that they would never work for Jacqueline again."

Babette reappeared with his drink and he grabbed the glass with one hand and Babette's arm with the other, his slender fingers caressing his wife's skin. "Thank you, Chérie. I'm so thirsty!"

Marcel resumed his earlier sipping strategy, and once the glass was three quarters full he continued. "Once Jean brought up Jacqueline's obsession with the food that evening, I remembered other guests commenting. Babette and I only noticed her absence with the guests, and that usually she preferred to be in the...how do you say? Oh, yes! She preferred to be in the thick of things."

"Marcel's correct, Evangeline. Jacqueline prides herself on being the consummate hostess, flitting from guest to guest while her staff manages the food. But that evening she dominated the kitchen, fulfilling the role as caterer rather than hostess. She even served the sandwiches herself—she insisted upon it."

"What? Jacqueline served the po'boys herself? Including Chantilly's? There's her means—she made sure she had exclusive access to the murder weapon."

Marcel lowered his glass just slightly, enough to respond. "Yes, Shorty picked up on that as well. Now Jean and Jacqueline aren't friends by any means, but he didn't appreciate your friend calling her a po'boy poisoner. Really, Evangeline, that crossed the line."

"Oh, dear! Well, I'm sorry about that. Please continue."

More sips—Babette should have brought him the entire pitcher. "Jean did bring up a couple of things, rumors really. Normally I don't like to gossip, but..." He stopped to stare at his wife as she covered up her giggles with a cough. "What? I don't, I really don't! Chérie, all I do is encourage information. That's not gossip." Marcel resumed sipping, and smoothing his ruffled feathers.

"Jacqueline had an affair with Beau Romero, twenty years her senior. Of course, she prefers older men—she married René Dubois, a man in his sixties, when she herself was only twenty-three. At twenty-five she played the widow in mourning, and Beau comforted her as only a dear friend could. But many nights the neighbors spotted Beau's Alfa Romeo pulling into Jacqueline's garage. Oh, Chantilly knew about the overnight consolation sessions, but she was too busy with her own love affairs to care."

My teal pen worked overtime. "*Was Jacqueline in love with Beau?*"

Babette appeared with the tea pitcher—the woman was a slow learner. She filled Marcel's glass. "I'm brewing more tea, in case anyone's interested."

But we were all engrossed in the love triangle, so Marcel picked up the tale. "After Beau's death, Jacqueline went about town claiming Chantilly killed Beau. Or rather she'd had Clifford kill him. But he died at Ami Fidéle, the distillery, which is outside the city limits. Sheriff Ray headed the investigation, and it went nowhere."

Until that point Elizabeth had remained in the shadows, keeping her lips on her tea glass and her fingers curled around her pen. She'd filled three pages of her notebook. "What about the kitchen couple? You know, the couple lurking by the kitchen that night? Did Jean know anything about them?"

"I have to go to the bathroom. Excuse me." Could we wait until he returned? The suspense was killing me—or did I need a turn at the facilities? Fortunately, men didn't spend as much time in the bathroom as women. Thank goodness! He returned before any of us could speculate further.

"Where was I? Oh, yes! Elizabeth, your question about the kitchen couple. No, I'm afraid Jean didn't know anything about this mysterious couple. But he's going to check with his staff, the ones who worked that evening. He'll get back to me."

Babette appeared with a full pitcher of tea and filled all our glasses. Marcel covered his glass. "Thank you, Chérie, but I've had enough. We'd better get ready for the visitation. Ladies, please make yourselves at home. We'll be back as soon as we can, but we'll do our best to keep our eyes and ears open."

My hand cramped from all the writing. "Oh, yes! You'd mentioned the interview wasn't exactly a success. But from our conversation, I think it went very well. Did something else happen?"

Marcel shifted on the couch, then stood up. Did he deliver bad news better while towering over people? "It was fine, I'm sure. But during our conversation, Shorty commented several times how someone who owned a restaurant might want to serve food to his guests, especially guests visiting from out of town. Jean finally offered him a table tonight at The Blue Moon Eatery. A table on a Friday night in the French Quarter is a gift! Especially during Mardi Gras. But your friend expressed disappointment that Jean wasn't providing a free meal. So the poor man threw in an appetizer and dessert. I think his gesture soothed Shorty's irritation, but I was just so embarrassed. I don't know if Babette and I can show our faces in Jean's presence. Excuse me. Babette, we need to go home and get ready."

Babette laughed, but only after she heard the front door shut. "Oh, don't mind him, Evangeline! Marcel has no reason to be embarrassed. He asks Jean for free food and drinks all the time! He even tries to take people to the restaurant and wrangle free meals out of our poor friend. Marcel's just upset that someone else is getting the same perks—*and* during Mardi Gras!" She laughed all the way out the door.

CHAPTER 9

"I can't stand this! Shorty and Annabelle are out on the town, dining in an exclusive restaurant in the French Quarter. Babette and Marcel dressed up and they're also headed out on the town. What are we doing, Ev? Why are we just sitting around staring at each other!"

"Elizabeth, this is what we do every Friday night. Well, you stare at Cliff and I stare at a book. And since when did a funeral visitation count as being *out on the town?*"

My bestie plopped on the couch, still dressed in her black slacks and jade ruffled shirt from our interview. Did she entertain the ridiculous notion we were going out? One glance at my purple plaid happy bottoms and black t-shirt would squash that idea.

"Exactly my point, Ev! Cliff and I spend every Friday evening staring at each other or the television. Or the grandchildren, if Cal and Annelise have plans. We're in New Orleans on a Friday night! I never pictured us sitting on a couch."

My happy bottoms tugged at my sleeve. *Ev, this is our time. You promised we'd hang out together until tomorrow morning.*

Please don't put us back in your suitcase tonight—you gave us your word! We'll never forgive you for going back on your word.

But what was more important, happy bottoms or happy best friend? "All right, let's go out! I'll change into pants and a shirt too, and give my friend Curtis a call. He owns The Mercado Club on Bourbon Street."

The legendary music club was one of Bourbon Street's oldest live music attractions. The name comes from its previous business—the building used to house hundreds of booths selling anything from shoelaces to canned preserves. Curtis' grandfather purchased the abandoned building and transformed it into an upscale nightclub. The walls in the entryway showcased photos of all the stars who frequented the club as patrons and performers. Most had autographed the spaces next to their smiling mugs. Tourists had streamed into The Mercado Club for two decades to have their photos taken with the wall and enjoy their favorite performers.

A couple of weeks before our trip, I'd called Curtis and promised to stop by the club. And I would keep that promise, if I didn't lose my hearing to Elizabeth's squeals, or pass out from her hug. Was this how it felt if a boa constrictor had wrapped itself around me? Was the sensation of cracking ribs identical?

"Eeeee! Oh, Ev, that sounds amazing. Cliff and I tried to get in there one time, but the guy at the door said we needed reservations. But Ev, you know people! Oh, I've got to change clothes—this is a slinky black dress occasion!" The squeals finally died down after she'd shut the door.

Doug and I had spent many evenings before kids, whirling around the tiled dance floor just in front of the glass-brick stage. We'd stop by after 10 p.m. most nights, after the so-called old folks left, when the live music ended and the venue transformed into a dance club for the younger crowd. Now I *was* one of the old folks, and by ten I planned to make an encore performance with my happy bottoms. "Now don't you fret," I whispered as I placed my pajamas back into my suitcase. "Mama's gonna see you again real soon, and that's a promise. I just have to pop out for a bit, but I'll be back in a jiff. You'll hardly know I'm gone." Was it strange I talked to my pajamas the same way I spoke to my dog?

"Ev, who are you talking to? Let's go, girl—this woman is ready for some authentic live music, courtesy of The Big Easy!" And we were off.

"Evangeline! Girl, it's so great to see you. And this must be Elizabeth—ma'am, it's a pleasure." One of Doug's first homicide cases was Clem Delacroix, Curtis' cousin. Doug solved it fairly quickly and the judge handed down a life sentence. Curtis and his family showered us with blessings, mostly the culinary kind. We, that is I, had a lifetime of free food at several local restaurants, courtesy of the Delacroix family. And instant access to The Mercado Club, owned by Curtis.

"Ladies, I have a table right up front. And, if you like, I'll take you backstage to meet tonight's performers. This evening we have Marcella LaPeer, a promising singer from the toe of the boot. Pay attention, mes amies, this young lady is making a name for herself!"

"What's Marcella LaPeer's style of music, Curtis? Cajun, zydeco, swamp pop, R & B, or jazz? Or a combination?"

Louisiana's shape resembles a boot, so the term *toe of the boot* means the southernmost tip of the state. America seized the land between the Mississippi and the Pearl Rivers from Spain, and Louisiana adopted it. That area has its own culture and history, including Cajun and Creole.

These two cultures have contributed Cajun dance music, Creole zydeco music, and swamp pop, and they all started with rhythm and blues. Swamp pop combines R & B, Cajun, zydeco, and country music. A strong horn section and honky-tonk piano sets it apart from other styles. Jazz is also a regional favorite from that part of Louisiana, so my question was genuine.

Curtis pulled out our chairs. "Marcella's style? Why don't you tell me? Because I can't figure it out! But she calls her act *The Gumbo Girl from Plaquemine Parish*—thick and robust, with thousands of variations. And you'll love every one of them!"

Elizabeth studied the menu. "Well, she sounds charming. Ev, let's get an appetizer—Curtis, what do you recommend?"

"Either the crab cakes or the sweet potato bits. Since they're on the house, I'll get you both. Oh, and some drinks? Perhaps our signature Sazerac cocktail, with purple and gold coloring for the season? It's the official drink of New Orleans, not the Hurricane, as some restaurants claim. How about it, ladies?"

"Ugh, no! Whiskey gives me a headache. Just some iced tea for me, unsweet. Coffee, Elizabeth? The heat from your glare tells me you want a cocktail. But remember, we've got a murder to solve. I think you should stick to coffee."

Elizabeth's lower lip stuck out like the Great Wall of China. Well, if the Great Wall architects had constructed it out of a gigantic lip. "Fine! Curtis, give me a cup of coffee." She touched his elbow. "But if it had a splash or two of whiskey in it, I wouldn't complain."

Who was this woman and what had she done with my friend? New Orleans had that effect on people.

Why hadn't anyone told me The Mercado Club had dropped the ten o'clock switch to dance club? How could the old folks make a graceful journey home and be in bed by 10:30 p.m.? Marcella didn't leave the stage until well after midnight. And my best friend wasn't leaving before her new favorite musician.

"Oh, Curtis! The Gumbo Girl from Plaquemine Parish didn't disappoint—she was amazing, simply amazing! Yes, just fantastic! When can we meet her?"

As Elizabeth came up for air, Curtis took a chair, his ebony skin shiny with perspiration. He pulled out a starched handkerchief and dabbed his temples. "Let me catch my breath! One of my servers lost his lunch just before coming on shift. And guess who covered for him? Oh and let's not forget my *favorite* customers tonight, at Table Seven. Yes sir, they claim the record for most complaints in a single night—we couldn't do anything right! I had to comp the entire meal and they still weren't happy. So I gave them all bread pudding—on the house. Then they had the nerve to tell me I'm living the good life, because I'm a small business owner—I don't have a boss. Well, that's rich! Yes, sir, I have a boss, several in fact. You're looking at every single one of them! You bet your sweet Aunt Hortense I do! I work for everyone in this room! And let's not forget my banker! But hey—I'm living the American dream, right? Hey, Louisa!"

A skinny brunette twenty-something flew across the room, standing beside her boss. At least she only had one. Curtis rubbed his temples as he put in his order. "Child, get me the usual, and make it a double. And get one for yourself—you've earned it."

More dabbing. "Ooh-whee! I'm gonna take a shower and climb right into bed. But first, let me take you backstage and meet Marcella. She'll knock your socks off—if you were wearing any, that is. After I get my drink, which should be right...now."

Louisa appeared, each hand holding a drink. "Mine's just water, boss. I don't live over the club—I've got to drive home tonight. Stu says he's closing down the bar, but he can bring you the bottle."

Curtis waved her away with one hand as he sipped his drink. "No, child, tell Stu not to bother. I'd rather sell the whiskey than drink it. Ladies, let's head backstage."

As we rounded the corner Elizabeth shrieked like a banshee. From the open mouths and blank stares of the band, I'd say most fans had less dramatic reactions. But Marcella recovered, her dark skin and eyes radiated delight. She shook her tight black curls in a quick nodding motion. "Oh, Curtis, are these your guests? Ladies, I'm Marcella LaPeer, it's so nice to meet ya'll."

Our new favorite singer couldn't be more than twenty-five, but her firm handshake reflected the experience of a woman beyond her years. Good—she'd need that maturity and professionalism. The career she'd chosen was difficult, full of long nights away from home. Hopefully, she had thick skin and a heart that rejoiced at every blessing, large or small. And a mama who prayed for her every waking moment.

"Oh, Miss LaPeer! We just loved your show! My name is Elizabeth Trahan, and this is my friend, Ev Delafose. We're on vacation and stopped in to see your show. You are amazing, simply amazing! Isn't she, Ev? Isn't she simply amazing?"

Elizabeth's words spilled over Marcella like a tsunami, almost drowning the poor girl. After drenching her for a good twelve seconds my friend slowed her speech, dialing it down to a steady current. The singer took it all in, every word, like a parched garden rejoicing at the sudden rainstorm.

"Oh, thank you, thank you, Miss Elizabeth, you're too kind. Oh, yes, my parents are proud of me, they are indeed. No ma'am I'm not sure how Ella Fitzgerald started out, but she is one of my favorite singers! Yes, ma'am, she is an inspiration, that's for sure. Oh, of course, I'd be happy to take some photos with you."

After three and a half minutes of being a fangirl, I cut off my friend. She'd had enough, we all had. "Elizabeth, I'm sure Miss LaPeer appreciates all your, uh, raving and gushing. But she's tired, and she needs to get on to her next place. Marcella, thank you for a spectacular performance. I've already purchased your two albums on my phone and added them to my playlist. Thank you again for a wonderful evening! El, let's leave the poor woman alone."

I'd never had to drag anyone anywhere, until the night my best friend became a groupie. Where was Cliff when I needed him most? Oh yes, sitting at home in his happy bottoms dozing in front of the television.

Curtis took the other arm while I continued pulling. For a skinny thing, my best friend sure was strong. Marcella took her cue and headed for her dressing room. At last, some traction!

"Ya'll didn't have to push me off the stage! I was going. I just wanted to bask in a star's light for as long as I could." Yes, New Orleans had that effect on people.

We planted ourselves at a table in the dining room. "Curtis, thank you for a wonderful evening. I'll admit, it was worth it to get out of the house and catch Marcella's show."

Elizabeth was somewhere in the land of social media, posting her gazillion selfies with The Gumbo Girl from Plaquemine Parish. I'd hate to type in the hashtag for that nickname.

"Oh, Ev, before I forget. Earlier in the evening, when I seated ya'll at your table, you mentioned something about a murder? You told Elizabeth *we've got a murder to solve, so you should stick to coffee.* What was that about?"

"Oh, that. You heard that? Uh, well, since I moved back to Graisseville, I've kind of been working on some cases for the sheriff. Just a few, well four. Marcel and Babette asked me to look into Chantilly's death, for their own peace of mind. That's all, nothing too dangerous."

Curtis waved his hand, and Louisa took his empty glass. "Yeah, I heard someone killed her. Chantilly and I weren't the best of friends, but she gave me a good deal on her whiskey. And I sure liked her husband, for what that's worth. A lot of people think she killed him. I'm happy to help ya'll with whatever you need."

Curtis took each lady by the arm. "In fact, let's go into my office, where it's more private. I might be able to fill ya'll in on some details. And the couch in there sure is comfortable." He led us to the end of a hallway, just past the bathrooms, and unlocked a narrow door marked *private*.

Elizabeth put her phone away, because murder always trumps social media. We sat in the two chairs facing the desk, and our host offered us bottled water. "I'm gonna lie down on the couch, if you ladies don't mind. I've been on my feet all night, and I ain't as young as I used to be." We sipped while Curtis stretched out, his five foot six-inch frame molding itself into the cushions. From the looks of the fabric, Curtis had spent many an evening unwinding on the crushed red velvet.

"Did ya'll know Beau's kid sister Bea was starting her own distillery? Yeah, my banker's her banker, and he's not supposed to say anything, but he always does. Her loan's almost approved, and she plans to be up and running by the end of year. Course it takes a good long while to age whiskey, anywhere from a few months to twenty plus years. It just depends on your taste. Bea's gonna start with small and large barrels. She can bottle and sell the smaller ones in a few months, because they'll age faster. Then, she can sit on the bigger ones until they're ready. She's in the process of buying out a little bitty distillery right outside the city limits, and that'll give her some cash flow to keep her loan going."

When would I learn? Someday I'd remember to bring my notebook and pen everywhere. The notes app on my phone would have to do. "Did Chantilly know about this?"

The raised eyebrows screamed *silly question, Ev.* "Okay, I guess she did. How'd she take it?"

Oh no! Eyes shut and slow breathing—my window of opportunity was closing fast. "Mmmm, not good. Chantilly doesn't like competition, but she does like putting it out of circulation. Bea had to pull together a lot of collateral to get her loan, and she had to get it from people willing to get on Chantilly's bad side. That's a short list."

Talk fast, Ev. Time's a wastin'. "Okay, real quick, you said Bea thinks Chantilly killed Beau. Is that really true? And does Bea know anything about poison?" "Mmmuhmmm..." Curtis was going down for the count. A not so gentle nudge to the sole of his foot brought him back for round two. "Huh? Uh, well, Bea has this weird hobby—she collects elements on the periodic table. You know...that table full of weird words we had to learn back in high school science. Hydrogen, Helium, Lithium, Burr..." Round two was over.

Another nudge to Curtis' feet, even less gentle. "Uh! Beryllium, Boron..."

"No, I don't need the periodic table, Curtis. What does this have to do with poison?"

Did crossing his ankles improve Curtis' brain waves? Hopefully. "Didn't you hear? Chantilly had arsenic in her system, which is an element on the periodic table. Number thirty-three with the symbol 'As.' And Bea has arsenic in her collection. Yeah, she calls it her *toy box*, gets her kicks out of waving all those poisons around. She's mental, that one."

Yes, I definitely should have paid more attention in chemistry. But that would have cut into my reading time, which wasn't going to happen. Obviously, Curtis had paid a lot of attention, thank goodness. "You mean to tell me that the periodic table has poisons on it?" Hmmm, that might be why my chemistry teacher, Mr. Boudreaux shuffled around the room rubbing his hands together like a mad scientist. And that could explain the mysterious disappearance of Miss Freeman, the history teacher, who went home after school in the middle of spring semester and never returned. Word around the lockers was that Mr. Boudreaux had a mad crush on Miss Freeman, fifteen years his junior. Oh sure, Mother claimed Miss Freeman had run off with the bank teller at First National Bank in Zachary. But no one knew for sure. In fact...

"Ev, honey? I think Curtis fell asleep again." At least one of us was paying attention.

Another nudge, this time to the ribs. "Curtis, do you think Bea Romero murdered her sister-in-law with the arsenic she kept in her own home? It's a stretch, don't you think? If I was going to kill Chantilly, I wouldn't use something from my house, especially if everyone knew I had it. For example, in my last case the killer used a statue from his kitchen, but he hadn't bragged about it. To my knowledge he hadn't discussed it with anyone. The weapon was part of the kitchen décor, it was kind of cute, actually. If I was a fan of Paris, I'd probably put it in my kitchen too. His wife had decorated it just like a little French Café, you see, because she'd always wanted to go to Paris. But he'd never taken the time..."

Curtis rolled over, his back facing me. "Yeah, well, who else knows about poisons, especially arsenic? The only other person I could see killing her is the sheriff. And Doug Ray doesn't have enough sense to come out of the rain. You think ol' Barney Fife on *The Andy Griffith Show* is a doofus? Wait'll you meet the sheriff. Nah, he don't know a thing about poison, except maybe what he's learned catching criminals.

And even then he's not real good at that. Yeah, the last time he…"

"Ev, honey? I don't think you're getting any more out of Curtis, at least not tonight." Elizabeth stood up and picked up a CD. "Do you think anyone would care if I took this? It's pretty beat up and it's got scribbles on it."

I pried the case from my friend's hands—yes, pried. "Uh, Elizabeth, these so-called scribbles you mentioned are actually a signature. Yes, this is an autographed CD from Buckwheat Zydeco! He performed on the *Tonight Show* and at the closing ceremonies for the 1996 Olympics. Girl, he's collaborated with U2 and Eric Clapton! So yes, someone would care if you took it. Now let's go before you find something else to steal."

As our Uber driver skimmed the ten minutes to Sweet Magnolia Manor, Elizabeth scrolled social media, delighting in all the likes and comments. Yep, New Orleans had that effect on people.

CHAPTER 10

Fifty-somethings who crept into bed after midnight must drink coffee first thing in the morning. There has to be a federal law on the books somewhere. My body started in on me, before my first cup. *Ev, if I've told you once I've told you a thousand times—you're not as young as you used to be.* Most days I listened, and my body thanked me. This time my body was not thanking me at all.

I don't care what you say, I had fun last night. And I don't do that very often—most times I'm in bed by ten. So give me a little grace, will you? New Orleans has that effect on people—we all know this. Lighten up.

My body would not listen to reason. *Oh no, Ev, I won't lighten up. See, I'm crossing my arms and planting my feet. See that? Nope, I'm not cutting you any slack. Because of your shenanigans, I'm forced to drink coffee this morning in order to function properly.*

Oh, leave me alone! Drink your coffee and stop belly aching. You got what you deserve—serves you right!

"Good morning, Gumshoe Krewe. Ev, honey? Are you having a conversation with your body again? And is it helping? Because if it is, have your body talk to my body. And thank you for talking me out of that cocktail! I'm struggling as it is, with too little sleep."

Babette poured coffee into a cup the size of a teapot and placed it into Elizabeth's grateful hands. We resembled twin statues, motionless except for our slurping.

"Ya'll had a big night, huh? Me an' Annabelle got home aroun' eight o'clock, an' ya'll two weren't nowhere t'be seen. Now what I wanna know is this: Were ya'll traipsin' all over town, or were ya'll workin' the case? Cuz Annabelle an' I were workin'."

Should I put down my cup and dignify Shorty's question with an answer? Mmmm, not worth my time, and the coffee's jolt of caffeine was stirring life into my soul.

Clunk! That was the sound of Elizabeth's tankard hitting the kitchen table. It was worth her time. "For your information, Cleophas Cormier, Ev and I did both! We traipsed via Uber to The Mercado Club, and met a fabulous singer. Her name's Marcella LaPeer, and she's The Gumbo Girl from Plaquemine Parish. We also dined on fabulous food! After the show we met Marcella, and I got a lot of pictures with her. So there!"

Oh, boy...Shorty's face reminded me of my father's, when I was about twelve, and I helped out around the house by putting Dad's stethoscope in the dishwasher. Not only did Shorty hate being called his given name, he knew I was the one who'd told. Yeah, I'd catch an earful of anger over that. *Sorry, soul, you'll have to finish the waking up process on your own.* Down went the coffee cup. Maybe Babette would fill it back up while I fixed the situation. I had to admit, her coffee tasted better than any I'd ever had.

"And after we went backstage, we followed the club owner back to his office, and he shared information crucial to the investigation." As I repeated what Curtis had told us, minus his dozing and my nudging, Shorty's eyes lost their dark clouds. He even smiled—just a little, but I could see it. Maybe my ear wouldn't endure the wrath of Shorty Cormier.

"Hey, that's real good, ladies, I'm proud of ya'll. Yeah, that Curtis feller sounds like a right good source of information. H ey, *Bab-Bet*, do ya'll think ya'll could get a coroner report? It'd be real handy t'see that thing." Shorty had waved off Marcel's French roast, and the poor man hadn't recovered from the insult. Yes, because of the free food from Jean and refusal of gourmet coffee, Marcel's face resembled Shorty's bull, Romeo, when the veterinarian drove up to the fence. As my father would say, those two didn't geehaw. My PI's comment about fancy drinks for fancy people hadn't smoothed the road either.

"No, Shorty, I don't think so. Sheriff Ray's office won't give us the coroner's report, so we'd have to get someone else to request it. Wait!"

Babette's stopped pouring in midair, much to my heart's dismay. "Maybe I could talk to Chantilly's mother, Sophie. We haven't spoken in a while, but I've always considered her a friend. She could request the coroner's report, since she's next of kin. But let me talk to her after the funeral—she couldn't request it until Monday, anyway." She refilled my tub of caffeine. Was it a bucket, maybe? Whatever my large cup resembled, I drained it almost as quickly as Babette had replenished it.

Shorty sipped his chicory coffee with cayenne pepper, the only kind he drank. Come to think of it, coffee was the only liquid I'd ever seen him savor. When Maggie opened her coffee shop, she'd hooked Shorty on espresso shots in his drink—the entire village still gave her grief for handing out extra caffeine to someone with ADHD. But Maggie insisted it could help with focus and concentration. The rest of the community agreed that the jury was still out.

My PI purchased an espresso machine and began adding five shots of caffeinated overkill to every morning cup. In his haste to get to New Orleans, he'd forgotten his machine, and the Bouviers hadn't stocked Sweet Magnolia Manor with that luxury. The bed and breakfast included all the amenities a tourist could covet, so why not an espresso maker? Thank goodness for that...but wait! What was Shorty pulling out of the pantry? It couldn't be...

"Hey, whatcha know! Ya'll gotta 'spresso machine! An' it's pretty much like mine at home. Ya' know, I was missin' my extra caffeine this mornin', an' feelin' mighty sluggish. Yes sir, nothin' goes better with chicory than 'spresso. Yep, this is gonna do the trick!"

Immigrants brought chicory to the United States from Africa, Asia, and Europe in the eighteenth century. It's a naturally caffeine-free root that's roasted for coffee, also referred to as New Orleans coffee. It has a dark, slightly sweet and rich flavor, and is a great option for people staying away from caffeine. Chicory also has a high amount of inulin, which is supposed to improve gut health, reduce cholesterol, and control blood sugar.

When Shorty was a teenager, his mother, Madie, started brewing it. Shorty's father, Mack, had visited the doctor and paid fifty dollars to receive a lecture about his cholesterol levels and pre-diabetic state. "Mack, you're going to die if you don't cut down on the sugar and reduce your cholesterol. Here, I'm sending you home with a diet plan. Give it to Madie so she can start cooking healthier." The stapled stack of paper never made it out of the parking lot. Unfortunately for Mack, his doctor sang in the church choir with Madie. Poor Mr. Cormier never stood a chance.

"Mack Cormier! What's this about a list of foods Dr. Miller sent home with you? He says you've got to lower your cholesterol and sugar, or we'll be putting you in an early grave." Madie spent a good month trying to cook off the doctor's list, but Mack pushed his plate away and dug into the pantry for peanut butter and crackers. Madie had to become devious, something she didn't enjoy. But she wanted to grow old with her husband.

Madie learned to substitute applesauce for butter, sneak pureed cauliflower into scrambled eggs, and even make pudding with avocados. And she began using ground chicory instead of coffee, for the health benefits. Mack never figured it out, but he lost thirty pounds. Then he bragged to the entire village how easy it was. "Yes, sir, just changed one thing. I cut the salt in my grits by half. I tell ya', it's the little things."

Madie never said a word, except to my mother. And lo and behold! My father started dropping weight too. He also gave credit to less salt on his grits, but Mother and Madie knew better. It wasn't long after that when most of the village cut the salt in their grits too.

By the time I'd strolled down Memory Lane, revisiting my father and Mack Cormier and their miracle diet, Shorty had the espresso machine all set up and percolating.

"Oh? You like espresso then? Did you know in France the favorite drink is espresso? Oui, if you ever visit my home country, you could sit outside a café and drink espresso all day long."

Shorty stood by his adopted machine, casting a long look at Marcel. "Ya' don't say! Well, *Mar-sell*, I might jus' travel tuh France, iffen I could drink 'spresso all day. An' ya'll don't put nothin' in that 'spresso?"

The tightness around Marcel's eyes relaxed and his shoulders dropped half an inch. "No, monsieur, nothing. A true Frenchman drinks it straight out of the machine, with nothing in it." And there it was, a glimmer in Shorty's eyes and a hint of a smile. Marcel had finally impressed him.

"Well, I'll be! Apple Dumplin', ya' hear all that? Those French people drink big ol' cups uh 'spresso straight up! Now I gotta tell ya' somethin', *Mar-sell*, the French ain't never impressed me too much, with yore fancy words an' yore little *burr-ray* hats an' such. An' America saved yore behinds in World War II. Yeah, which ya'll seemed t'forget real quick. But I'll tell ya' one thing—if ya'll can drink big ol' cups o' 'spresso with nothin' in 'em, well, sir! That's real impressive. Say, ya' know what, I think I might not've had the right idea about ya'll. Tuh the French!" Shorty lifted his cup of caffeinated madness in the air and clinked Marcel's cup. And not one of us mentioned that espresso arrives in tiny cups for customers to sip, one shot at a time.

"Evangeline, Marcel and I can't attend Chantilly's funeral and scope out suspects. That would be too disrespectful. We couldn't even do it last night at the visitation. No, I'm sorry, we just won't do it." We'd adjourned to the living room, killing time until the funeral. Babette perched on the side chair, wringing her hands.

"Babette, it's okay. We don't need you to wear your detective hat today. Don't worry about it." Actually, we did. It would be ideal if the couple would snoop around and ask questions. But the shrillness in my cousin's voice told me not to push it. Shorty was too busy enjoying his espresso and beignets to protest my decision.

"But I will tell you, Marcel and I saw every single one of our suspects at the visitation last night. And I'm sure they will all be at the funeral. Everyone appeared solemn and respectful, and no one danced in front of the casket." Babette threw out her last comment with a twinkle in her eye, and Marcel chuckled. At least my cousin had found her sense of humor.

"Good, I'm glad. Shorty, did you two have any luck at the Blue Moon?"

My PI paused mid drink and wiped his mouth—with a napkin, much to my relief.

"We talked tuh some o' the staff, tryin' t'figure out who worked the night o' the party. Annabelle did better'n me—she talked tuh someone in the bathroom. Honeybun, go ahead an' tell everyone what ya' found out."

Honeybun stood up and reached for her notebook, then flipped it open and found her page. As my father would say, she looked as happy as a tick on a fat dog. "I spoke with a young lady, about twenty-two...maybe? We spoke in the ladies' bathroom, by the sinks, at approximately 7:20 p.m." She looked up from her page, nose crinkled like a discarded piece of paper. "I'm sorry, Ev, I didn't get the exact time. Shorty said it didn't matter, but I wasn't sure."

"It's okay, Annabelle, really. Go ahead." I pressed my hands into my lap, then my lips into a tight line. Don't laugh, Ev, it's not funny. It's wonderful that she's taking it so seriously.

"Monica, the server I spoke with, worked Jacqueline's party the night of the murder. She remembers Clifford Benoit arguing with Chantilly about five minutes before the screaming started. You know, the screaming, because Chantilly collapsed and started foaming at the mouth. Oh, I'm sorry!" Annabelle looked toward the Bouviers. "That was too graphic, wasn't it? Oh dear, I hope I didn't offend you."

Babette clasped Marcel's hand. "No, it's okay. You're trying to solve Chantilly's murder, so these things have to be mentioned. Go on, please."

Annabelle returned to her notebook. "Uh, well that's it, I'm afraid. Monica doesn't know exactly what the argument was about, but she thinks it's because Clifford wouldn't take a test bite of Chantilly's po'boy." To Shorty's credit, his lips were more tightly sealed than my grandmother's canned peaches. He wasn't about to ruin Annabelle's chance to shine.

"Clifford usually tries all Chantilly's food, because she's convinced people are out to get her. Why he refused the po'boy, Monica didn't know. But Chantilly started screaming and Clifford started screaming, and then he stormed off. Five minutes later he returned when he heard the screams. The other screams, you know, from the people around Chantilly. Shorty and I think the killer planned the murder from the beginning—I mean, who brings poison to a party unless they intend to use it? Maybe that's why Clifford wouldn't eat the po'boy."

"Good work, Honeybun. Let's review the elements board." I dodged a pink pen as I walked by Annabelle. Shorty's glare hit the mark, but caused no damage. "Jacqueline Dubois...she had an affair with the victim's husband, and she may have been in love with him. Either way, she thinks Chantilly had her bodyguard kill Beau. We don't know whether she had access to arsenic, but we do know she didn't let the po'boys out of her sight. I'd say her motive and opportunity are strong, so I'm underling those with red. But Jacqueline's means is weak, so I'm leaving it green."

Murmurs of agreement kept me going. "I'd say Jean' Breaux's motive is medium—he used to be in love with Chantilly, but we don't know how he feels in the here and now. I'm underlining that, orange, I guess, because we don't have a yellow. He has no means, so that's green. But he was standing next to the victim and gave her CPR, so opportunity is red."

"Ev, how much do you know about arsenic?" Elizabeth had a point. "Babette, I hope Chantilly's mother can get you the coroner's report. It would be nice to read more about what they found. Say, Ev, you still know a lot of people on the police force, don't you? Maybe you could get some information."

"Nah, those cops can't do that. Any o' them that handed out stuff about an open case would get fired quicker'n my hogs can eat a batch o' my homemade feed. Yes sir, I make it with cotton seed meal, corn chops, an' soybeans. Then I grind it up in my daddy's ol' grinder, that he got from his daddy an' his daddy had it before that. Yes sir, that..."

"And thank you, Shorty, for that useful family recipe for hog feed. But yes, he's right. I'm not going to ask, and no one would give it to me, anyway. But I do plan to call Doug's former partner, Brad Cox, and see what he knows about the case. He's with the New Orleans police, not the Orleans Parish, but I'm sure he's heard some things. I'll call him today. Now let's continue."

Annabelle charged towards the board, nearly flattening it. "Oh, me! Let me do Clifford Benoit." She grabbed the markers out of my hand, leaving a faint scratch on the knuckle. That girl was having too much fun.

"Now Clifford has been loyal to Chantilly in the past, and rumor has it he's even killed for her. But people saw them fighting five minutes before the victim died. I'd say motive is, uh, yellow?"

"Good, Annabelle, yes! I'd say yellow as well. Please continue." The woman was having the time of her life, and Shorty couldn't be prouder.

"To our knowledge, Clifford doesn't know anything about poison. That makes his means green. But for opportunity, well, he refused to take a bite of Chantilly's po'boy. Was it because he'd poisoned it? It's definitely suspicious, so I'm going to underline it orange. But Elizabeth's right, we need a better understanding of poison. Think, everyone! Do any of us know someone who could help?"

Who was that oddly interesting professor I'd befriended at Loyola? She taught in the chemistry and biochemistry department, but we'd met on a bench under my favorite tree on campus. "Dr. Luci Lirette! She's a chemistry professor at

Loyola, and her passion is poisons. I'll give her a call too and set up something. Yes, she'd be perfect. Okay, let's continue. Elizabeth? Would you like to take a turn?" Annabelle held out the markers, like a relay runner passing off the baton.

Elizabeth stood up and took the markers. "Thanks, Annabelle. Let's see, Sheriff Doug Ray. Honestly, we don't know much about him at all. He was first on the scene for Beau Romero's death, so he could have had a hand in covering up a murder. But that seems weak to me, so I'm going to leave it green. We haven't uncovered any knowledge of poison, so I'm going to leave that green as well. And he was the first officer on the scene of Chantilly's death, but that doesn't mean anything. The guests and staff had already contaminated the crime scene. Correct me if I'm wrong guys, but I think the sheriff's green all the way across."

Nodding heads confirmed Elizabeth's assessment. And we definitely needed more information. "Go ahead, El, take the next one—you're doing great."

My bestie shook her head. "No thanks. I mean, no offense, Ev, but it's more fun to watch it on television, or listen to you talk about it. I don't even like to do crossword puzzles, or the word jumble—no wonder I don't want to solve crimes."

"Oh, I'll take the next one—here!" Annabelle rushed the keeper of the markers. Hmmm, was LSU looking for a middle linebacker?

"All right, Beatrice Romero suspected the victim of killing her brother, so I'm giving that red." The marker squeaked as Annabelle pressed on the board, creating double red lines under each word. "Bea has arsenic in her element collection, so means is strong." More squeaking, like nails across a chalkboard. On second thought, no one used chalkboards anymore. Everyone used whiteboards with dry erase markers, just like ours. So what should I say to describe a marker squeaking on a whiteboard? I couldn't use the same description for the analogy...

"Ev, are you listening? Bea wasn't near Chantilly when she died, but I don't think that matters. All she needed was access to the po'boy. What do you think?"

"Huh? Oh, yes you're right. All the killer needed was access, which Jacqueline guarded like a, well, a guard." Darn outdated chalkboard analogy had me all messed up. "Let's leave it green, until we find out more about arsenic. But I think we need to do some digging, find out if anyone else could have snuck some arsenic into the kitchen. And we've got to find out more about this mysterious kitchen couple. Right now all we have is a bunch of gossip."

The theme from *Cops* filled the air. "Ethan! I'm putting you on speaker."

"Hey, Ev, hey everybody. I just emailed you the guest list and the staff list from Jacqueline Dubois' party."

"Oh, thank goodness! Our interview was less than perfect. There was no way I could go back and ask for them. What else do you have?"

"I'm sending you some news articles from some, well, let's say the sources rely more on gossip and less on fact. I can't vouch for their authenticity, but you always tell me where there's there's fire." Out of the corner of my eye I spotted Marcel bobbing his dark curls in agreement. "Several of Chantilly's, uh, business associates died from poison. There's a lot of chatter that her bodyguard Clifford Benoit handled her dirty work. The media linked him to the New Orleans mafia though, and poison wasn't really their style. Still, you never know."

"Thanks, Ethan, what's next?"

"I found a commercial real estate listing. Chantilly had Ami Fidéle distillery on the market to sell. She'd made an offer on a house in Dallas, Texas, contingent on selling the distillery."

"Ethan, this is Shorty Cormier. Did she have any offers on that distillery? Thank ya'."

Only Annabelle and I had taken part in the complete Shorty experience. Oh sure, we'd tried to describe it after the fact. But we could never do it justice. We locked eyes, basking in our delight. By the end of the weekend, three other people would complete their initiation. If they survived.

"Uh, no sir, the contract reads, active listing. No pending contracts. Oh, one last thing. Sheriff Ray has a serious gambling problem. He owed a significant amount of money to Chantilly, and she was trying to collect. If she was moving to Dallas, it makes sense she'd want all her money. I found some messages between them, where she threatened to report the sheriff to his superiors."

"Ethan, this is Shorty Cormier. Son, her gamblin' operation wasn't legal, why'd she want t'report the sheriff? Thank ya'."

"Uh, well, I'm sending you copies of the messages, but it sounds like Sheriff Ray looked the other direction for a lot of illegal operations, not just Chantilly's. And that's probably what she was going to report."

"Thank you, Ethan. Please keep looking. But thank you so much."

"Ethan, this is Shorty Cormier. Ya' did good, son. Thank ya'"

Everyone inspected their fingernails, too afraid to look up. If anyone flashed an eyeball in another's eyeline, we'd all burst out laughing. "Hey, why's everybody all clammed up? An' are we eatin' before this funeral?"

CHAPTER 11

"Shorty, honey, you can have my leftovers from last night. The funeral's at eleven, and Babette's making French toast for breakfast, so you should be fine until lunch after the funeral, right?"

"Why thank ya', Marmalade, but when I got up at six, I ate yore leftovers. That's okay, I'll jus' double up on French toast."

Babette turned toward the four loaves of bread. I could only see the back of her head, but I guessed she was dividing her inventory by the number of guests, then probably tripling it. "Could you...oh, thank you, Cher!" Marcel's lanky frame disappeared out the front door, presumably to get more bread. Eggs too, if he was smart. By the end of this case, I might owe the Bouviers money. Hopefully, they would call it even.

"I'm going to call Dr. Lirette and see if she's available tomorrow. I think today is all booked up. We've got the funeral and our interviews with Clifford and Beatrice. And let's not forget girls' night tonight with El's friends."

"Before you call your friend, Ev, I'd like to talk to you about the funeral. Marcel and I don't think it's a good idea for everyone to tag along. I mean, none of you even knew Chantilly, so we think it would be in bad taste for ya'll to make an appearance. I hope you understand."

Babette's tone reminded me of my mother's, when she had made up her mind. There was no room for discussion—she was telling us out of courtesy. And no case was worth hurting my relationship with Doug's cousin. "Of course, we understand. But do you know if there'll be a jazz funeral?"

New Orleans was the jazz capital of the world. When a loved one passed from this earth, people flooded the streets with jazz music to honor and celebrate the life of the deceased. These jazz funerals had been a New Orleans tradition since the late 1800s. Not every funeral in New Orleans had one, though. High-profile men and women normally received the long procession accompanied by music, but families could request one.

A typical jazz funeral was a band leading the mourners from the church to the gravesite immediately following the service. The procession could also begin at the home of the deceased, or a family member, leading mourners and the casket to the funeral service and then the gravesite. The music started out slow and somber, as guests cried and mourned their loved one. But after the graveside service, the band played joyful jazz music to symbolize the transition to a better place.

Doug had a jazz funeral, from the church to the cemetery. At first I'd said no. I'd never taken part in one, and all I knew about them was the scene in the James Bond movie *Live and Let Die*. An MI-6 agent watches the band and mourners coming toward him and asks the man beside him, "Whose funeral is it?"

"Yours." Out comes a knife and down goes the secret agent. The pall bearers put the casket over the dead body to pick it up and carry it down the street. The band switches from a mournful tune to "When the Saints Go Marching In" and the crowd dances down the street. I couldn't imagine walking with the crowd without remembering that scene. But after Doug's partner explained the significance of the tradition, I changed my mind. Thank goodness, because it was a beautiful way to honor my husband.

"Of course, Evangeline!" Babette said, "Chantilly was a pillar of this community. It really is a lovely tradition."

And a perfect opportunity to flush out a suspect or two.

"Ev, it's so good to hear your voice! I've missed you, and our lunches. Are you in town?" Luci Lirette's voice floated through the phone, her rich, mellow timbre reminding me of a cello in a symphony. Luci expressed excitement by accelerating her words, never raising the volume. My friend was single, but I'd conjured up her soulmate. He was always a man matching Luci in stature and reserve. They wouldn't raise their voices when fighting. Instead they'd create a perfect harmony of soothing tones.

"It's good to hear your voice as well, Luci. Yes, I'm in town, and I have some questions about poisons. Could you find

some time tomorrow afternoon to discuss your favorite topic?"

"Ah, of course, I can always make time for you. How's five
o'clock tomorrow?"

"Perfect! How about our favorite coffee shop? Do you still
enjoy café americano? I'll buy you a cup, in exchange for your
knowledge."

Luci's chuckles resonated deep tones, leaving me with a
feeling of wholesomeness. "I'll take a free coffee, sure. Is
there any particular poison you want to discuss?"

I'd reviewed my notes, not trusting my memory. "I've been
helping out law enforcement on some cases, and I'm working
one now. The victim suffered nausea, then began vomiting
before she died. So, any types of poison that would cause
those symptoms. I've heard it could be arsenic, but that's not
confirmed."

"You're working the Chantilly Romero case, aren't you?"
Luci sprayed some starch on her conversational tone.

"Uh, yes, will that be a problem?"

"No, not really. But I didn't know about your new career,
and I certainly didn't know you'd come back to help out with
the case." Luci's words gave off an innocent vibe, but they
felt stiff against my ears. "I offered to help out, because of
my knowledge of poisons, but the sheriff's department didn't
accept my help. How did you get on the case?"

Doug used to call me The Gusher. When I became upset
or embarrassed, or especially flustered, I'd spew words like a
rainstorm. "Oh, Luci! I didn't mean to step on any toes. Please
forgive me. I'm just helping out some friends, I haven't joined
the case officially. Gosh, I'm so sorry! Never mind, just never
mind. I sure hope you're not mad..."

The cello solo interrupted me. "Ev, it's okay. I'm not mad, just jealous. In fact, I'd love to help you with the case, if only to show up the sheriff. I'll see you tomorrow at five o'clock. And yes, I still enjoy a large cup of café americano."

My favorite part of Luci's friendship was the warm, soothing feelings that lingered long after our conversations ended. It felt good to reconnect. I promised myself to maintain my connection with Luci—New Orleans wasn't that far away.

My thoughts now turned to Doug's partner. As much as I loved Brad, talking with him never produced the same pleasant feelings I had with Luci.

Conversations with Brad reminded me of my husband, which reminded me that I no longer had a husband. Brad and I talked once a year, on the anniversary of Doug's death. Brad was right beside his partner, and took a bullet himself. But Brad lived and Doug didn't, and there was a part of me that couldn't quite forgive him for it. I suspected there was a larger part of Brad that couldn't forgive himself, either. Our annual conversation always made me nauseated—what would this one do to my stomach?

"Hey, Brad, how are you? Good, I'm glad. Yes, I'm sure this is a surprise. Actually, I'm in town, doing a little work on a case." During our call eleven months ago, I'd mentioned my new side hustle. "Uh, well, it is an active investigation, but not one for the New Orleans police. It's a parish case, but I'd hoped you could tell me a little bit about it. Which one? Um, the victim's name is Chantilly Romero." For a second, I thought I'd lost the connection.

"Gosh, Ev, that's a high-profile case. Even if I knew something about it, I couldn't say anything. Not much anyway."

Which was exactly what I thought he'd say. But I knew Brad. "Oh, of course, of course. How about we meet for lunch tomorrow? For old time's sake."

"Uh, sure. Yeah, there's no harm in that. For old time's sake. We're due for a chat in a couple of weeks anyway—we'll just do it early. How about Bistro Brigitte? It'll just be me—Carol's out of town visiting her mother."

"Sounds great. Two o'clock? Remember to leave early for the Mardi Gras traffic." I'd hoped to corner Brad alone, so Carol's travel plans fit perfectly.

"Works for me. I'll see you tomorrow. Have a good day, Ev."

My promise to Babette echoed in my brain. As my lips had formed the words, my conscience had waggled its index finger. No, to host a stakeout during a funeral was inappropriate and disrespectful.

And yet, too tempting to pass up. Looking back I questioned the outcome of the afternoon. Did our stakeout run like a well oiled machine? Hmmm, not exactly. But to be fair, it was my second time, and my first one didn't go so well. During my initial surveillance, the Remy Robichaux case, our target spotted us within ten minutes after setting up. And his neighbor almost called the authorities because we were trespassing. She was all set to do that too, if Shorty hadn't assured her that we worked for the United States Post Office. I was pretty certain that impersonating a government employee was a felony, but Shorty claimed I was overreacting, as usual.

My PI was our official expert on stakeouts and trailing suspects, having completed over forty-seven stakeouts on his own. His office, in the renovated supply closet of the Graisseville Gas n' More, secured a lot of traffic, mostly clients concerned about wayward spouses. Shorty had tailed most of the women to the Stone Outlet of Baton Rouge, spending his day looking at women's shoes and purses. The money was pretty good—Shorty charged $200 a day plus expenses, just like Jim Rockford. As a bonus, he'd found several gifts for Annabelle, and gave excellent recommendations on the restaurants in the food court. The men gravitated toward gun shows and sporting good stores. According to Shorty, most clients were disappointed to learn the truth. Yes, they expressed relief there was no cheating involved, but they were less than pleased that their spouses were out spending money. And how could they stop the flow of cash without admitting how they'd discovered the truth? Shorty said that was *their* problem, not his.

For Annabelle and Elizabeth, this stakeout was an inaugural event. No one expected the ladies to know what they were doing. Why Shorty expected more from *me*, I'd never know.

"Doc'll cover the northeast corner; Buttercake, the southeast. I'll take the southwest, and Elizabeth'll handle the northwest. Let's take a few moments t'review our suspect's photos. We got five minutes."

"Sweetie, I can't remember 200 people's faces. What if I took a video on my phone? In fact, what if we all did that? It could come in handy later."

"Honeybunch, that's a great idea! Jus' pretend like yer takin' pictures o' the church, or some o' the other buildin's. Do ya'll got any more questions?"

Why did Shorty think this was a good plan? Yes, of course I had questions. "Uh, well I have one. Which way's north? And while we're on the subject, which way is east? If I'm standing on the northeast corner, I need to know both."

Elizabeth squirmed. "Yes, I've got a similar question. I also need north, but I need west too."

Annabelle tugged Shorty's shirt sleeve. "Uh, me too. Which corner is both south and east?"

My PI mumbled. We all strained to hear his words but Annabelle voiced our frustration. "What was that, Sweetie?"

"I said, why don't these public schools teach useful stuff, like how t'read a compass an' tell which way is north an' which way is west? Why do they teach dumb stuff like *pass particles* an' *al-gore-rhythms*?"

"Shorty, I think you mean past participles and algorithms. But you're right—balancing a checkbook and knowing which way is east are more practical." Changing the oil in my car and sewing a button back on would have helped me out a lot more in life than dissecting a frog and square dancing in P.E. class. But I had more important things to ponder than the quality of my public school education.

"Beautiful day for a funeral, isn't it?" A man of medium height stared at me, his brown eyes reflecting friendliness.

"Uh, I'm just here for the Mardi Gras parade. I'm admiring the church while I wait. Why? Is there a funeral going on?"

My new friend pulled out a blue handkerchief and dabbed his forehead. He had just a little hair, on the sides, black and shiny. He continued up towards the top of his head, mopping off perspiration. "Of course there is, Evangeline. Isn't that why you're here?"My team had scattered, leaving me alone with a chatty and possibly dangerous stranger. My fingers curled into my palms, feeling the dampness of perspiration.

"Uh, how do you know my name? Who are you?" Down the street I heard the music and shouts signaling the parade. The sidewalks overflowed with people, as if someone had opened a dam. A dam of people, that is.

The man returned his handkerchief to his pants pocket. "My name is Davis Dugoux. I'm a private investigator. Pleased to make your acquaintance." He extended his hand. "Chantilly Romero hired me three years ago, right after her husband's death. She believed someone killed him. I found evidence supporting her theory, but Mrs. Romero asked me to hold on to it. Shall we step away from the crowd a bit?" He directed me to an empty spot behind us. "Mrs. Romero asked me to keep the evidence because Sheriff Ray was involved, and she couldn't risk going to the authorities. We're not sure how far up the chain this coverup goes. Gum?"

Davis held out a pack of Wrigley's stick gum, spearmint, and I took a stick. "Thank you. But why are you telling me? Shouldn't you go to the state police, or a federal judge, or someone? Why me?"

He chewed his gum slowly. "Because you're not affiliated with any local law enforcement, that I can tell anyway. Your late husband worked for the New Orleans police, and you've kept in touch with his partner. Who's clean, as far as I can tell. And you're dating Sheriff Dupre, but he's clean too. Dr. Delafose, you have connections outside of this area, honest people who could put this information in the right hands."

Davis glanced at the church. "After her death, I decided to turn over my files to someone I could trust. And I choose you." Davis smiled, but it didn't reach his eyes.

He fished into his burlap messenger bag and produced a scrap of paper "This is the contact information for my friend who's keeping my evidence safe. I've instructed him to hand it over. You can read it at your leisure soon, but I'll give you a summary. Mr. Romero uncovered several of Sheriff Doug Ray's secrets. The biggest one, the one that would put him in prison, is that he murdered his wife and dumped her in a swamp just outside New Orleans. He's got a buddy, owns one of those airboat tours, who took him out in the middle of nowhere and helped him get rid of the body."

My senses reeled from the news. Or was it the noise of the crowd? More important questions swirled inside my brain. Had Doug seen any of this? Was Brad involved? Just pretend it's old news, Ev. Keep talking. "Oh, yes! I know all about men and their buddies. My colleague, Shorty Cormier, has a cadre of buddies who help him out with a moment's notice. They'd probably help him with a dead body too—they're all pretty tight." Hmmm, let's hope Annabelle doesn't make him mad. Who was I kidding? To Shorty, Annabelle walked on water. And his moral compass wouldn't allow for dumping bodies. Well, at least not bodies of innocent people.

"Dr. Delafose? Are you listening? I've got the name of the friend who helped Sheriff Ray get rid of his wife, and with some coercion he'd probably testify. Beau gave that information to his wife before he passed, and she handed it over to me. But I've got strong evidence that the sheriff murdered Beau Romero."

A couple strolled by, oblivious to their screaming toddler. Davis used the cries to muffle his words. "The sheriff shot Beau with his personal firearm—a Glock nine millimeter. He filed it as an accidental shooting, claimed Beau was cleaning his gun and it went off. Beau also owned a Glock nine millimeter, exact same weapon. No one performed a ballistics test on Beau's gun, since the sheriff said he found it at the scene and the shooting was an accident. That's when Mrs. Romero hired me."

Davis spit his gum into the silver wrapper and dropped it into his messenger bag. "I talked to some people, did a little digging, and found a witness. Someone saw Sheriff Ray drop a bag in a trash can at the park near his house in Metairie. I got over there quick, and found a nine millimeter Glock wrapped in a bag with dog poop. I'm gonna hang on to that, Dr. Delafose, for security. The Glock, that is—I disposed of the dog poop. But I'm giving *you* the rest of the evidence. Call my friend and get with him soon."

He stood up, tucking his bag over his shoulder. "Good luck, and be careful. You carry a gun, don't you?" With that parting question, he blended into the crowd around us. Just another anonymous body on the street.

My mind reeled at the break in the case—it was hard to focus with the throngs of people. Mourners climbed the steps to St. Augustine, adding to the confusion. I fumbled to click the video button. I hadn't even asked for a business card! Evangeline Delafose, you had a lot to learn about the private investigator business.

CHAPTER 12

"Doc, I got jus' one question for ya'. Even though there was that big ol' crazy group of Mardi Gras delinquents runnin' around, the resta us got good video o' all those mourners goin' in an' comin' outta the church. But not you. Why not? An' after the funeral, an' the street had cleared, we all got good video o' all those people marchin' down the street in the jazz funeral. Same for the graveside service—all t he *resta us* got good video, but somehow *you* didn't? Can ya' answer me that? But this stuff yer tellin' us? Well, I don't even know what it is. So can ya' tell me exactly what happened?"

Judging from Shorty's outburst, I should have mentioned my conversation with Davis Dugoux earlier. When was the appropriate time to repeat the conversation? Definitely not on the street, where people could overhear. Certainly not at the cemetery—we'd spent our energy ducking behind gravestones while trying to get decent footage. In the Uber with Elizabeth? No, I needed to share with the entire team.

"First, that was at least three questions—you claimed to have just one question for me. Which one do you want me to answer first?" Honestly, I'd lost track of all the questions and needed a refresher.

Cue the horse snort—it'd been awhile, so we were due. "Doc, ya' gotta get yore head in the game! Annabelle an' I stopped an' bought a little camera last night, so I could get some recordin's today. So, we all got the tools we needed t'do our jobs."

Shorty stopped to gulp down some orange soda—chewing me out was thirsty work. But at least he'd explained the empty box in the kitchen trash. I knew the new video camera was Shorty's but I hadn't asked. My mother always said, "Evangeline, never ask a question unless you're prepared for the answer. And with Shorty Cormier, well most times you wish you hadn't asked the question." I still had to ask a question, because I knew the answer. Shorty owned a prepaid tracfone, so he needed something else to take photos or shoot video. But at least the government couldn't track him or his phone calls.

"An' I know yer an expert with that recorder on yore phone. Know how I know? Cuz yer always takin' video o' yore dog! We all got some good video today—so why'd ya' record yore feet? An' how does that help us find the killer?"

Elizabeth perched on the couch cushion beside me, touching the top of my hand. "Honey, what's going on? You've been acting strangely since we left the church."

The scrap of paper with Davis' contact fit neatly inside my pocket, hidden from my friends. I reached in, wrapping my fingers around the paper edges. "While we staked out St. Augustine, a private investigator approached me." As I repeated my encounter with Davis, Shorty tucked away his scowl. Elizabeth's tender touch became a vise around my fingers. Annabelle's eyes revealed a...what? Jealousy perhaps? No problem—she could have the next conversation about murder and a coverup with a stranger on the street. I'd had my fill for a while.

"Doc, ya' brought yore gun, right? An' I've got mine. No-body's leavin' this house without me, got it? In fact, we're all goin' home. This is gettin' too dangerous, an' there's too many movin' parts. I can't keep all ya'll safe, so we jus' need t'pack up an' get the heck outta Dodge."

"Nice cowboy reference there, Shorty, but we can't leave. We've got a corrupt sheriff! And who knows how many others are involved, and at what levels? No, we've got to keep going, we've got to get that evidence. Davis said he trusted me, trusted us. We owe it to the Romeros to bring Sheriff Ray to justice."

"Now hold on a minute, Doc! Accordin' tuh you, this Dugoux fella wants ya' t'get this information, go back tuh Graisseville, an' give all this evidence tuh yore boyfriend. Cuz he's an honest guy an' he can get it tuh the right people. An' that's what we're gonna do. I'm not stayin' in this lawless an' corrupt town one more minute. C'mon, honeypot! Ya' best go pack, an' I'll start loadin' the car. Hey, I wonder if we got room for some o' that chicken salad? An' if we got room for that, then we gotta take some sourdough. Yeah, an' that Louisiana crunch cake, but not the strawberry ..."

Thank goodness Shorty made time to pack the refrigerator. Normally I'd roll my eyes, but my body felt heavy, lifeless. My feet couldn't move. I remembered how as a child I'd tried to pull up a sunflower stalk, and it wouldn't budge. Just like my feet. I couldn't leave town, not yet.

When Doug died, I hated his killer, Rocky Ragusa—I still did, God forgive me. But part of my anger pointed toward Doug. Why couldn't he let SWAT execute the warrant? Why did he die and his murderer lived? Did he have to sacrifice *his safety* to pursue justice? I spent a good three years angry at life, angry at Doug, angry at God.

After my first case I started to understand Doug's passion—all the victims needing justice, and not enough good guys to make that happen. My resentment took a new direction, focusing on the criminals. Why were there so many bad guys and so few good ones?

When Nate asked me to work a case for the first time and the killer threatened my life, her actions only fueled my fire. I was going to solve the crime and bring justice to Michael Cook. And that's when the clouds parted and I saw the light, so to speak. Doug couldn't help himself—he had a servant's heart. God gave him that heart so he could live out Micah 6:8, "What does the Lord require of you but to seek justice, love mercy, and walk humbly with your God?" My anger towards my husband melted like butter on a bowl of grits. I asked God to forgive me for channeling my bitterness into the wrong locations. I asked for His love and peace towards my memories of Doug, and to use my passion for solving crime.

"Elizabeth, Shorty, and Honeypot, you do what you need to do. But I can't leave. I need to solve these murders, both Beau's and Chantilly's. I'm not going anywhere."

What did I expect? Well, a couple of things. I expected Shorty's anger to reach far beyond a horse snort. What that might look like I couldn't imagine. Maybe an F1 tornado, or possibly an F2? And I expected Elizabeth to pack my suitcase while Shorty hog-tied me and dragged me to his truck. How would that feel, being hot-tied? I didn't know but figured my PI would remedy that unknown ASAP. And what would Annabelle do? Well, I expected Annabelle to pack up all the food she could for the trip home—for her fiancé, of course. But I wasn't good at reading my friends.

Shorty pushed the air out of his lungs, sounding like an F1 tornado...possibly an F2? "Sweet Pea, Elizabeth, why don't ya'll go pack up yore things an' load 'em in Ev's car? Sounds like the doc an' I are stayin' a bit longer."

And how did someone hog-tie a person, anyway? That was not the day I'd discover the answer.

The Gumshoe Krewe was breaking up, which made me a little sad. We'd helped Elizabeth load my car. My best friend wavered between Southern etiquette and speeding back to her comfort zone. "I think it's best I go home now—I don't want to worry Cliff. But what should I tell my friends? I'm supposed to meet them for coffee tonight after supper."

"Just tell them you had to scurry back home, family emergency. And your best friend would like to keep the meeting, and get to know everyone. In the interest of fellowship and...and feminism." Yeah that last part stretched so far it almost touched the horizon. "El, it'll be fine, I promise."

Of course it would—how suspicious would my greeting sound? "Hi, I'm Ev, Elizabeth's friend. Oh no, she had a family emergency. Something about her father. Oh, she said it was her mother? Yes, that's what I meant. Mmm, no, we're quite close. Well, not so close she'd confide which parent had the emergency, I guess. But we're pretty close. So close, in fact, that I'd like to ask ya'll a few questions. Just a couple, really, nothing major. How about we start with...who do you think killed Chantilly Romero?" Yes, that would win friends and influence people. Hmmm, I should probably work on my opening line.

Getting rid of one friend was easy—Elizabeth wanted to get as far away from danger as she could drive. To our great surprise, however, Annabelle insisted on staying. After some initial arguing, in the end, Shorty agreed she would be safer with him than home by herself. Annabelle dug in her heels. "I can find a dress in Zachary, or I can come back to Babette's store another time. I want to stay and put this dirtbag behind bars. But I do have a question—would the deep discount still apply, if the killer is Babette or Marcel?" She checked our eyes, round with disbelief. "No, I suppose not. Especially if I helped put them in the slammer."

Seriously? When did my favorite librarian turn into Dirty Harry? Not to mention her eagerness to lock away my extended family. Annabelle's mind had worked overtime to point fingers at my cousins. Was I too close to see the obvious? No, shake it off, Ev. They had no motive, means, or opportunity. Or did they?

Shorty sided with Annabelle, at least about the part where she stayed too. "I think the best place for my two favorite females is right by me. We'll all have each other's backs. Now, Doc, don't worry about yore cousins. They don't have no motive. An' before ya' get all sore at me, I had Ethan run some checks on them too, jus' in case. Good news, he didn't find a thing, so Doug's relatives are...Umph!"

That was the sound of my arms squeezing the air out of Shorty's lungs. "Good gravy n' biscuits, Doc! Well, I'm sure glad yer still speakin' tuh me. I mean' I had t'do it! Cuz ya' jus' don't know 'bout people. Okay, ya' can stop squeezin' me! Ya' know, Doc, iffen ya' keep doin' all that sweet stuff, like huggin' an' cryin', people are gonna talk. They're gonna think yer in some sorta competition with muh girl. Except yer datin' the sheriff an' all, mebbe not official like, but people know. An' those people are gonna talk, so ya'd best stop that." Shorty talked the talk of a prickly private investigator pushing off his colleague. His shuffling and sniffling didn't fool me at all. I knew better.

The Cormier home had been full of love, but short on physical affection. Mama Madie, raising six kids, showed her love with homemade biscuits and gravy, pot roast with little potatoes from the garden for supper, and quilted blankets on the beds during those few but chilly Louisiana nights. She had laundry to wash and food to cook and clothes to mend. Madie woke up at 4 a.m. every morning, already an hour behind. What if she took a breath to hug a child or kiss a forehead? Well, she'd be that much further in the hole.

Mack worked his kids hard, passing down the belief that idle hands were the devil's playground. He'd grown up understanding that his wife took care of the tears and the pains. His job? Put food on the table, and make sure his children respected the Bible and their parents. God had saved his soul, and the best thing he could do for his family was to provide that same path, in the way of a God-fearing church and parents. What greater love could there be? He believed in the Bible verse, Proverbs 13:24, the one about spare the rod and spoil the child. But he never beat his kids. He taught them to embrace hard work, especially labor on the farm that provided for the family. Everyone pitched in, because that's what a family did.

I'd only seen Shorty cry a handful of times–at both his parents' funerals of course. But the most memorable time was the day he'd joined the Army. My family—me, Nate, Mad, my parents—and all eight Cormiers attended the swearing in ceremony. Mack walked up to his oldest son, wrapped his arm around Shorty's shoulder, and announced, "I will never be prouder of my son—never! He's serving the greatest country in the world, and keeping us safe. God bless him." Shorty excused himself to go to the bathroom, but I saw his tears. Of course I did—they shone through my own.

And now, here in the driveway of Sweet Magnolia Manor, my PI covered his mouth, swiveled towards the house, and hopped towards the steps. But I saw the tears. He didn't weep in joy and gratitude, like when his father expressed pride. He wondered if he'd make it through this case and stand beside Annabelle, to repeat his wedding vows. In my zeal to discover the truth, to bring justice to the victims, would Shorty die protecting us? No, I couldn't let that happen.

The plan included calling Davis' contact, then for me to meet with Brad while Shorty and Annabelle kept Marcel, and Babette safe. And they were to do that without giving off a bodyguard vibe. Shorty didn't like the plan.

"I don't like this plan, Doc. I don't like you goin' off by yoreself. An' whatcha know about this Brad fella? Sure he was Doug's partner, but is he clean? Mebbe he's involved in this whole mess, an' he's jus' meetin' with ya' so he can go back an' tell his boss what we know."

"Yes, you've made that abundantly clear—you're not a fan of the plan. Davis said Brad isn't involved. I can't believe that he'd say that unless it was true. I'm meeting a cop in a public place, and I'll take my SIG. I'll be fine." Shorty sat on the couch, scooting his boots towards the coffee table then pulling them back until his heels knocked against the seat. My PI fidgeted a lot as a kid, which had improved as he'd aged. But when he was anxious, he couldn't keep still. Annabelle perched beside him, stroking his arm.

"Besides, I should be worried about *you*, Shorty. Please keep Diane close, and my family closer. By the way, you're family now, Annabelle." My friend managed a smile as we watched Shorty's knees bounce up and down. Was that an improvement over the feet scooting? How long would it take for Marcel and Babette to figure out something was up?

The future Mrs. Cormier tried a harsher approach. "Shorty! Stop being so jittery. Take a deep breath and plant your feet. No, you can't move your knees either. Just focus on staying still."

The couch slid back half an inch as my PI jumped to his feet. Yes, there it was, his other nervous habit. At the height of his anxiety, Shorty paced. "Ladies, I tell ya', I jus' don't like it, not one bit!" Back and forth across the living room. My cousins wouldn't stop by until supper, and it was just 1:30 p.m. Plenty of time for Annabelle to soothe Shorty's nerves, maybe.

"Shorty, should you and Annabelle tail Marcel and Babette? What if the killer attacks them while they're at the wake, or helping clean up afterwards, or even consoling Chantilly's family? Gosh, if the killer was smart, he or she would follow them back home, wait until they'd changed clothes and laid down for a nap. You know, killing someone in their sleep would be a lot easier." Wonderful, Ev, you'd developed the mindset of a murderer.

"Yeah, well, here's the thing, Doc. No offense tuh yore cousins, but I'm more concerned about you. Yore daddy'd kill me if I let ya' get murdered. An' then he'd have t'come up here tuh the city, an' ya' know how much he hates drivin' in traffic. Nope, I'd never hear the end o' that one!"

Shorty stopped pacing long enough to focus on his monologue. "An' don't get me started on yore brother! He'd probably have t'take off work, so he'd be real sore at me. Now I'm hopin' he'll get some sort of pay for comin' t'fetch his sister's body from the big city, take her tuh the funeral home in Zachary. But he'd be right sore at me, an' you too, I'd reckon. Yeah, keepin' ya' safe would be in all our best interests."

My PI cast an eye in my direction. "Say, Doc, is that who ya' want takin' care o' yore body? Bill in Zachary? He handles mosta the people getting' buried in the Graisseville Cemetary. 'Course Doug's buried here in New Orleans, so ya'd wanna be next tuh him, I s'pose. So mebbe yore daddy won't have t'drive up here t'fetch yore body. Well, that's somethin' good, at least."

He resumed pacing, then stopped. "Oh, now hold on! Iffen yer buried here, then they'd still have t'take off work for the funeral, Bonnie too. Yeah, an' they'd have t'pull the kids outta school. Yore daddy's gotta go an' find Mad. I mean, ya'll aren't real close or nothin', but I'm sure ya'd want yore sister at the funeral."

Annabelle opened her mouth to stop him, but he was on a roll.

"Say, who ya' want as yore pallbearers? I'm happy t'do it, an' I can think of a buncha people that'd do it too. They're all in good shape, I s'pose, an' ya' can't weigh more than…what? A buck fifty, sixty at the most? With a casket that'd be…well, probably double that. Yeah, I know a few guys, even a coupla women. But I gotta tell ya, Doc, if those pallbearers gotta drive here tuh New Orleans, then they probably won't come. Hey, when ya' have yore coffee with Brad, why don'tcha ask 'im if he's got a few guys that could handle, say three hundred seventy-five pounds. I'm roundin' up, jus' in case."

My head tilted just a hair as I studied Shorty's features. I'd narrowed my eyes, beckoning the logic of planning my funeral to join the conversation. Nope, no logic peeping out from behind a corner. So many questions dancing in my brain. But should I bother? No, there wasn't time to hop down rabbit trails. Best to block the trails and guide my PI towards another route. "Yes, Shorty, I'll add that to my list of questions for Brad. Thank you for being so helpful. Wow, look at the time! Let me call this Miles Miller and get our interview set up. Then I'd better head to Bistro Brigette. Don't worry—I've got my SIG. She'll stay in the car, so I'll only be in danger from my car to the bistro. Hopefully, I'll get to recruit some pallbearers before anything happens."

Miles Miller was a retired cop who couldn't say enough nice things about Davis Dugoux. We scheduled the meeting at his brother's cabin off Lake Pontchartrain. "Dr. Delafose, I can hardly find that place when I'm actually looking for it! It's the perfect spot to visit. Come hungry—I'm grilling burgers." I hung up the phone, lightening Shorty's mood with the meal invitation.

Bistro Brigette's lemon walls and turquoise furniture hadn't changed in my year and a half absence. Brad's wife, Carol, and I used to meet for coffee, bonding over our husbands' love of fighting the bad guys. Occasionally we'd drag our husbands along, and listen to their war stories. We'd heard them a thousand times, but in stereo they appeared larger than life. I'd never shared my thoughts with Carol, but those times with all four of us made me even prouder of Doug, and the career he'd chosen. After his death, Carol's schedule mysteriously became full, making it impossible to ever meet me at Bistro Brigette. I couldn't blame her, I wouldn't want to spend time with a cop's widow. It hit too close to home. Next time it could be Brad, and no wife wants to waste time thinking about what could happen. So Brad and I started meeting, filling our time with stories about Doug, Brad's new partner, and our kids. Spending time with Doug's partner kept me connected to my husband, helped me cling to the good times and push away the bad ones. Brad needed the meetings too, to keep the memories alive. Bless Carol's heart, she never complained about my weekly time with her husband. She could tell how much we needed it.

Brad greeted me from a table. "It's so great to see you–Carol sends her love. You're looking good. Come join me—I came early, for *our* table." After my move, Brad never called. Neither did I—it didn't feel right. Coffee once a week to talk about Doug and old times made sense. Phone conversations felt...inappropriate? Perhaps. If Brad had passed, I wouldn't want Carol calling my husband just to chat. Giving me those precious hours every week with her husband had been enough.

"Evangeline, how are you?" Both Brad's tone and greeting warmed my heart with memories. Doug had always called me Evangeline, never Ev. "You're an angel fallen from Heaven," he would say, "And angels have beautiful names like Evangeline. Mere mortals have names like Ev." His friends and family picked up the habit, and they chuckled at the comparison to an immortal being.

"I'm well, Brad. How's Carol?" I glanced at my phone, watching the allotted time for small talk to pass. We caught up on kids, home repairs, Brad's latest homicide case, and my blossoming dating life—it took exactly forty-three minutes. "Do you want another cappuccino? I'm going to get another chai latte. C'mon, I'm buying this time."

I pulled my credit card from my purse and stood up. So far so good. "Uh, sure, Evangeline, that sounds great. So, is this the part where you casually ask me about the Chantilly Romero case?"

Where had I gone wrong? My mind replayed the last forty-three minutes. No, Brad led the entire catch up period. He'd asked me why I was in New Orleans, and I'd mentioned my girls' trip, Annabelle's upcoming wedding, and the search for a dress. All true statements, so he couldn't have spotted any lies.

"Don't look so surprised. New Orleans is a big city, but we operate like a small town. Why don't you sit back down?"

What was that thumping? Was that my heart? "Evangeline, do you remember Captain Pilcher, Doug's boss? He's still my supervisor, and his cousin's married to Sheriff Ray. Well, I don't know how, but he heard about our coffee date today. He called me into the precinct this morning, told me to shut the door and sit down. He said some crazy things. Are you investigating the sheriff?" Brad's pupils grew dark and wide, like a pool of ink. "Honey, this isn't one of those little cases you've been playing with in hick town. You can't run around New Orleans, spreading rumors about an important government official like Doug Ray."

My stomach hardened, like Brad had punched me in the gut. "Now, one of your girlfriends packed up her things and headed home. The rest of your so-called team better do the same. Captain Pilcher was pretty serious when he called me in this morning, asking me if I knew anything about your shenanigans. I assured him I had no idea."

Shenanigans? I thought only old people used that word. Oh, and my brother. Maybe Davis was wrong—maybe Brad *was* involved in the case. At the least, he was taking Sheriff Ray's side.

"Anyway, the captain says since you're Doug's wife and all, he's not going to haul you in, start a formal investigation. You know, for slander and obstructing justice. But he made it real clear that you and your friends need to drop what you're doing. And you've got to leave town."

CHAPTER 13

As my uncle Earl used to say, Shorty was angrier than a herd of feral hogs at a neighborhood yard sale. No one ever explained that saying to me, but if Earl could see Shorty, he'd nod his head. "Yep, yep—you're right, Evangeline. That fella's just as angry as feral hogs at a yard sale."

"I wish I'd've been there, Doc. That bully wouldn't o'pulled that bullshi..." He glanced at Annabelle's furrowed brow. "Uh, well if I'd been there he wouldn't've been so ugly.. Gimme his address, I'll go have a talk with 'im."

"While I appreciate your chivalry, threatening a police officer isn't the way to go. Forget about Brad—let's focus on our next interview. What do we know about Clifford Benoit?"

Annabelle jumped into our conversation, eager to be of service."Mr. Benoit is an unemployed bodyguard, and I doubt he'll ever get another job. Think about it, guys! The last two people who used his services are dead! And the guy before that, Anthony Carollo, died in prison. Let's face it, no one wants to put *that* on a job application."

Shorty squeezed Annabelle's hand. "Huh! Well, there ya' go! Good job, pumpkin. But why did ol' Clifford kill his employers? That really messes up his job opportunities."

I cleared my throat. "Ahem. Thank you for applying, Mr. Benoit. Before we start the interview, I noticed the area for listing references is blank. And next to your previous employers' you wrote DEC. Were they all born in December?"

Yes, it's always good to find humor during dangerous times. Shorty joined in on the fun. "No ma'am, I ain't real sure when Mr. an' Mrs. Romero came into this world. I put those three letters beside their names cuz they're deceased. Ya' know, dead. An' that's why I ain't got a single reference t'put on that application. I mean, I could put my mama, she'd vouch for me. Oh, I could put the guy I worked for before the Romeros, but he's dead too. He died in prison though, o' natural causes, y'know. I mean, it's kinda hard t'protect someone if they're in prison an' I ain't."

Laughter really is the best medicine. We all let the chuckles trickle down to giggles. "We needed that—thanks, Shorty, for playing along with me. But what else do we have? Anything?"

Annabelle leaned forward."That server I met in the ladies' room, she saw Mr. Benoit arguing with Chantilly just' before the murder. Maybe talking to him will shed some light."

"Good idea, honeybun. Let's see what he tells us, an' if it passes the sniff test."

We both snapped our necks toward Shorty. "Uh, the what? What's a sniff test?"

But my PI had disappeared to retrieve his mid afternoon snack. We had to wait for his return, a good two minutes. "Huh? Oh, ya' know. Does the guy's story make sense, or does it smell fishy? He worked for the mafia, so he's good at lyin'. But we're pretty good too, so we'll see."

Annabelle giggled but I couldn't resist commenting on Shorty's appetite. "Oh okay. And I see this afternoon's snack is leftover pecan chicken salad on sourdough with some *Zapp's* Crawtators. No dessert?"

Shorty waited to gulp down his bite, which I appreciated. "Nah, I'm gettin' married soon. I gotta watch what I eat." He shoveled a handful of chips into his mouth, followed by a swig of orange soda. His actions sent Annabelle into a round of giggles. At least someone found his ravenous appetite amusing.

Before I could take another step down the rabbit trail and question my PI's definition of watching what he ate, my phone rang. "Hello, Babette. Yes, we're doing fine, just getting ready for our interview with Clifford. Oh, that's fine—I didn't expect ya'll to come with us. Oh? Well, that's unfortunate. Not surprising, but it is unfortunate. Uh, could you hold on Babette?"

I put my phone on mute and glared at my PI. "Are you swatting a fly, or trying to get my attention? Honestly, I can't tell."

Shorty washed down the contents of his mouth—two thirds of the sandwich had disappeared. "What's goin' on? What's unfortunate?"

Yes, the patience of...well, of someone who had the opposite of the patience of Job. Maybe a three year old? I had compared my PI to toddlers before, so that analogy fit. And what was more annoying—Annabelle's bursts of giggles or Shorty's...well, just Shorty.

"Babette says the sheriff has canceled on us, but no surprise there. I'll see if Miles can move up our meeting to the sheriff's spot, tomorrow at two. I think that'll be an even better interview than with the sheriff. Do I have permission to finish talking to my cousin?" A wave as he turned toward the kitchen gave me the answer.

"Sorry about that, Babette. Where were we? Oh yes, the canceled meeting. Yes, I'm sure it is for the best. See you soon. I love you too."

My PI reappeared. He'd found a box of chocolate chip cookies and opened another soda. "Shorty, I'm going to call Miles—would you like to speak to him?"

Gulp! "Mhmm. Nah, Imma jus' gonna listen. All this crime fightin's makin' me hungry. An' these cookies are pretty good—do either of ya'll ladies want one?"

Annabelle reached for a snack, but I waved off the box. "No thanks. But I know what you mean. Do you think Batman has this same issue, keeping up his strength while fighting crime?"

Crunch! "Well o'course he does! Why do ya' think he's got his buddy Alfred aroun'! T'make all the food an' bring it to 'im. An' then, they'd go fight crime together. Yeah, that Alfred's a pretty good friend. Wish I'd had a friend like that. But now I've got Annabelle, an' she takes mighty good care o' me."

Should I? Should I dash Shorty's illusion that Alfred hung out with Batman out of the goodness of his heart? Yes, yes, I should. "Uh, Shorty, you realize Alfred is Bruce Wayne's butler, don't you? Sure he's a loyal employee and helped take care of Bruce when his parents died. But he's an employee—he gets paid."

"What? Nah, that can't be true...can it?" My PI chewed on a cookie, glancing at Annabelle as he worked through the trauma of his shattered childhood dream. The nod of her head confirmed his memory lay on the floor of his brain in pieces.

"Well, I'll be hog-tied an' fed tuh the coyotes! Yeah, I guess yer right." His teeth crushed the dark chocolate chips. "Now that ya' mention it, I always wondered why Alfred wore a suit an' tie most every day. I jus' thought he liked t'dress up. Ya' know, like ol' James Bond. Aw, geez, I'd better call my brother Bart an' let 'im know we was wrong." More crunching and pondering the revelations of Batman and Alfred.

Annabelle patted his shoulder. "Sweetie, for what it's worth, I think Bruce and Alfred shared more of a friendship than a work relationship. I mean, Alfred's Bruce's right hand. Even more than Dick Grayson."

But Shorty had already dialed his brother. "Hey, man, there's somethin' I gotta tell ya. Are ya' sittin' down? Ya' ain't gonna believe this..."

Miles and I changed our meeting, so the only thing left to address was Shorty's traumatized Batman memories. "Well, Bart took the news as bad as I did! He said I should break it tuh Merle an' Clovis, but Doc, I jus' ain't got the heart! Mebbe in a coupla weeks, after I recover from the bad news."

Annabelle rubbed her fingertips on Shorty's arm. The woman had the patience of a saint, whereas mine had packed a bag and left town. "Shorty, we're still talking about Alfred working for Batman, correct? Instead of just being his friend?" If I didn't know better, I'd think someone died. Wait, someone, or something did...a part of Shorty's childhood.

"Yeah, yeah, I'm jus' havin' a hard time dealin' with it, is all. Bart an' Merle an' I'd run aroun' the house, playin' caped crusader. I was Batman, cuz I had one o' those black magician's cape. Bart was Robin, an' Merle was Alfred. Clovis was jus' a little ol' thing, he sat in his playpen an' clapped an' cheered."

Shorty shook his head for perhaps the thirtieth time. "I don't know what I'm gonna tell Merle! All these years, Alfred's been his hero. Merle'd run into the kitchen, make us baloney sandwiches an' pour us water in those little paper cups. 'Member those?"

Annabelle nodded her head while I rubbed my temples. "Mama'd let him use the big ol' lid from her roastin' pan t'serve us. Man, we thought those three guys were like, ya' know, what're those guys with capes an' swords? They're on a candy bar?"

Annabelle's rubbing turned to patting. "Honey, I think you mean The Three Musketeers."

Would it further traumatize my PI if I mentioned the musketeers came first, out of a book? The candy bar came many years later. No, my friend had enough dreams shattered in a twenty-four hour period.

Shorty grabbed Annabelle's hand and squeezed it. "Yeah, that's it. Those *Mus-kuh-tears*. We kept hopin' somebody'd make a candy bar with Batman, Robin, an' Alfred on it. Heck, we even wrote a letter tuh that candy bar company. What's their name? Saturn, or Pluto or somethin'?"

My turn to fill in Shorty's blanks. "Mars. The candy bar company that makes Three Musketeers candy bars is the Mars candy company."

Annabelle went back to rubbing Shorty's arm. "Yeah, yeah, Doc,, that one. Merle even drew a picture o' the new wrapper. We told 'em they should get rid o' those three goofy men, put some real heroes on their candy."

I continued to rub my temples. "Well yes, I can see your point. No one considers men with swords and capes heroic."

Shorty raised an eyebrow. Oops! Best to revisit my statement. "Well, what I mean to say is, capes are wonderful. Batman wore them, so yes," Rein in your enthusiasm, Ev! "Super heroes wear them, I mean. So yes, capes are the best. But swords? Nope, nothing exciting about stabbing the enemy."

In another situation, Shorty would see through my sarcasm like weak iced tea. But he was still processing his trauma. Should I pour out my knowledge on the French historical adventure novel written in 1844 by Alexandre Dumas? Nope, my lips pushed together, like my mother's china cabinet with her heritage dishes. My friend had endured enough reality for the day. "Uh, Shorty? We'd all best head for our next interview. I guess you're driving since Elizabeth took my car."

Clifford Benoit, former enforcer for the New Orleans mafia, bodyguard to the Romero family, welcomed us inside his home. My first impression was that, well, he was old.

I'd expected someone like Robert De Niro from *The Untouchables*. Slicked back hair, white shirt with dark tie, maybe even a vest, and a dark suit with a white handkerchief tucked neatly in the pocket. When we rang the doorbell, Mr. De Niro didn't greet us.

To be fair, Clifford was just a kid, in his early twenties, when he worked for Anthony Carollo. Oops, I meant *allegedly* worked for Mr. Carollo, who passed away February 1, 2007 while serving time. According to Ethan's intel, Clifford had just turned a spry seventy-three last month. In short, Clifford was old.

What was that new saying? Yes, the one that my kids told me all the time... "Mom, fifty is the new thirty, and sixty is the new forty. But I'm not sure about you. I mean, you're pushing sixty, right? But you act like you're seventy-five, maybe older. You're in your pajamas by nine every night, and you don't do anything interesting. Not to mention...you don't even know who Jimmy Fallon is! Now Mr. Shorty, he's definitely the new forty—maybe thirty!"

At fifty-three, I was pushing sixty? I was too tired to argue, which confirmed just how old I was. But my kids talked to me, and that was a blessing in this day and age. Many of my friends reached out to me, tugging at my heartstrings. "Oh, Ev, please pray for my son! He's so far down the wrong path, he won't listen to reason! What can I do?"

My answer? Always the same. "What can you do? Pray! All we can do at this point is pray. I'm sure you want to step in and give advice, but children think they know everything. They're not going to listen."

My response bumped into a forehead of wrinkles, sometimes even a scowl. "You don't like my answer, I can tell by your face. But I'm still going to say it...teenagers and adult kids hardly listen to their parents. As parents we want them asking our advice and taking it, but most times they won't. All we can do is pray, and be there to pick up the pieces..."

"Hey, Doc, yer daydreamin' again! Mr. Benoit's askin' us t'come on in. Do ya' wanna go in? Or do ya' wanna jus' stand here on the porch, jus' starin' out into the house across the street? I mean, it's a nice house, nice neighborhood. But I think we should go on in."

Ah, my PI, always the voice of reason. "Yes, of course. Thank you, Mr. Benoit. Let's all go in. Thank you so much for having us."

Just a few minutes from the outskirts of the city, Clifford embraced the niceties of suburbia. "Ya'll come into the dining room. I've got sweet tea and a cherry cobbler." Wow! Clifford's mama raised him right. He understood the definition of Southern hospitality. Shorty's eyes brightened in appreciation. He loved a good cobbler.

"Now cut yourselves off a big hunk. My housekeeper made it for me, when I told her I'd have company this afternoon."

As I admired Clifford's four foot Mardi Gras tree, Annabelle represented our Southern manners. "Thank you so much. We always appreciate a good cherry cobbler in the afternoons."

My PI began slicing, so I sat patiently for my slice. "Oh, thank you, Shorty, that's awfully kind of, oh, well, I guess not."

Shorty sliced off almost a quarter of the cobbler, presumably for the four of us. When he tried to fit it on one of the dainty dessert plates, I realized he'd only cut *his* serving. My PI had a solution—he cut his serving in two, and placed the second plate side by side with the first one. The lineup reminded me of two people waiting at Maggie's coffee shop to place their orders. Here, the cobbler stood in line waiting for Shorty's mouth.

I wrestled the serving spoon from Shorty and cut myself a slice small enough to fit on the dessert plate. Clifford's housekeeper set out four plates—presumably for me, Annabelle, Shorty, and our host. Instead, Annabelle donated her plate to Shorty's meal, a beautiful sacrifice. As my fork rose to bring the cherry cobbler into my eyeline something tickled my brain.

What was that tidbit of intel Ethan had mentioned? "The crime boss before Anthony Carollo, Frank Todaro, officially died of natural causes. But rumors circulated that Carollo had Todaro poisoned, so he could lead the crime family. No one could prove it. Ev, it could have been Clifford!"

Down went my fork and Clifford commented. "Dr. Delafose, is something wrong? Mr. Cormier is enjoying the cobbler—don't you like it?"

The cherry juice puddled around the mound of...what's the non fruit part called? Cake? Pie? Cobbler? Yes, it's got to be cobbler. Anyway, my mouth sent a letter of complaint to my brain, demanding to know why it wasn't filled with cherry cobbler. One glance to my right confirmed the second helping had moved to the front of the line. No waiting for Shorty's mouth.

"Uh, I'm trying to watch my weight, so I shouldn't have any. But thank you." What about the tea? Do people poison iced tea? Why, Ev, of course they do! "Uh, I'd best stay away from the sweet tea as well. Just in case. But again, thank you so much. And, do thank your housekeeper for me." Should I warn my PI? Shorty had eaten so much cobbler, nothing I could say would help him. But there was hope for Annabelle–she'd barely touched her iced tea.

At about the words I *shouldn't have*, Shorty reached over and moved my dessert up to the front of his line. How did the second piece feel about my piece cutting in line? I pulled out my notebook and pen. At least I could take notes.

"Uh, anyway, thank you for taking some time to see us. We're looking into Mrs. Romero's death and we wanted to ask a few questions."

Clifford put down his fork and grinned. "Well, I'm pleased to have you here. I don't get much company, and now that Miss Chantilly's gone, I don't have any place to go anymore. I'm really not someone who enjoys checkers in the park, if you know what I mean."

Oh, I knew what he meant! Clifford preferred poisoning people to board games. "Of course. One question I have is, well, no offense, but why did Mrs. Romero have a bodyguard old enough to collect Social Security?" Yes, it was a good thing I hadn't touched the food or drink. I wasn't going to leave the meeting with a new friend.

But Clifford laughed until he coughed. Also, a good thing he'd put down his fork to answer our questions. Well, *my* questions–Shorty's line was back down to no waiting. Maybe Annabelle would join in soon.

"Yes, that's an excellent question. Miss Chantilly liked to call me her bodyguard, but really she indulged an old man. Don't get me wrong–I'm pretty fit for a guy my age. And I'd take a bullet for any of the Romero family. But yes, she should have hired someone younger and stronger."

Yay Annabelle! "Mr. Benoit, would you mind telling me why you and Mrs. Romero were arguing just before she died?

Witnesses claim it was a heated argument." A gleam of pride shone from behind her eyes.

Clifford fiddled with his iced tea glass. "Please call me Clifford, and I hope I can call you Annabelle. Now don't get me wrong, Annabelle. When I said I'd take a bullet for the family, I meant it. I'd do most anything for them. But I'm allergic to shellfish! If I take just one taste, my throat swells up and I head to the hospital. Miss Chantilly knows that, so she has someone else taste her food. But that night, the night she passed, someone tried to run her off the road. That scared her, convinced her someone was going to kill her. She wanted me to taste her po'boy, because all those people had access to the food. Sure, Jacqueline told us no one had touched the food but her. But we didn't trust that woman any farther than we could throw her."

He took a sip. "We argued because I wasn't going to the hospital, possibly dying, just so Chantilly could eat a po'boy. I told her, take whatever you want off the appetizer stations. I'll eat any of it, as long as it doesn't have shellfish. The woman lost it, started screaming at me to do what she said or she'd fire me. I said go right ahead. It's not like I needed the job! Then she demanded I take off the tomatoes, but I refused. I can't even touch shellfish without breaking out in hives. So Jean grabbed the sandwich, took it back to the kitchen, and brought Chantilly another one without tomatoes."

Annabelle was chugging along, a real pro. "Did Jean bring a new sandwich, or did he just take the tomatoes off the original one?"

Clifford put the glass back on the table. "Well, I'm not sure. I mean, I thought he brought another one. But he could have taken off the tomatoes. Does it matter?"

Shorty focused on the third piece of cobbler, as usual. But this time I had my favorite librarian. "I'm not sure, honestly. But it might. Did Jean know anything about poison?"

More fiddling—why couldn't Clifford look at us? "Uh, I know he took some horticulture classes at the community college. He loved plants—you should see his yard! In fact, he mentioned to Chantilly he took a couple classes about poisonous plants. And he enjoyed the professor so much, he took some of her other classes. But I don't remember what they were."

Annabelle glanced in my direction, feeling guilty for taking the lead. My smile encouraged her to keep going. "Mr. Benoit, uh, Clifford, what was Jean's relationship with Chantilly?"

Clifford moved his hands to his lap. "Look, I don't enjoy speaking ill of the dead, especially my friend and employer. But I will tell you this: Jean pursued Chantilly after Beau passed. But she just didn't feel that way about Jean, so they agreed to be friends. Wait a minute!"

Clifford's knees bounced under the tablecloth, making it dance. "One time we went to Jean's house, and they closed the door to his study for a private meeting. I wandered around a bit, not opening any cabinets or drawers. I wasn't snooping—honest! But I saw a couple of books on Jean's bookshelf about poisonous plants, and household poisons. I asked Miss Chantilly about them later, but she told me to stop being so protective. She said those were from the classes Jean took and I had nothing to worry about."

Clifford's knees slowed down from a gallop to a walk. "I'll tell you one thing, there was no love lost between Jacqueline and Miss Chantilly. Jacqueline owed Chantilly and Beau a lot of money, from the poker tournaments at Ami Fidéle.

That woman also took classes from that same professor, ones about poisonous food. She's a good suspect, I'll tell you that."

My pen scribbled furiously while Annabelle continued. "What about Sheriff Doug Ray? Did he have any knowledge of poison?"

Clifford's tea glass became a source of great interest. "Mr. Benoit, what about the sheriff?"

"Huh? Oh, I think he has some knowledge of poison. He had a couple of cases, before he got elected sheriff, where the victim died of poison. But you shouldn't get mixed up with Sheriff Ray, Dr. Delafose." With that, Clifford slammed shut his door of hospitality.

"Say, I hate to be rude, but my son calls me every Saturday before supper. I'll walk you to the door."

"Well, Shorty, what did you think? We're awfully good at getting thrown out of homes. I'd have to say though, Clifford's one of the nicest people to throw us out. Oh, and great job on the line of questioning, Annabelle. You're really getting the hang of this."

Annabelle glowed from the praise as Shorty made a right onto the street. "Yeah, great job, Pudding. And yeah, for a mobster ol' Clifford's a pretty good guy. An' we're about right on schedule, as far as the case goes."

"How so?" We reached the end of the street and Shorty turned left.

"Well, this is about the time we munch on toffee apples an' ride ponies."

"What? Shorty, I never understand your analogies." And why did they often revolve around food?

"We're on a merry-go-roun', Doc. Yeah, we're jus' goin' round an' round in circles. Which means we're due for a break in the case."

CHAPTER 14

"Thanks for that carousel reference, Shorty—now I'm craving toffee."

Shorty pulled the truck into the Big E-Z. "Ya' know, I don't care about gas bein' cheaper in the big city. It's still too dang crowded here, an' all the crazies jus' hang out on the corner an' stare at ya.'" Ever the small town guy, he nodded to the gentleman on the corner as he filled his gas tank. The gentleman not wearing any pants yelling at the cars streaming by. Say what you will about Shorty, his mama raised him with good Southern manners.

Annabelle opted for the interior of the truck, but I got out to keep my friend company. Not surprisingly, my actions proved to be a mistake.

"Know what I think, Doc? I think one o' our so-called leaders made a deal with someone, an' boxed up all the crazies an' bused 'em here tuh The Big Easy. Yeah, mebbe that's why this crazy place is called The Big Easy—cuz it was a pretty big, easy thing t'sell out the city!"

I leaned against the truck bed, but straightened up at Shorty's glare. Not a single part of my person touched my PI's truck.

"Okay, I get it—you're ready to go home to Graisseville, your hometown, where people stop to help you change a flat and chat about the weather. I'm right there with you, Shorty! Let's get this case solved and I'll pack the truck. Oh, but first I'm going inside, to see if they have a toffee candy bar, maybe even a toffee covered apple."

I mean, I hadn't eaten the cherry cobbler, so I could splurge on a toffee candy bar, or a toffee apple. I even grabbed four moon pies and an orange soda, a bottled water for Annabelle, and a candy bar for me. When I returned, Shorty had the truck running and the air conditioner blasting. My phone noted a coolish sixty-three degrees and a not even remotely bearable seventy-four percent humidity. New Orleans' proximity to the ocean made for buckets of sticky oppression. Annabelle was chatting with her sister on the phone. I knocked on the window and handed her the water.

For some reason I decided to try my skills at throwing plastic grocery sacks onto truck consoles. And from the back seat no less. I hadn't practiced as much as Shorty and it showed—the plastic grocery bag slipped off the console and landed at Annabelle's feet. She kept right on chatting with her sister. *Dear Lord, please make sure the drinks didn't squish the moon pies. Or my candy bar. Amen!*

"Geez, Doc, thank goodness ya' don't play for the Pelicans. They got enough troubles! They don't need yore lousy shootin'."

As Annabelle regaled her sister with the sights and sounds of New Orleans, she reached down for the sack and handed it to me. Yes! All four moon pies and my lone candy bar remained unscathed. *Thank You, Lord, for small blessings!* "Uh, Pelicans? That's basketball, right?" The horse snort echoing throughout the cab confirmed my guess. Or did the snort mean I'd guessed wrong?

"Doc, how can ya' live in Louisiana an' ya' don't know the sports teams? 'Course the Pelicans are a basketball team." I'd guessed right, but the exam wasn't over.

"Say, what's the name o' our NFL football team? An' no lookin' on yore phone."

"Uh, the Tigers?" Shorty pulled out his scowl and sat it smack dab in the middle of his face.

"No, that's LSU. All their teams are the Tigers, even badminton." He lengthened the word *no*, to emphasize how wrong I'd been. "An', while we're on the subject, those teams that aren't even on television, why should they get t'use the same mascot as the football team? Or any o' the other teams that bring in revenue for LSU?"

Would this conversation never end? Would Annabelle ever get off the phone?

"Guess ya' don't got an opinion. An' for the record, Doc, our professional football team is the New Orleans Saints, the only thing good about this Sodom an' Gomorrah town." He merged into the traffic circus, and I distinctly heard a "those dang drivers can kiss my assets." Shorty might be right about government officials busing all the crazies to New Orleans.

"Doc, ya' teach at LSU! How come ya' don't know the difference 'tween the college teams an' the professional teams?"

The landmarks around me, familiar from the time I lived here, promised we were just a short five minutes from Sweet

Magnolia Manor. And hopefully that much closer to a sports reprieve.

"Shorty, I can't believe we're having this conversation! When have I ever known anything about sports, professional or otherwise? We went to high school together—you know I never attended a single sports event."

Oh no, a sore subject for Shorty. He and his brothers had to work on the farm every day after school. There'd been no time for extracurricular activities. But he'd gone to almost every sports game Graisseville hosted. Except for the badminton games, of course. He listed badminton in the same category as tiddlywinks and checkers.

Now, over thirty years later, the man bled, uh, purple and gold? Maybe? Gold and black for the Saints? Or was it black and blue? And don't even ask me about the Pelicans' colors! Anyway, if you looked up the definition of a fan, Shorty's face would be there.

Annabelle tucked her phone back into her purse. "If you two are finished squabbling, my sister says 'hi'. She had a lovely conversation with Harper and Breaux. Oh, I miss those two something awful!"

"Who the heck are Harper and Breaux?" The words flew out of my mouth before I could grab a hold of their coattails. The names rang a bell but that bell was old and rusty.

"Geez, Doc, where ya' been? That's Annabelle's grandkids. They live in Natchitoches with Annabelle's daughter Caroline, an' her husband, Ray. Don'tcha know nothin' about yore friends?"

We pulled into Sweet Magnolia Manor, and not a minute too soon. Never had a driveway made me cry tears of joy. "Oh yes, I knew that! I'm sorry, Annabelle, I'm a little scattered.

That's right, they do. We had lunch with them last time they came to visit you. Anyway, I hope you like the bottled water, and Shorty, I got you some moon pies, and an orange soda, and I think..."

"What the Hello Dolly? Doc, are ya' drinkin' the devil's bathwater? Yore mama an' daddy raised ya' better n' that!"

Oh, goodness! It was official—this conversation of misery would never end. Yes, I'd be on my deathbed, my loved ones surrounding me...hopefully grandchildren too, although at this point things didn't look so good. Matty wouldn't even discuss his love life and Ellie...

Anyway, Shorty would be there, of course. The guy would outlive us all. My nurse would fluff my pillows and smooth the wrinkles in my sheets. In my version of my last hours, my nurse's name was Blade, and he looked a lot like Jean Claude Van Damme. Hey, it was my story and my nurse resembled whomever I pleased! And I daydreamed elaborate stories to check out of uncomfortable conversations.

So yes, my nurse Blade would fluff my Chamberlain down and feather dual-chamber pillows, and smooth my Boll and Branch 100% organic cotton sheets. Would Boll and Branch ever allow wrinkles in their sheets? According to their ads, definitely not.

Uh, well, getting back to my story, I'd sink into my version of Heaven on earth, comfy cozy in my bed with a bowlful of nurse candy lounging just within my sight.

Amongst my family and my friends, and my nurse, Shorty would lean over, as if to stroke my hair. But then he'd change gears, and blurt out, "Ya' know, Doc, ya'd be up dancin' an' havin' a real good time, iffen ya' hadn't drunk the devil's bathwater for the last twenty-five years o' yore life! An' don't get me started on yore lack o' sports education. Yore daddy tried, he shore did, but..."

Blade would shake his head as he wrote out some sort of letter. Oh no, he'd given notice! He'd hand it to Matty, who'd shake his head. Oh goodness, my eye candy gave notice to my son? No parenting book had ever prepared me for that situation.

What could I do? Well, I'd have to orchestrate a quick death. Yes, that was the only way out. It was all just too much! My embarrassment knew no bounds. Yes, I'd die fast, the victim of shame.

Why was my PI bringing up this insane conversation? Did he want me to die, just like the Billy Joel song? What was it? "Only The Good Die Young?" Well, of course, Ev! That was pretty obvious.

And could someone literally die of embarrassment? No doubt I'd find out the truth, and probably sooner than I'd hoped. Question: could Blade still tag along, if I languished in bed, dying of embarrassment? I mean, he'd be so handy. Nope, in the real world my son would never allow a Jean Claude look alike near my death bed. Unless... "Hey, Mr. Van Damme? Uh, or the man who looks like Mr. Van Damme?"

Who was I kidding? In my world, it would be Jean Claude, hands down. "Uh, yes sir, you can act as a nurse to my mother, but here's the thing...you've got to put her on your YouTube Channel. You know, film yourself taking care of my mother. Then, yes, I'll let you care for her. Oh, and I get fifty percent of the revenue stream. My sister? Who? I don't know what you're talking about, I don't have a sister..."

No, shake it off, Ev. Matty wouldn't deny his sister! Or would he? At any event, I had to re-engage in this never-end-

ing conversation with Shorty, for the sake of our friendship—and my sanity.

*Lord, please help me word my response correctly. Please
calm my nerves and soften my tongue. Oh, and if it's within
Your Will, please throw in those grandchildren. I mean, if You
don't mind. Not right now, but sometime down the road. In
Your Name always, amen.*

And back to Reality Road. "Okay, I'm going to stop you
right there, Shorty. Yes, we're still on the right side of the
Mason-Dixon line, and yes, everyone considers sweet tea
the house wine of the South. But I'm counting calories and
watching my sugar! Drinking unsweet tea is not, nor will ever
be, the equivalent of drinking from the bathtub of the Prince
of Darkness. So please stop calling my tea by that outrageous n
ame!"

"Hush, Shorty, leave Ev alone. Honestly I don't know how
you two ever solve a case with all your bickering back and
forth. You're worse than my kids, when they were teenagers."
Yes, we had to solve the case soon, before we all drove each
other crazy.

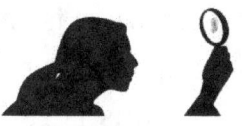

Shorty and I had passed through the living room to separate
corners. We needed a small break, to calm nerves and eat
sweets. Truth be told, Annabelle probably needed a break
from us too. Five minutes later we sat in the living room, our
friendship restored. Good friends can't stay angry.

But first I'd texted Marcel and Babette—*Elizabeth had a family emergency, and drove home in my car.* Some things were best left unsaid.

We had fifteen minutes before our interview with Beatrice Romero. Time to review the elements table.

I stood by the white board, markers in hand. "Know what I think, guys? I think Clifford's afraid of Sheriff Ray. He's not the killer, but he thinks the sheriff is."

During our break I'd consumed a quarter of my toffee candy bar and tea, and Annabelle was working on her second bottled water. Shorty had three moon pie wrappers and an empty soda can to show for his break. If eating were a sport, Shorty'd have a wall of trophies.

"Mebbe. But poison's a great weapon for a geezer. An' Clifford said it himself—he spent a lot of time with Chantilly. But hey, yer entitled tuh yore opinion. How're we doin' with the elements?"

Annabelle studied the board. "Is it okay if I add that Jacqueline owed Chantilly money for gambling debts? Her motive's still red. She took classes about poisons, so her means changes to red. She's now red across the board."

I studied the board. "Jean's motive is still yellow/orange—was it a broken heart, or a quest for revenge? He also took classes on poison, so his means is red. And now, we know he brought Chantilly the po'boy with the poison. He could have doused the sandwich with arsenic." Annabelle changed the colors to match my words.

"Doc, I know yer sweet on the ol' geezer, but a lotta people in his life died o' poison. But I'll give ya' green on motive and opportunity—if the shellfish allergy holds water. He was fightin' with Chantilly cuz he didn't wanna swell up an' all. An' he refused t'take the test bite cuz of the shrimp, not cuz he'd poisoned it. But I'm still givin' his means yellow. Or orange, whatever."

The *swoosh* from my phone confirmed a text. "I asked Ethan to double check Clifford's allergy story. He found proof, so yes, it's true. Clifford Benoit's allergic to shellfish, which makes him our weakest suspect. And please don't call him a geezer."

Another *swoosh* but not from a text. It was the sound of my PI consuming his last moon pie. "Doc, it's a sign o' respect! Know what's the opposite of a geezer? A dead man! Clifford's outlived all those other mobsters, an' a lotta other people his age. He's proof that bein' seventy plus doesn't mean yer knockin' on death's door!"

Once again, Mom broke up the squabbling. "Okay, children, let's move on. Next is Sheriff Doug Ray. Chantilly suspected that Beau's death wasn't accidental, and she hired Davis. He found the murder weapon, which he's holding for safekeeping. And he's sending us to his trusted source to hand over the evidence proving that Sheriff Ray killed Beau. That's a definite motive."

The memories flooded back in my mind, drenching my soul. Oh, it was so uncomfortable! And frightening—Davis had kept his cool, but I could sense the fear oozing from his body. "You're right, Annabelle. Of course, the means is weak, and so is opportunity. Sheriff Ray worked some poison cases, and he was first on scene for Chantilly's death. But I can't make them any other color but green. Oh, I don't like that man !"

"Doc, nobody likes that man, not even his own deputies, I bet! But he's got files on so many dirty little secrets that he's not goin' anywhere. This is a good time t'bring up somethin' that ya'll don't wanna hear. But I'm gonna say it."

My PI, no, my *friend* hopped across the room and first took Annabelle's hand, then mine. "We gotta let this go. It's too much for a disabled Army vet, a librarian, an' a doctor o' books. We need t'pack up our stuff, head back home, an' turn over the name o' this guy tuh Sheriff Dupre. Let's let ol' Mitch take over this case, an' go through all this so-called evidence."

Shorty made all his points and Annabelle's head bobbed up and down. Even I was thinking about giving up. In fact, I had one foot in Shorty's truck, and my bag tucked under my arm. Okay, not literally, but my mind kept pondering how quickly I could pack my things and throw them in the back of Shorty's truck. The theme from *Cops* interrupted my logistics.

"Ev? You asked me to do some digging into Davis Dugoux, the private investigator you met today. Well, I've got my eyes on, uh, anyway.... local police just found his body in a vacant lot over in the Seventh Ward. Dispatch reports four gunshots to his chest."

My shoulders shook with dread. Someone *murdered* Davis? I'd just spoken with him, what? Less than twenty-four hours ago. The fact the police found his body in the Seventh Ward made my heart race. Only three percent of the population in that community was caucasian. It was a known fact.

"Ethan, this can't be right. Davis Dugoux was middle class and white. No one goes to the Seventh Ward unless they're invited. And even then, they would need protection. Why would he be over in a place that he didn't belong?"

"Yeah, I know, it doesn't make sense. The police chatter's suggesting he was on a case. I only report the facts, Ev—it's up to you to solve the mystery. Oh, that reminds me, I'm working on the coroner's report. And I'm sorry it's taking longer. But I've never done that before, and it's a different database. But, to be fair, you've never asked."

"You're right, cousin, I haven't. I'm still new at asking you for things that you shouldn't ever give me. Tell your mom and dad I said hi. And keep me posted."

My thoughts raced around the track in my head. Davis tried to right a wrong, bring a killer to justice, and his actions got him killed. That could have been me, or Shorty, or even Annabelle. My eyes sought out my friend, the one who insisted we get out of town. But strangely enough, a murdered private investigator planted Shorty's feet in New Orleans. "I jus' can't believe this, I jus' can't! It's not right, it jus' isn't."

Shorty hopped back and forth, clearly agitated. "Yeah, criminals murderin' cops, that's wrong, so wrong. But now they're killin' private citizens? Nope, we've gotta get justice for this Davis Dugoux. It's wrong, jus' so wrong." He turned to Annabelle. "Puddin', I hate t'do this to ya', but I changed my mind. We gotta get justice." Puddin's eyes shined with tears, but she nodded her head.

I rallied our team. "So, we all agree? We're staying until we solve the case?" Would Babette and Marcel continue to host us? Nope, best to put those questions in the back of my mind. I had Shorty on board now and that was something.

Annabelle's timekeeping skills came in handy. "Uh, guys, look at the time! You're late for your interview with Beatrice Romero! Go—I need to stay here and call my mom back. Let's hope I can leave out the parts involving dead bodies and talking to potential murderers."

According to the Bouviers, Beau Romero stood at six feet, one inch. His sister, on the other hand, wasn't quite as tall. Uh, well...she was petite.

At only 4 feet 8 inches tall, people in Graisseville would call Beatrice *a tiny mite of a thing*. Yep, probably here in New Orleans too. The woman owned a bakery, Bea's Bites. How did she reach the counters? Maybe that should be question number one?

"Thank you so much for meeting us, Beatrice. We're like everyone, we're trying to get to the truth."

Bea walked us into her home. "Come, sit. I've brought some food from my place. I hope you don't mind, but I haven't eaten all day and I'm starving!" Mmmm, free food? Yes, please!

But why did tiny people fuss about being hungry? They had access to food just like the rest of us—all they had to do was eat it.

"Oh, yes, thank you so much, Bea! We've heard great things about your bakery. But we never made it over there. Thank you."

Bea studied us, much like a cat observes a mouse. "Let's examine the facts. Yes, I told people that Chantilly killed my brother. Yes, I told people she tried to run my life, and she took whatever she wanted. Even meals from my restaurant, even my brother. And what could I do to stop her?"

Hmmm...well this conversation wasn't going as planned. I tried another tack. "Uh, well, Bea, I guess that's all you could do then—nothing. So you're admitting you had issues with your sister-in-law?"

Bea ignored my comment as she served our plates—generous helpings, even by Shorty's standards. Maybe murderers could have respectable Southern manners? And why hadn't my mother covered this, in her endless lessons on etiquette south of the Mason-Dixon line?

"Yes, *always dress up when paying a visit to a Southern murderer. Should you bring a gift? That's up to you, but most rules say yes. Especially if the host doesn't have formal charges of murder. What if our blessed courts dismissed the charges, or even acquitted your host? Well, then you've committed a most grievous sin! Yes, best to always bring a gift.*" Maybe Shorty had some uneaten moon pies left in the truck?

Of course my PI had to step in, always up to the fight. "Miss Bea, didja kiss an' make up with yore sister-in-law, before she died? I mean, ya' seem like a right nice young lady. I bet ya' geehaw'd with Miss Chantilly, before her death?"

Yep, Shorty conveyed supernatural powers over women between the ages of twenty until death's door. He'd probably serve as a Blade to more than one woman's death bed...if he wanted. Or if Annabelle wasn't around.

Cue the nauseating giggle. How did Annabelle put up with this? Maybe Shorty's flirtations amused her. She definitely had nothing to worry about. He only had eyes for Annabelle.

"Oh, why Mr. Shorty! You're so perceptive! Yes, of course I forgave Chantilly. I mean, I couldn't ever prove she killed my brother. I hired a private detective, but he couldn't find a single blessed thing. My mama always told me, forgive and forget. And Beau? Why he'd tangled himself in all sorts of not-so-ethical things, I'll never know. Chantilly wasn't my best friend, by any standards. But my new distillery, Counterblow, stood to shatter all records. It was my way out. I'd paid for it, out of my inheritance. Why would I muddy the waters by killing Chantilly?"

That was a new one! Beatrice owned a distillery? I turned my back to text Ethan. *New distillery Counterblow owned by Beatrice Romero?*

My phone shrieked in anger. *I'm working on a crappy laptop in the mountains on my winter break! Sorry, but this isn't a paying job. I'm doing the best that I can.*

What the heck, Ethan? My fingers flew forward furiously, then stopped. Was that the Holy Spirit staying my angry hands? I held my thumb over the backspace key until the message box was empty. *I'm sorry, Lord. Of course, You're right. Let me start again.* I took a deep breath, then replied.

You're right, Ethan, and I'm sorry. Consider this the last case I give you for free. Cousin, I will figure out a way to pay you in the future.

Ethan's response both hurt me and humbled me. He was right—we'd never paid him. Shorty and I had other revenue streams. But Ethan didn't. If we wanted to continue using our cyber source, we should offer him compensation. Except, I was in the middle of an interview—Ethan had to wait.

Maybe Shorty should conduct all our female interviews? "Yer a gemologist, right Miss Bea? Ya' got a hobby, collectin' all those pieces off the periodic table? Arsenic's in there, right? Ya' got some arsenic stored in yore home?"

Gone was the good old Southern hospitality. "Mr. Shorty, I really don't know what you're talking about! Okay, at the Mardi Gras party, I went to the bar. But once I got my drink I was right there behind Chantilly, just talking to some of my friends. That's when I saw her wobbling. Oh goodness! Chantilly's face turned pale as a peace lily bloom. Then she started sweating."

Bea's face softened, like my grandmother's quilt. "Mr. Shorty, I asked Chantilly if she was feeling alright, maybe she wanted some water? But she couldn't answer me. She was throwing up all over the place! I screamed something about calling an ambulance."

Yes, my PI hooked Bea. Except for her last remark.

"But just so you know...*anyone* can purchase Crystalline arsenic from the internet. It's not that hard."

CHAPTER 15

"How was the interview? And do we think Beatrice killed Chantilly?" Shorty couldn't wait to call Annabelle—I was a little concerned for her safety too. Our favorite librarian liked honesty and reason. And it was an honest and reasonable question. In any other world, anyway. And why, in a crazy big city like New Orleans, did my PI drive like, uh, what was that film? Mama Dora? Mrs. Dana? Miss Debbie?

Why didn't any of those names sound quite right?

My Aunt Ruby drove faster than Shorty—while he drove in New Orleans, anyway. My aunt worked hard to drive five miles under the speed limit. Aunt Ruby had given me a lecture—several lectures, in fact.

"Evangeline, the speed limit is exactly that, a limit. We shouldn't drive more than the limit. In fact, we should drive under it, to maintain a balance with people driving more than the limit."

Aunt Ruby had always made up her own rules, especially when she'd been Graisseville's mayor. Fortunately, I'd resided in New Orleans during that short but traumatic dictatorship.

Ev, focus on the case. And yet...

"Shorty, before you answer Annabelle's question, which was whether you think Beatrice killed Chantilly, please answer this one."

Take a breath, Ev. The following question was crucial. "Why is everyone around us passing your truck and blaring their horns? They're pretty angry at your snail's pace." Both questions were important, but the second one intrigued me more.

Shorty gripped his steering wheel with both hands, knuckles white and tense. His shoulders curved up towards his ears, and his jaw tucked into his chest. If Shorty's nose was just a couple inches longer, it would have touched the steering wheel. How could that position even be comfortable?

My PI's eyelids scrunched toward his cheeks, creating slits. What was that sound? Was Shorty praying?

"Amen! What'd ya' say, Doc? I didn't hear ya', on account o' I was prayin' that the good Lord would let us live long enough t'get back tuh Graisseville. Now what was yore question?"

Shorty's voice strained, struggling to force a carefree attitude into his tone. But the stress of big city driving took his tone by the coattails and shoved it out the door, then slammed and locked said door. His fingers had become one with the steering wheel, and I feared his shoulders would never smooth back into their rightful place several inches below his chin.

"Uh, never mind." I said. "But do you think you could go a little faster? People are screeching by us, yelling words unfit for anyone's ears." My Glock and Shorty's girl Diane rested nearby, but that didn't mean I wanted to take them out for a stroll.

"Uh, I guess so. But we're turnin' off the main road—look, I got my blinker on." Yet another difference between the big city and small towns. In Graisseville, residents rarely used their blinkers. Why? Well, that was Ken Crocker right there in the blue pickup, and Ken lived on Blunt Mill Road. He'd turn left just about...yep, there he went. And up went his hand, executing the small town wave in the rearview mirror. Why would Ken need to signal, when we all knew where he'd turn?

"I think I'm gonna say a prayer every time we leave the driveway. Normally I don't bother the good Lord with somethin' small like gettin' from Point A tuh Point B. But I think that, right here in this den o' iniquity, we're gonna need all the prayers we can send up tuh Heaven! Now Sunshine, I'm gonna let ya' go. We're in the driveway, but I'll be inside in jus' a minute. We'll all sit down an' talk about ol' Bea Romero—she's quite a character, ain't she?"

As Shorty turned off his truck, the color returned to his knuckles. Even his shoulders reclined into their favorite position, straight and level. Annabelle greeted us at the door, her frownlines smoothing at our return.

Lord, thank You for bringing us back safely. Please help us solve this mystery soon, before Shorty's shoulders remain a permanent fixture half an inch below his ears. Amen.

Miss Daisy! It was the film, *Driving Miss Daisy*. At least I'd solved another mystery.

"It's so good to have ya'll back! I worried so much while you were gone." Annabelle gave us a group hug, wrapping her slender arms around us at the same time.

After our harrowing ride home, Shorty needed sustenance. So did the rest of the team. He emerged from the kitchen, arms bulging with sustenance. "Hey, I know what my problem's been! I ain't been gettin' my recommended daily allowance o' Crawtators!" He hopped to the coffee table and dumped two bags of *Zapp's* Spicy Cajun Crawtators. "See, I been *suh-come-in'* tuh the round crunchy cookies dipped in chocolate, huggin' all that creamy marshmallow goodness. All that sugar's been throwin' me off muh game!"

Annabelle and I took the bottled waters offered and watched Shorty plant himself on the couch, practically in his fiancée's lap, orange soda in hand.

As one woman stroked Shorty's arm, the other addressed the moon pie accusation. "Let me get this straight, Shorty. You believe that you have succumbed to the sweet temptations of moon pies, thereby sacrificing the savory saltiness of Crawtators? And that's what has kept us from solving the murder of Chantilly Romero?" I opened my water and took a few sips, contemplating the logic. It made almost as much sense as my aunt Ruby's theory on speed limits.

Annabelle glared at me. "Well, Ev, it can't hurt, switching up his afternoon snack. It's almost seven o'clock, so there's a nice window for digestion before supper."

Annabelle had done her best to head off the bickering. What she didn't understand is that Shorty and I thrived on it. "Huh, Doc? I can't hear ya', on account o' the noise from openin' my Zapp's. Say, ya' got yore ladies' gossip session in an hour an' a half—what're we havin' for supper?"

Swoosh! I reached into my phone to check the text message. "Good question. Babette and Marcel won't be coming over until tomorrow, when they pick us up for church. We're on our own for supper, and they'll be in the driveway tomorrow at 10:00 a.m."

A sigh escaped from Annabelle's lips. "Well, I saw some salad in the refrigerator. The chicken salad's all gone, but there's some roast beef and' bread left. Shorty and I can eat some leftovers, and Ev, you'll have supper with Elizabeth's friends."

Having a buffer for me and Shorty was nice, especially one who'd take care of Shorty. "Mmmm, Annabelle, sounds good. For now, I'm content drinking my water and listening to your fiancé crunch and slurp. Tell me, though—what do ya'll think about Beatrice? Is she our best suspect?"

Amid the munching and gulping my PI weighed in with his opinion. "We know the sheriff killed Beau Romero, an' we know Chantilly had proof. It doesn't seem a far stretch that Doug Ray'd kill her too, an' now Davis. But that's a lotta bodies, even for an underhanded sheriff. Nah, I think Bea's real glad her sister-in-law's dead. But I still think ol' Clifford did it. He knows how t'kill people with poison, so it'd be real easy for him t'do. An' he was with her all the time! Yeah, he's allergic tuh shellfish, but that don't mean nothin'. My sister Dottie's allergic tuh peanut butter an' she makes sandwiches all the time for her kids! She jus' puts on some latex gloves t'protect her skin, an' she wears a mask so she don't breathe in no fumes. Ol' Clifford coulda done the same."

Annabelle stood up. "My money's on Jacqueline. Maybe it's because I really don't like her. Maybe it's because I just can't imagine sweet little Clifford Benoit killing people. I'm really missing my grandkids—I'm going to call them real quick, before they all sit down for supper." Annabelle and her phone disappeared down the hallway.

Shorty swallowed but didn't shove any more chips into his mouth. Had his sustenance level reached capacity?

"Look, Doc, I wanna say a few words, while it's jus' the two of us. This case is takin' some twists an' turns, an' we're up tuh two dead bodies—three, iffen ya' count Beau. I wanna say get some things out in the open, jus' in case I don't get another chance."

Shorty took a gulp of orange soda and cleared his throat. "I asked ya' t'be my best, uh, person. But I didn't make any speech or nothin' about why."

I touched Shorty's knee. "You don't have to say anything. It's an honor reserved for a special person, and I'm touched you chose me."

"Uh, yeah yeah, that's all true. Look, I'm jus' gonna say it. Annabelle's my girl, an' she'll always be my girl. Heck, she's gonna be my wife, an' I didn't think anyone'd ever wanna put up with me! But you an' me, Doc, our relationship is jus' as important tuh me as the one I got with Annabelle."

Shorty cleared his throat. "Ev, we've known each other since we were young'uns—we played together while our mamas drank coffee an' laughed an' talked most every day. Yore mama an' daddy are jus' like another set o' parents tuh me—ya' saw how much I cried at yore mama's funeral!"

Shorty picked up my hand and held it between his palms. "Yer every bit as kin tuh me as anyone o' my brothers an' sisters. Heck, Doc, I'd trade ya' in for ol' Clovis in a heartbeat! Probably Dottie or Ceci too. Mebbe Bart or Merle, even. Yeah, even those two."

If only he'd stopped while he was ahead. "No, hold on a minute. Ceci bakes me an' Ooey Gooey cake for my birthday, so mebbe not her. But yeah, definitely Dottie."

Once again we'd stepped into the land of quasi-compliments. Shorty always started off with a bang, doling out praise like moon pies. But then he'd start to analyze his words, out loud, which produced mixed results. Best to take the win, Ev—Shorty considered me the equivalent of a sister. And that revelation brought tears to my eyes.

"Now jus' relax an' have some fun! Doc, ya' gotta have confidence in yoreself, like I do. Don't worry about what other people think. Yer real smart, the smartest person I know. Jus' sit back an' listen to what everyone says. And whatever ya' do, ya' better not get a scratch or dent on my truck." A glare from Annabelle caused Shorty to shift a little. "I mean, I got great insurance an' all, an' roadside help, so I know yer gonna be safe. But I got a real high deductible, an' I jus' don't wanna use it. Know what I mean?" Shorty's speech played through my head as I parked his truck. Once again his lecture had sped out of the gate, destined for greatness.

"But don't take that silly notebook an' green pen, okay? Ya' look like some kinda note taker, all official like. That makes people nervous, an' they don't trust ya'. Oh, an' don't make any silly jokes, or give out too many compliments. People get real suspicious when ya' start handin' out compliments like free tires or somethin'. Nobody trusts free stuff."

My response hadn't helped the situation. "Who hands out free tires? Because I could use some—have you priced tires lately? And I'd definitely trust someone who gave me free tires—I'd thank them mighty kindly too."

Cue the horse snort—it had been awhile. "It's jus' a figure o' speech! Look, jus' be yoreself, except don't do those things. Yer gonna do jus' fine. As long as ya' 'member what I said an' watch what ya' say. Oh, an' watch where ya' walk too. Don't trip over nothin'."

Once again Shorty's speech had produced a jumble of good advice mixed in with a bit of not-so-helpful information. Maybe I should have stopped listening after the left turn into the land of unconstructive criticism?

My arrival in the parking lot brought waves of relief to my soul. I'd sent a steady stream of prayers upward from the time I left Shorty and Annabelle in the rearview mirror. By God's grace Shorty's truck and I arrived without a smudge. Well the truck did anyway. My inspection in the mirror turned up smeared lipstick and garish eyeshadow. Why did I let Annabelle talk me into fancy makeup? It only made me feel more awkward and out of place.

A quick trip into Shorty's console produced paper napkins, which traded in their pristine white for red and blue. Nope, lip balm was more my style.

I pushed open the doors to Charm Cafe, yet another tiny pretentious overpriced eatery in New Orleans. The Elizabeth I knew wouldn't set foot in a place like this. Thank goodness I'd left my notebook and teal pen at home. Don't trip, Ev, and don't make silly jokes. And don't hand out compliments like free tires. Just relax, but don't be yourself.

"Ooh, Sweetie! Come over here! Sit right on this side, right by me, Sugar!"

No, these couldn't be Elizabeth's friends. What had she told me about them?

"All our husbands graduated veterinary school together, Ev, so we have that in common. They're all nice ladies, but they do love the big city life. You know, tracking who's on the front page of the society news, who's hosting a party at the country club. Cliff says the husbands are all pretty much the same as they were twenty plus years ago, when they graduated. But maintaining a successful practice, human or animal, requires getting and keeping new patients. It's not like Graisseville, where everyone brings their animals to Cliff because he's a nice guy and they grew up with him, or his daddy or his cousin. No, these guys have to go where the money is, make an appearance, shake hands and hang out with their clientele. And let's face it–for veterinarians, the money's with the rich people and their pets. These veterinarians take care of every expensive animal from tiny ankle-biting mini dogs to cats with unpronounceable names eating food costing more than my wedding ring. And let's not forget racehorses. With the Fair Grounds Race Course in New Orleans, the rich love to buy and race horses. And they'll pay a lot of money for someone to take care of them."

Even through the phone Elizabeth's voice stretched tight, like a clothesline. "If you can sit through the name dropping and the constant competition over who paid the most for their new high heels, you might hear something interesting. I'm sure they'll take you to Charm—it's the place to see and be seen. Order the honey lavender lemonade, a large. Then sit back, sip on your lemonade, nod and smile. Good luck!"

"Here, Sweetie! Evangeline, isn't it? Delilah, will you flag down our waitress? Here, sit right here."

Why did El give them my full name? "Oh, thank you. I'm Evangeline, as you know. But what are your names?"

"Oh, where are my manners? That's Delilah, but you know that. This is Sabine, and this is Georgia. And these two are Josette and Lisette. And I'm Mary Louise. We're so excited to meet you—Elizabeth has told us so much about you!"

Of course—Ev would've stuck out like a sore thumb. And it wouldn't be a gathering of Southern ladies without a woman bearing two first names. "It's so nice to meet you—Elizabeth has told me many things about you too." Not a lie, exactly, although a more truthful statement would have been *Elizabeth has warned me about you*. Let the name dropping, and the shopping competition begin!

"Oh, that's a precious blouse, Sweetie. I understand your little village is miles from a decent clothing boutique. So where in the world did you score that find? Elizabeth tells us she has to make do with the clothes in, what's the name of that town again? Zuckerville?"

"It's Zachary. Sabine, isn't it? But no, I acquired this and my shoes in Graisseville. They have a darling upscale women's shop called Southern Sass."

More half truths—Elizabeth lent me the shirt. "Trust me, Ev, you'll want to wear it. Yes, the blouse cost more than your monthly mortgage payment. But I got it in a thrift store for a fraction of the price, so don't worry about spilling anything on it. And you'll fit in better if you're wearing a label they recognize." Normally I wouldn't care about women putting more value on clothes than manners, but the Zuckerville remark hurt my heart. No one makes fun of my small town, or the not-as-small-town just down the road. *Forgive me, Lord, for my fibbing. Please put a shield around me, and guard my heart. Remind me that the words of these women mean nothing. Amen.*

"Oh? Well, I may have to run the road down to your part of the state, and check out this Southern Sass. But ladies, let me show you this! NOLA Couture just got in their spring collection! Isn't this bracelet beautiful? And it matches my earrings."

The ladies oohed and ah'ed, and dished on their recent excursions to Pilot and Powell, Friend, and Hemline. Had they visited luxury women's clothing stores or quaint little Louisiana towns? Maybe I should have left the lipstick and eyeshadow? No, these women could definitely spot makeup purchased at a designer store. I glanced at my phone—what? I'd only suffered through ten minutes? Dana the server came to my rescue.

"Yes, ma'am—what can I get you?" Waiting for a honey lavender lemonade soaked up another four minutes. I nursed my sugar rimmed glass of manna, stretching its life to another twenty minutes. When would I learn something useful, other than...hmmm, it was official. I hadn't learned anything useful.

The exchange of information flew across the table, as Elizabeth's so-called friends left Lila's book club in the dust. But at least Lila's gossip helped me solve murder cases. Nothing Delilah, Sabine, Georgia, Josette, Mary Louise, or Lisette gushed about had given me any insight into our suspects.

At nine thirty I waved the white flag of defeat. I'd spent thirty-two dollars on three honey lavender lemonades, plus tip. My happy bottoms texted me—or was it my PI? "*Where are you? Don't stay out too late.*"

Mary Louise accepted my white flag. "Evangeline's right—it's time to go. Ladies, it's been a pleasure! I'll see ya'll tomorrow at church. I'm going to walk our guest to her car, see her off as a proper Southern woman should."

My escort guided me to Shorty's truck. Yes, I definitely didn't fit in. "Look, I'm parked right here. Thank you again, Mary Louise. I'll be sure and tell Elizabeth how much fun I had." And that she owed me thirty-two dollars...plus tip.

"Oh please! My kettle boiling for iced tea is more interesting than this evening. The only fun I ever have is when Elizabeth blows into town."

Mary Louise linked her arm with mine. "I'm sorry you had to sit through that, Evangeline. I really am. Truth be told, they all hated Chantilly, because she worked for her money. Several people in our merry little band inherited money. But all our husbands built their veterinary practices with hard labor and sweat. You'd think we'd all appreciate hard work. But no. The wives, you see, we've earned nothing—unless you count knocking down your neighbor to grab the last Max Mara silk shirt."

Mary Louise unlinked and stepped back. "Just talk to any ethical person in New Orleans. They'll tell you the truth about Sheriff Ray, how he's so crooked that if that man swallowed a nail he'd spit out a corkscrew! Someone somewhere has got to have solid evidence to back up all these rumors. Of course they're spending all their time looking at Clifford Benoit. From what I understand, he's the number one suspect in the investigation."

Miles Miller's words floated in my head. "*I can hardly find that place, even when I'm looking for it!*"

"Shorty, are you sure you know where you're going? We won't be much good to the case if we're lost." Annabelle patted Shorty's leg in agreement. Did she always pat Shorty's body parts, or was it a nervous reaction? And, did I really want to know the answer to my question?

"Huh? Oh yeah, we're about there." Obviously, Shorty's mind reflected on Miles' other words. "Come hungry—I'm grilling burgers."

"Yep, here we are, an' I can smell them burgers!"

"Really? In an air-conditioned truck at the edge of the driveway?" But all I heard was the slam of Shorty's door. Annabelle hopped out and trailed behind him.

I didn't move as fast as the rest of my team. By the time I stood on the front porch I could see through the open front door. Miles had slid the glass back door open and stepped onto the deck, my team right behind him. I walked through the open front door, and my father's voice rang through my head. "*Child, were ya' born in a barn? Close the door!*" I shut the offending door, then stepped into the living room.

Another conversation floated through my head—the one with Marcel and Babette after church.

"Just be careful, Evangeline. We've told everyone you're off the case, just tying up a few loose ends and you're leaving tomorrow."

"What? No, that's too soon. We've got so much more to do."

Babette squared my shoulders, so that we were eye to eye. Well, actually her eyes were at my neckline, but she stared up at me. "No, you must leave tomorrow. Take your evidence to your sheriff. Hopefully, he can find an agency not connected to Sheriff Ray. Promise me, cousin."

Annabelle called my name and I crossed to the open sliding door, right into a paper plate of potato salad and a bacon cheeseburger.

"Folks, I don't want to rush you, but the the burgers are ready. And I'll save you some time—ninety percent of what you've heard about Doug Ray is true. The other ten percent is probably true too, but only a few people are brave enough to talk about it."

I wiped my fingers on a paper towel and picked up a file folder on the outdoor table. Miles nodded. "Davis built one of the best cases I've ever seen in my thirty years of law enforcement. He said you're taking this to your sheriff, right? I'd tell him to go straight to the FBI, definitely one of the federal branches—bypass any state involvement altogether. We're not sure how far these dirty cops go up the food chain."

Miles observed Shorty shoveling a hamburger into his mouth. "I sure wish you had the murder weapon, but a good D.A. can make a winnable case out of what you do have.

Before you leave, let me get you what I got. There's some juicy stuff in my Doug Ray file too."

Shorty licked his lips, hamburger number one gone. For the sake of our case, I set aside my bacon cheese and goodness burger. "Mr. Miller, what can you tell me about Clifford Benoit? Do you still have sources on the local police force? Isn't he the official suspect?"

Miles had turned his back to me as he flipped his burgers, but he flinched. "Call me Miles. And yes, I've heard that. Clifford wanted to leave Chantilly after Beau's death, open a bar in Florida. Chantilly said no, that she'd expose his sins, make sure he landed in prison. She was good at that, running tabs on people—money, secrets, you name it. Then she'd threaten to collect. Clifford wanted to spend his golden years with his grandkids. But I wonder..."

Annabelle nibbled on her burger as Shorty thrust his empty plate toward Miles. The swish of the spatula signaled that burger number two had landed on the bun. My PI positioned his plate before him—no matter he still had three, no two bites left of the first...never mind.

"Keep eating, everyone. There's plenty more where that came from. Where was I? Oh yeah, I don't think Clifford would have gone far anyway, not from Chantilly. A lot of people whispered that he was in love with Chantilly, but that's not true. I have it on good authority that Clifford took a DNA test about ten years back. He's Chantilly's father. Yeah, I know. It was a shock to me, but I don't think many people know. And the ones who've heard the rumor don't believe it. Clifford won't comment on it, but my source is pretty solid."

Miles watched his patties. "Do either of you have children? Then you know what I mean. Clifford wasn't in love with

Chantilly, like a man loves a woman romantically. He adored her in the way a father adores his child."

What was that gagging sound? Shorty choking on food? Had that *ever* happened before? Miles' burgers towered well above the plate, especially when loaded with condiments and vegetables. Perhaps Shorty had met his match. Annabelle just kept nibbling, with an occasional sip of water. The woman truly was a saint.

Annabelle's mouth was the least full. Most empty? Anyway, she was the most qualified to ask a question. "If Clifford is Chantilly's biological father, how could he kill his own daughter? I can't believe that's possible."

Miles turned off the grill and squeezed ketchup on his bun. "The mafia has its own set of rules. A father loves his daughter, until she becomes a problem. If Chantilly was threatening to expose him, then yes he could justify killing her as the only way to survive. The act would break his heart, but he could bring himself to do it. One key piece of evidence in the case is a witness who will testify that Clifford asked around about any updates on killing with poison. He'd been out of circulation for a while, and wondered if there were any new or improved ways to kill. The witness will testify he specifically asked about more humane poisons. Ones that caused just a little bit of discomfort or suffering."

My father had the best ringtone, "All My Rowdy Friends Have Settled Down" by Hank Williams—but the absolute worst timing. "Dad, I'm kind of in the middle of something. Could I call you back?"

"Evangeline, this here's your Daddy. Fed-Ex delivered a package to you this morning, and I picked it up when I came by to feed Zydeco. Now I would have called you sooner, but

I went to church, and then we had a potluck afterwards. I brought my baked beans—you know, the ones your mother used to make. People sure go on and on about them. Why just yesterday, Brother Tom stopped me at the post office to make sure I was bringing my beans."

"Dad, what kind of package is it? What's it shaped like?"

"Well, I don't know who it's from—do you want me to open it?" No matter what anyone said, Dad insisted that he wasn't losing his hearing. I punched the speaker button. "Yes, Dad, please open the package. I've got Shorty here with me, and Annabelle. What's in the package?"

Why did it take my father forever to open a simple plastic envelope? Yes, he was eighty plus years old, but still... "Okay, I got it open. I wish I'd grabbed my seven-inch blade from the workshop. I had to use my four-inch pocket knife, because it was handy and all, but it sure was..."

"Skeeter, this here's Shorty Cormier, Can ya' discuss yore knife collection later, an' jus' tell us what's in the package? Thank ya'."

Don't laugh, Ev, don't laugh. "Well, ya' don't have to get your britches in a twist, Shorty! If you're going to be that way, then ya'll can get someone else to open packages."

"Dad, I'm sorry! You know Shorty can be impatient sometimes. I really appreciate you taking the time to call and let me know about the package. Please, just tell us what's in it." Annabelle's eyes danced with laughter. Thank goodness someone was having a good time.

"Well, that's better. I know your mama and I raised you right, Evangeline, with good Southern manners. Shorty, your mama and daddy are rolling right over in their graves at this very moment, on account of you're being rude. Thank you, Honey. Now let's see what's in this package."

Good grief! He didn't even have it open? "Huh, now that's mighty strange. Evangeline, why would someone mail you a Glock all wrapped up in a plastic bag? Child, did you sign up for some sort of monthly subscription? Like a weapon of the month club, or something?"

CHAPTER 16

I instructed my father to hightail it over to Mitch and hand over the Glock.

"Tell Mitch I'll explain later. And for the last time, no, I don't have a subscription box for gun enthusiasts. But yes, it would make a lovely Christmas gift for you. I'll be sure and look into that. Goodbye, Dad."

"Miles, apparently Davis mailed the murder weapon to my home. My father's going to take it to the sheriff. I appreciate your time, and both yours and Davis' file. But I think it's time to leave."

"Doc, ya' want that last burger? Dumplin'? Miles? No?"

Or maybe it was time to eat more food. As Shorty always said, solving cases made a person mighty hungry.

"No, no, take it. While you're eating, why don't we just go through the file? It's as good a time as any to look at it."

As my PI devoured his third burger, Miles flipped through the Beau Romero file. "As I said, Davis is real thorough, a credit to his profession. Or he was, anyway, God rest his soul. He's got background information on all three Romeros, including the sister. And tabs for Clifford, Jean Breaux, and Jacqueline DuBois."

He closed the file. "Everyone knew Jean had a crush on Chantilly a long time ago. But they both pushed the story that nothing ever happened and Jean had moved on. According to this file, there was definitely no love between them. In fact, Chantilly teased Jean about his limp, and he accused her of sleeping around. Neither one of them had respect for the other. Wow!" Miles slapped his knee with the file. "Those two kept their hatred under wraps. According to friends and business associates, they got along. How in the world did Dugoux dig that up?"

How indeed? "Maybe Clifford spilled the beans. He spent most of his time by Chantilly's side. That would be hard to hide."

Our host stacked the empty plates and dumped them in the trash. "Why don't we go inside? I've got chocolate cake and vanilla ice cream. They're store bought, but I think they're pretty good."

Once again Shorty disappeared at the words *chocolate cake*. Annabelle and I helped Miles with the remnants of our cookout. "You've got strong motives with all your suspects, especially because many people thought Chantilly killed her husband. I'm curious what will happen when charges are filed on the sheriff for Beau's murder. There are several people who wanted Chantilly dead. But if her killer was either Jacqueline or Bea, then Chantilly died for the wrong reasons." He opened the sliding glass door. "Of course, there's no good reason for murder. But if the murderer was Bea or Jacqueline, I wonder how she'll take that news."

I shut the door. "That's a good point, Miles. Is there any-thing in the files about Counterblow Distillery? Bea told us she'd be opening soon, paid for with her inheritance from Beau. She claims it takes away her motive for wanting Chan-tilly dead, because it will make all her dreams come true."

Miles moved to the counter and opened the cake. "Here, Miss Annabelle, you slice and Ev, you serve. And I'll go over some more of the file. Paper plates are in the far cabinet, by the stove."

As we worked on dessert, Miles sat at the table. "Let me read you this section on Counterblow, LLC. There aren't any notes on it being a distillery—looks like it's just got money in it. Bea claims she's about to open the doors? According to the file, the money's just sitting in the LLC bank account, no activity for the last six months. But maybe she's just waiting for permits or something." He squinted at the file. "It's not much money—just a few thousand. Oh, but let me read you something interesting."

Shorty had the ice cream out thawing while he rummaged for a scoop. "Oh, Mr. Cormier, uh, Shorty? The ice cream scoop's in the top left drawer by the fridge." When it came to food, my PI did his part to hurry along the eating process.

"What else is in there, Miles?" After that burger, how was I going to eat chocolate cake and ice cream?

"In the back of each tabbed section is a miscellaneous area, with random items of interest Dugoux discovered." Miles squinted at the file, then pulled a pair of glasses from his front shirt pocket. "I suppose you've heard about Chantilly's pregnancy before she married Beau? Some thought the baby was Beau's, some thought it was a local judge, and others believed the father was a famous jazz singer. But the notes under Jean's section tell a different story."

Miles took his bowl of cake and ice cream. "Thank you, Shorty. Now, the story has always been that Chantilly went to Jean to prepare a prenuptial agreement—that was the first time they met. She returned a month later, pregnant and hysterical. Jean took pity on her and offered to marry Chantilly and adopt the baby, but Chantilly refused. The young lawyer regretted his words as soon as they cleared the air, and he expressed relief later they'd never married."

Miles demonstrated amazing reflexes, eating drippy ice cream and cake while reading—and keeping his reading material pristine. Could I do that? Who was I kidding?

"But according to this file, *Jean* was the father. Now Chantilly loved Beau, so she refused to marry Jean, and she gave the baby up for adoption. Jean searched for his child, but never located the baby."

The twists and turns in this case made even Shorty put down his spoon. "I don't understand, Miles. If Chantilly hired Dugoux t'find out who killed Beau, then why's he got all these files on other people?"

All four spoons rested in our bowls. "Because Bea Romero *also* hired Dugoux. She asked for evidence that Chantilly killed her brother. The PI figured both cases had the same goal, to find out who killed Beau, so he took them both. He never told his clients of course."

I should have known—Shorty put his spoon down because his bowl was empty. "Hey, I'm gonna get jus' a little more. Keep goin' Miles—this is good stuff."

As Shorty filled his bowl, our host returned to the folder. "Bea insisted that Chantilly killed her brother, but suggested

Jean as another suspect. Clifford's in here too, but more as an informant." He flipped a few pages. "Bea mentioned her alliance with the sheriff, so Dugoux never told her what he'd discovered—that Doug killed Beau. He wanted to protect her, so he reported that he'd found nothing and eventually closed her case."

Annabelle pushed away her barely eaten dessert. "Wait a minute! Bea mentioned she'd hired an investigator who'd found nothing. So this makes sense. But what's this alliance between her and the sheriff?"

Shorty seated himself at the table, spoon in the bowl, then his mouth, then the bowl again. "Yeah, Miles, what's this alliance?"

"Bea had been bugging the sheriff to solve her brother's murder. In fact, there's a copy of the official investigation from his office. I'm sure she mentioned she'd hired a PI, which is probably what got Dugoux killed. Maybe Chantilly confronted the sheriff with Dugoux's findings? That woman had no fear—she'd take on an alligator. And that's probably why Davis gave her the truth about Beau's killer."

I stared at my puddling mess of brown goo in a bowl. I'd forgotten to take out my notebook! But everything Miles had said was in the file.

"Anything else you want to tell us? We'd better get going."

Miles flipped the pages. "The miscellaneous sections are interesting. Did you know Chantilly was pregnant again when she died? An unnamed source thinks Sheriff Ray is the father. Oh, and the sheriff's sister is a pharmacist. That might give you means for Chantilly's death. Oh wait, here's something."

I gathered our sticky bowls and stacked them in the sink, running water and dishwashing soap over them. "Did you know Chantilly has a half brother? Yeah, his name's Maurice Gentry, and he's partners with her in Ami Fidéle. He's been putting pressure on her to buy him out." Nothing surprised me anymore.

"That takes care of all the dishes—thank you again so much for the amazing food. Not to mention your time, Miles. You've helped us more than you can ever know."

We gathered our files and said our goodbyes. "Be careful, you three. My advice is to leave town today. You've got enough evidence for any ethical law enforcement agency to open an investigation. Good luck."

I remembered my promise to Babette, and pulled up my phone to look for other accommodations. We couldn't leave town, but we needed my cousins to think we had.

"Doc, ya' think when this is all over, we can sell the rights tuh Netflix or Prime or somebody? Cuz I watch a lotta television, an' I ain't never seen anythin' like this before!"

We packed up the truck and said our goodbyes. I texted Ethan with wide-eyed emojis, begging for him to work his magic. Maybe he felt guilty for snapping at me, maybe he was just that good. A *swoosh* confirmed, whatever the case, my cousin had come through for me once again.

Look for some pretty exposing video and photos coming tomorrow, cousin. What? Did Ethan have compromising digital evidence of my shortcomings? What were my shortcomings? I wore my happy bottoms more than any other article of clothing. Was that embarrassing? Probably, but how could Ethan have proof?

Another text...what, more awkwardness and humiliation? *Of the suspects, that is. But you probably knew that.*

Oh thank goodness! *Thank You, Lord, for giving Ethan a higher opinion of me than I deserve. Your blessings overflow. Amen.*

"Doc, can ya' take some time away from yore phone t'tell yore cousins goodbye?"

Good grief! My PI was giving me social cues. "Yes! Thank you, cousins! I love you, and can't wait to see you again." Please don't lecture me, please don't lecture me.

Babette released me from her death grip. Were those tears in Marcel's eyes? "Promise me, Evangeline, that you will drop this investigation. I honestly regret the day I got you involved in this crazy mess. It was fun at first, with the catchy code names and the colored pens and paper. But the local police are criminals? No, that's something for law enforcement to handle, accounting for each other. Civilians should stay out of it. "

Uh, she regretted the last two days? *Honey, if that's all the regret you've got, then you're doing better than most.* But I couldn't say that. "Babette, I promise I won't give this case a single thought. Love you, cousins!"

Annabelle added her own hugs to the mix. "Your rental is amazing, and ya'll are honestly the best hosts I've ever had. Thank you again for your hospitality. Ev and I'll be back soon, when everything's died down. I'm going to get to your shop and get my wedding dress!" This last bit of compliments and warmth soothed my cousins' emotions.

As we pulled away from Sweet Magnolia Manor, my stomach churned. Had I lied to my cousins? By worldly standards, not at all. I wouldn't give the case a single thought—I'd give it dozens of thoughts, probably more like hundreds.

Oh, who was I kidding? I definitely wasn't fooling God. No, I'd fashioned my response to deceive Marcel and Babette. And that was lying, no way around it. *Please forgive me, I know I lied. I'm going down a dangerous path, please keep me safe. I promise to come clean to Babette and Marcel after I solve the case.*

Yet my conscience tugged on my soul, and a saying from my childhood wound around my brain. *Oh, what a tangled web we weave, when first we practice to deceive.* Let's not forget Jeremiah 9:8 *Their tongue is a deadly arrow; it speaks deceit; with his mouth one speaks peace to his neighbor, but inwardly he sets an ambush for him.* But I had a case to solve—my soul would have to soothe itself.

"The Welcome Lodge? What were ya' thinkin', Doc?"

I'd kept the motel a secret, hoping to delay this conversation as long as possible. "The price was right, and it sounded, well, welcoming. Let's look at that—the name says it all! The Welcome Lodge—you can't get much more welcoming than that."

Shorty threw his truck into park and stared at the manila brick building. Annabelle pulled out her phone, no doubt looking for an alternative to the Welcome Lodge. "How many stars did it get? Annabelle says if a place has less than three stars, then it's best t'keep on drivin'. Right, Honey Bunny?"

Honey Bunny mumbled as her fingers flew over the keypad. Would Shorty believe I hadn't checked the ratings? Who was I kidding? Annabelle and I probably tied in the record for *most reliance on Yelp to determine life choices*. I glanced at my phone. "Uh, let's see. Well, I'm not sure this is a reliable site..."

Shorty grabbed towards the backseat, presumably for my phone. He missed so he looked towards the front seat. "Honeybee, how many stars did this place get?"

Could Annabelle look more awkward? "Uh, looks like, um, two and a half."

"What? Two and a half stars! Doc, I didn't bring enough firepower t'stay in this rat trap." He read the most recent review over Annabelle's shoulder. "*As we walked through the door, we literally found yellow crime scene tape strung along the carpet. We were visiting my sister, and she saw this motel on the six o'clock news. The place hosted a drug bust the night before we checked in, and three people died. Do not stay here, unless you have a death wish!*"

He swiveled his torso, so I could feel the full effects of his glare. "Doc, that was two days ago. We can't stay here—it ain't safe. Nope, Annabelle's already lookin' for a better place."

I scrolled through Yelp, which didn't produce a solution. "I can lay out our options, and they aren't pretty. And keep in mind it's Mardi Gras season, so we're lucky to even find any rooms. But first on the list, what I'd call *Door Number One* is, well, this place. It's forty dollars a night, and they prefer cash. You've mentioned the negatives, but let me state the positives. First, no one will ever think to look for us here.

Second, the price is a bargain. Third, we're close to all our suspects." Was that a positive? "Did I mention it's a bargain?"

"Now let me tell you about a place in, what I'd call, the next tier. Let's call it *Door Number Two*. It's called the Good Neighbor Motel. On the plus side, they rate four stars, and have a nice view of a lake. But they charge two-fifty a night, because of Mardi Gras, and only take credit cards."

I squared off against my PI. "As of this morning, I have one hundred and forty-two dollars in my bank account, and fifteen dollars left on my credit card. I don't know about you, but my finances are screaming *Door Number One*."

Annabelle looked up from her phone. "Ev's right, Sweetie. And we're saving for a wedding, so we're not flush with cash either." She tilted her head and studied our motel. "Besides, it has a certain, uh, nostalgic air about it. Reminds me of the places I stayed as a kid when we went on vacation."

To Shorty's credit, he carefully weighed our two options. Okay, maybe he didn't carefully weigh them. He shifted our options, and his torso, from one side to the other. If he'd been a four year old child, I'd declare he had ants in his pants. My PI didn't own a credit card, or a debit card, or any card—because the government tracked us with that pesky magnetic stripe. And don't get him started on the cards with chips, or the ones that took money out of an account with j ust a *tap*! But that was a topic for another time.

Shorty reached for his phone. Then he put his phone down. He looked at Annabelle, then he looked at me. "Yeah, none o' us have much money at the moment."

Annabelle reached over and squeezed his arm. "Besides, I'm not at all worried about our safety. Why, I've got my big strong honey bear to protect me. And Ev, too! I bet it's a cozy room—we'll all be as snug as a bug in a rug."

"Okay, ya'll win. But we're takin' turns sleepin', an' we're gonna keep both guns handy. Deal?"

My stomach lurched—was it from the feeling of danger or the presence of sickeningly sweet romance? I swallowed to keep my nausea in check. "Uh, yes, sir, it's a deal. How about I go in, tell the clerk I want a room for one night? That way we don't have to explain why two women and a man want a room."

Multiple and fervent nodding greeted my suggestion. "Great. Now I've only got twenty dollars. How much cash do ya'll have?"

Annabelle rummaged through her purse. "Okay, I've got twelve dollars. And about that much in my checking account. I don't have any credit cards—Shorty says they're tools of the government to monitor our spending." Et tu, Annabelle? You've fallen into the rabbit hole of government conspiracies?

More squirming from Shorty. Maybe he really did have ants in his pants. "A good bit."

"Huh? What denomination is that, Shorty, a good bit? Is it U.S. currency?"

Maybe Shorty had to go to the bathroom? I wouldn't be going in this sleeping establishment. My plan was to hike down a block to the gas station. Chances were good the bathroom had seen more disinfectants than the Welcome Lodge. Hmmm, on second thought, maybe I'd take Shorty's truck and drive a few miles closer to...well, closer to a better part of town.

Annabelle had become strangely silent so I hammered on Shorty. "Well? Are you going to share the amount of money in your wallet with us, or do I have to rob you to find out? Actually, that wouldn't be a bad idea, practicing for the inevitable. You know, like practicing to run a race before actually doing it. I'd probably do better in the real robbery if I had gone through it a few times."

"Hardee har har. Ya' know, Doc, I was jus' tellin' yore daddy the other day that yore sarcasm's gonna get ya' in a world o' hurt. How does yore boyfriend feel about that sarcastic wit o' yours? I bet he don't like it much." Even Annabelle had to chuckle at the response.

"First, Mr. Smart Aleck, good comeback, dragging my father into our discussion. Second, great use of words! *Sarcastic wit* is a wonderful choice. Third, we'd better exit this vehicle soon, or the cops will show up and arrest us. We're not in a part of town where a man and two women just sit in a car together and talk. So how about this? I'll get out and you two drive around the corner behind the motel. Then I'll call you with the room number and we'll all meet outside. And let's hope it's not the room with the homeless man leaning against the door talking to himself."

Annabelle couldn't stop chuckling. "Great plan, Ev. and be sure to ask for a room on the second floor. It'll be harder for a criminal to break into. And I hear that roaches prefer the first floor, anyway."

Poor Shorty! By the look on his face, he was doubting how well he knew his fiancée. I'd decided a few hours ago I'd seriously underestimated the woman.

Our collective forty dollars stepped out of Shorty's truck, tucked into my fist. My guess was Shorty had a great deal of money in his wallet, probably more in the truck. He paid cash for everything, so it made sense he'd brought several hundred dollars. And he'd sponged off my cousins and Jean Breaux, so he still had most of it. We could stay awhile if necessary.

"A room for one please, for one night. And I'd prefer the second floor around the back. And it's just me, I'll be the only one in the room. But I might stay another night. No, scratch that. I'm only staying one night." If anyone came in asking, I wanted the clerk to think it was just one night.

"I'm here visiting my sister and the baby's colicky, so I don't want to stay with her. I left my credit cards at home, so I only have cash. Your fine establishment is one of the few that takes cash anymore."

The clerk sent his evil eye through the plastic partition. "Lady, I don't get paid enough to repeat your tale to the police, or anybody else when they come asking about you. We're not real full right now, on account of the triple murder, so I can give you 207 in the back. You have to be out by 11 a.m. tomorrow, or bring me forty more dollars." He slid a key under the plastic partition. So much for my backstory.

CHAPTER 17

M y PI wasn't letting anyone out of his sight, playing bodyguard 24/7. He agreed to wait a minute or two before tailing me into Bruno's Coffee Shop to meet Luci, for what that was worth. After much discussion, he decided to bring Annabelle.

As I wrapped my friend in a warm Southern hug, I heard Shorty clear his throat. "'Scuse me, madam stranger. Do ya' know what's good in here? We don't know each other, but ya' look like ya' know a little 'bout coffee shops. Do ya' spend a lotta time hangin' around those places? Ya' know, coffee shops?"

Luci squinted at Shorty through her glasses. "Oh, you don't want her opinion. She doesn't even live here. My name's Luci Lirette, and I've lived in New Orleans all my life. Let me help you."

So typical—I'd spent less than five minutes with a woman before losing her to Shorty's charms. No one could explain why women found him irresistible. How could someone radiate enough charisma that a woman would abandon a friend she hadn't seen in over a year? Abandon her friend to help a stranger purchase coffee? And why did this wayfaring stranger need assistance with his coffee purchase, anyway? He ordered the same coffee drink no matter where he was: chicory with cayenne pepper and five shots of espresso, if they had it. And most coffee shops didn't carry chicory or cayenne pepper, so he'd order black coffee and five shots of espresso.

Oh, but to hear him talk, the man had never darkened the doorstep of a coffee shop. And now he'd drawn Annabelle into his little charade. Hmmm, how would this play out? Would Annabelle be his bride to be, with art imitating life? Or perhaps a hitchhiker he'd found on the side of the road?

"Oh, thank ya', ma'am. May I call ya' Luci? Muh sister an' I, we're jus' passin' through this fine town, on our way tuh, uh, tuh Baton Rouge. I don't know much about these fancy coffee places! Why, they sell more kinds o' drinks than I got cattle. By the way, the name's uh, Monty Gautreaux. This here's muh sister, Lulu. I'm mighty pleased tuh make yore acquaintance."

Annabelle was his sister? Thoughts of Abram and Sarai from Genesis floated in my head. Abram posed his wife as his sister, and that hadn't gone well. Thousands of years later I didn't see this ending any better.

But Luci bought it all, hook, line, and sinker. "And what do you do for a living, Monty?"

"Uh, I'm a police officer, ma'am." Shorty tossed my theory out the window, like yesterday's trash. Wait a minute, who threw trash out their window? No, Shorty tossed my theory out the window like a dead fly. Better but not great—note to self: work on my analogies.

Oh great, he'd used his buddy's name, a deputy with the East Baton Rouge Parish sheriff's department. And then he stepped right into impersonating a police officer.

"Ev, did you hear that? This is Deputy Monty Gautreaux. He's passing through on his way to Baton Rouge. Monty, Lulu, this is my dear friend Ev Delafose. Now, deputy, I simply won't t ake *no* for an answer! You've got to join us for coffee."

In what universe was this a good idea?

"I'd be mighty happy t'do that, Miss Luci. That's awfully kind uh ya." Hmmm, I guess in Shorty's universe it was a fabulous idea.

We placed our orders and grabbed the last table in the shop, near the back. For five o'clock on a Sunday, Bruno's boasted standing room only.

Annabelle couldn't stay out of the fun, and the deception. "In case anyone's asking, I'm a tree surgeon. Yes, I complet-ed four years of undergrad, three years of timber medical school, two years specializing in timber surgery, then I stud-ied another two years under the famous tree surgeon, Dr. Lawrence Shively. I have my own practice in Baton Rouge."

But Luci only had eyes for the single deputy sitting before her. "Monty, have you heard about the murder we had re-cently? Someone poisoned a local businesswoman, Chantilly Romero. Oh, it's just awful! I live alone, you see, being single and all, and I fear for my life—I really do!"

I glanced around. No, I still sat at a table in Bruno's, smack dab in the middle of New Orleans. But in my world, the real world, Luci had no fear of living alone. She laughed at fear, spit in its face, actually. Luci probably owned more guns than Shorty had cattle. Who was this woman and what had she done with my friend?

My PI was enjoying his new persona. "Do tell now? Well, I declare, what is this world comin' to, when a person can't sleep peacefully at night? Land sakes!"

Apparently in this upside down world I'd fallen into, Shorty spoke like an old Southern woman. Wait a minute! He and Annabelle had watched *Gone with the Wind* just before we left on our trip. Hmmm, yes, come to think of it, my PI sounded a lot like Scarlett O'Hara.

Here came Scarlett herself. "Why, I do declare, Monty! You're taking over the entire conversation. Would anyone like to hear about my latest surgery? I had to separate conjoined spruce trees, melded together since they sprung up as seedlings. Anyone?"

Luci waved off the titillating story of Siamese spruce. She leaned across the table, and brushed her fingers across the top of Shorty's hand before resting them in the space beside his wrist. Watching my friend flirt with an engaged man rated right up there with watching the illicit love scene between Jack and Kate in *Titanic* with my mother. That night rated right up on my top ten list of worst moments ever. I'd fanned myself as embarrassment took hold of me like a summer heat wave. My mother attempted a conversation with the words, "How in the world do you have sex in the backseat of a car? Evangeline, have you ever done that? How is that possible?"

I swore off all future movie nights and avoided my mother's eyes for a good two months after that horrific evening.

And when did Luci become the local gossip? "Well, I heard from a reliable source that Beau Romero had an illegitimate son, some relationship he'd had before he met Chantilly. The kid's now twenty and he's hanging around demanding a share of Beau's estate. Why wouldn't he just kill his stepmother and get everything?"

"Oh, land sakes! What is this world comin' to?" Two guesses on who made that comment. Hint: it wasn't Annabelle. She was too busy pouting because no one cared about her tree surgeon skills.

Could I rein in this conversation? "Uh, Luci, I'd like to talk to you about poisons."

But it was too late—my single friend wanted to make an impression. "Know what else I heard? Chantilly had herself all tangled up in a bunch of shady business deals. Mm hmm, you know that's right! It wouldn't surprise me if one of those people offed her." She leaned back, obviously impressed with herself that she'd inserted the word *offed* into her dialogue. *Luci Lirette, I fear I never knew you.*

Okay, Ev, if at first you don't succeed... "Uh, Luci, don't you teach classes on poison? At Delgado Community College, right?"

"Well, my goodness, that sounds excitin'! Yes, Luci, can ya' tell us about that?"

Okay, the syrupy sweet tone irritated the fire out of me, but at least Shorty got us back on track. And why couldn't he talk that sweetly to me, just once? And would Annabelle ever recover from the rejection of being a surgeon of flora? Or was it fauna? No, that might be animals and plants...

"Oh, well, of course, Monty, anything for a man in blue." Luci pulled her chair forward, interrupted only by the words, "Monty, your order is ready! Lulu, your order is ready! Ev, your order is ready."

Where was Luci's order? Hmmm, had my PI paid for her drink? Since we had no formal method to recoup costs for our case, Shorty was on the hook for at least seven dollars. *Why did I feel my PI's generosity would come back to bite me?*

"Well, that's a good question, but let's wait for Monty to return with our drinks. Isn't he dreamy, Ev? Lulu, where does your brother live—maybe it's not too far. You know I've heard long distance relationships can be a real turn on."

Flashbacks of Jack, Kate, and my mother flew into my head. "Uh, let me see if, uh, Monty needs any help. I'll be right back."

My heart raced—was it from the sprint to the coffee counter, or my fear of learning more about Luci's feminine wants and needs? At any rate I got my cardio in for the day.

"Look, you've got to nip this flirtation with Luci in the bud. It's not respectful to Annabelle, and it's making me uncomfortable."

Shorty balanced four paper cups with two hands and the crooks of his arms. "Now hold on there, Doc. I ain't said or done anythin' t'make that woman think I'm wantin' anythin' more than a friendship. She's the one makin' all the moves." His sideways grin caught me off guard. For a moment I saw it, that charm and appeal other women couldn't get enough of.

"Now quit yer bellyachin'—we're getting' some real good stuff here. In fact, ya' know whatcha need t'do? Ya' need tuh jus' sit back an' sip yore tea an' smile. Let me work my magic."

And like a Southern summer shower, the warm squishy feeling disappeared. Shorty was back to my irritating and frustrating friend and private investigator.

Luci gushed as she took her drink from Shorty. "Oh, thank you so much, Monty! Chivalry is dead around here, but obviously there's plenty where you come from. Where do you come from, by the way?" Luci focused on her paper cup, but her eyes shifted upwards to gauge Shorty's response. Annabelle had not given out any geographic information regarding her fiancé.

"Uh, well, ma'am, I hang my hat in Zachary, jus' about ninety-six miles from here. But my boss, Sheriff Mitch Dupre, he works in Baton Rouge. I'm headed over there tonight, tuh have an important meetin' with 'im. Ya' see, he relies on me for my opinions an' *ex-purr-tees.*"

When had Mitch ever relied on Monty for anything? The deputy didn't even write the monthly quota of parking tickets. No, the sheriff didn't count on Monty's so-called expertise. And since when did a sheriff have an important meeting on a Sunday evening? Not to mention, Shorty's logistics didn't add up. Luci caught Shorty's mistake.

"I'm confused, Monty. If you live in Zachary and you're headed to Baton Rouge, why are you passing through New Orleans? Baton Rouge is between Zachary and New Orleans."

Say what you will about Shorty, he thought fast on his feet. "Oh, that's easy! Ya' see, muh sister lives in Slidell, muh other sister Beaulah. So we hopped over tuh her house, an' visited with her a spell. Now I'm headed back towards home t'meet with the sheriff."

Luci's navigational skills knew no limits. "But wouldn't it make more sense to take I-12 from Slidell? It's a straight shot. Taking I-10 adds a lot of unnecessary miles to your drive."

Shorty tapped the first two fingers of his right hand on the top of his paper cup. "Miss Luci, ya' sure ask a lotta good questions. I don't see brains an' beauty in the same package very much in my line o' work. Ya' definitely got both."

Yes, there it was. Just a giggle and a hair flip later, and my friend had forgotten all about the navigational inconsistencies. Honestly, my PI amazed me with his super powers. One look at Annabelle told me a lot. For some reason, Shorty's antics didn't bother her one bit.

"So, Luci, ya' teach classes at Delgado Community College? What kinda classes? Didja say *poison*?"

Ugh, another hair flip. "Oh, yes, they're lots of fun! I teach about poisons and how to kill people with them. You should talk to your sheriff, since you have so much influence, and suggest he bring me down there to teach one. I could even stay a couple days afterwards, and you could show me around. We could even have supper."

Shorty's chin tipped down just slightly, indicating that was a possibility. Had Annabelle seen the chin tip? Her chocolate eyes said *most definitely*, and her fiancé would hear about it later.

"Oh, my class could benefit the entire department. Every law enforcement officer should know about poisons. It's so easy to kill people with everyday household chemicals."

Luci hesitated, a wild look taking over her eyes. Yes, in most potentially romantic situations, divulging that you know how to kill someone with items around the house was a definite *no*. Not to mention, everyday common Southern etiquette frowned on that as well.

"Yes, *bring flowers and compliment the hostess on her décor. Perhaps even bake a dessert to share, carrying it in a decorative container for the hostess to keep as a gift. Be sure and mention her table setting, and shower compliments upon her food. Ask for the recipes! But never ever mention that you can kill a person using common household items. Why, it's just not good Southern manners.*"

To her credit, Luci retraced her steps. "That is to say, uh, I have no firsthand knowledge of killings involving simple home cleaning solutions. But I've read about killers who have done just that. That's all I'm saying."

No, that didn't help at all, so my friend tried again. "Look, I'm just saying that it's possible." Luci tossed her hair, as if to throw off the awkward moment. "Let's talk about my classes at Delgado. Honestly, I have a waiting list for my poisons class — it's quite popular!"

No, not sure that was a good thing to advertise.

"Now that I think about it, Jean and Jacqueline were in my class. They must have pulled some strings to get in there. Now, did they kill Chantilly? I have no idea. Literally everyone in that class asks the million dollar question: how do you get away with murder? How do you poison someone and no one finds out? Jacqueline and Jean didn't stand out from anyone else in the class."

Lulu, uh, Annabelle jumped in. "But they had the knowledge to poison Chantilly, right? Regarding the three elements, they both had the means to commit the crime?"

Poor Luci. Her shoulders slumped forward and her chin dragged her chest. I suspected many of her dates ended in this same situation. The man fled the restaurant, afraid to date a woman who could kill him without detection. Was this why James Bond had remained single all those years? Should I tell Luci she had no reason to worry? Shorty/Monty wasn't single, anyway? And his tree surgeon/librarian fiancée was right by his side. Or would that make things worse?

"Yes, I suppose they did. I just never stopped to consider that I've been teaching potential murderers how to make their dreams come true!"

Ethan texted, his *swoosh* hitting my eardrums. Thank goodness I had a distraction!

Watched videos. Scanned photos of party. Nothing worth sending. Got the coroner's report. Chantilly was three months' pregnant. But you probably knew that. You're usually two steps ahead of me.

Ethan's text continued. *Social media says Sheriff Doug Ray could be the baby daddy—Chantilly just discovered her pregnancy. Also, deep digging revealed baby sister Bea can't stand Chantilly and wanted her money. I've emailed you everything—I hope this was helpful.*

Ethan's sign off brought tears to my eyes. *I'm sorry for being snappy before. My job fell through and I'm scrambling to find another one. If you know anyone who could use a good graphics artist, let me know. Mom and Dad say if I don't have a job at graduation, I have to come back to Graisseville and wait tables at the café or work at Big Ed's.*

Oh, Ethan! I remembered those days, leaving home and getting a taste of the big city, and wanting more. I'd set my sights on teaching at the college level, which required more education in a big city. Then I met Doug, and I never looked back at my small home town. I understood Ethan's desire to live a life beyond Graisseville.

Please, Lord, please remind me that everyone has struggles. Give Ethan peace as he searches for a job. Help him find a job in a big city, but please keep his heart tethered in Graisseville. And, if it could be Your will, please help him figure out at some point that his tiny home town is all he needs. Well, that and You. Amen.

"What's goin' on with yore phone, uh, what's yore name again?"

Would I ever exit this bizarre world? "Uh, nothing. My friend Ethan just gave me some information. It's no big deal."

Could I help Luci recover from this ultimate embarrassment? "Chantilly died from arsenic poisoning, at least that's what I heard. Could you tell us about that?"

Luci's face relaxed as she shifted into professor mode. I knew the stance well. "Arsenic poisoning occurs because of elevated levels of arsenic in the body. If it happens quickly, the symptoms usually include vomiting, abdominal pain, brain damage, and watery diarrhea with blood."

My friend ramped up, her speech quickening and her arms gesturing wildly. If only Bruno's had a white board! "Oh, but long-term exposure, that's different. That type of poisoning causes a thickening and darkening of the skin, abdominal pain, diarrhea. Many times we see heart disease, numbness, and even cancer. Dying of arsenic over time isn't pleasant."

Our resident tree surgeon jumped in. "Luci, did Chantilly die from long-term exposure to arsenic?"

My friend shrugged. "No idea. I haven't seen the coroner's report, since I wasn't accepted to be part of the team. But I can tell you that arsenic tastes sweet, and contaminated drinking water is the most common reason for long-term exposure."

I grabbed my phone. "Wait! I have the coroner's report."

We huddled around my small screen. "What? The coroner determined Chantilly suffered from long-term exposure to arsenic, but she died from nicotine poisoning?"

I locked on Luci's eyes. "Does nicotine mimic the effects of arsenic?"

My friend leaned back into her seat, eyebrows digging down in concentration. "Well, yes. The best poison to mimic those symptoms, or to even cause those symptoms exactly, is nicotine. Not to mention, nicotine's easily absorbed, especially through the skin. The onset for nicotine is fifteen to thirty minutes, depending on the dose. Acute symptoms are respiratory failure, but death occurs around a quarter to half hour after exposure. From what I read on social media, everyone ran around, trying to figure out what happened, mopping up the spilled drink around her..."

Luci's eyes brightened. "Wait! Nicotine absorbs into the skin, so no one would know Chantilly received the poison, if it was..."

Her eyes clouded in thought. "Originally, I thought it was Chantilly's drink that people cleaned up after she collapsed. But now that I think about it, someone could have spilled a drink on Chantilly intentionally. And they could have laced it with nicotine."

Annabelle, uh, Lulu, got her two cents in . "Luci, where is the best place to purchase nicotine if you wanted to poison someone and not get caught?"

No hesitation. "Oh, any vape or shop. A good dose costs less than ten dollars, and they come in lots of flavors. If someone paid cash, there'd be no records."

Luci poured her soul into Shorty's eyes. "Will I ever see you again?"

"So, Annabelle, how do you feel about some woman pushing her phone number into your fiancé's hand?"

Annabelle giggled and Shorty shrugged. "Oh, that's all right, Doc. I'll jus' pass Luci's number on tuh Monty. He'll call Miss Luci, all nice and polite, tell her he had a cold that evenin' in the coffee shop, an' this is his real voice. She'll never know the difference. An' let me tell ya', Doc—this woman's right up Monty's alley! He loves a woman that could kill 'im without a second thought."

"Huh! Well, Shorty, that changes my perception of Monty by, uh, well, by a lot. But I don't know about all this."

My brain placed two images side by side. On the left my PI stared at me, dishwater blonde hair touching his shoulders (although he'd promised Annabelle he'd get a haircut and a shave for the wedding), fifty-something face wearing his life well, with just a touch of lines around muddy brown eyes.

On the right Monty gazed at me, hair the color of midnight, his early to mid forties features showing no lines around his bright blue eyes. Should I ask? Yes, I couldn't keep my logic bottled up inside.

"But what if they set up a date, and they meet face to face? Shorty, you and Monty look nothing alike! You weren't even born in the same decade! How is he going to explain all that?"

Oh, Ev, how naïve you are to the ways of men. "Doc, women don't pay much attention tuh how a man looks. They're attracted tuh a man's personality. An' his bank roll. It's in all yore women's magazines—don'tcha read 'em?"

Why did I always fall for it? Why did I always ask questions when I should just zip my mouth, nod and smile? Would I ever learn? "Shorty, I don't read women's magazines, unless you count *Ellery Queen's Mystery Magazine.* Which I'm pretty sure appeals to everyone, male and female. And I'm going to stop you right there. If Mitch showed up at my door one evening, flowers in hand, looking ten years younger with dark black hair and blue eyes, then I'd know he wasn't really Mitch. In case you've forgotten, he has sandy blond hair and moss green eyes."

My PI shrugged. No, it wasn't a shrug, really. He tilted his head to the right, then threw it to the left side, his shoulders following right behind. What was that, exactly? A grimace? A convulsion? Hmmm, was Shorty having a seizure, brought on by my zeal for the truth?

What would the doctor say? "Uh, Miss Brochet, your fiancé convulsed himself to death, most likely because he had to face the truth." Okay, the doctor wouldn't say that, I would say that. The doctor would have no idea why Shorty's heart stopped.

"Annabelle, I'm just speculating. But let's face it. I'd just called Shorty out on a story he'd generated. That's when he convulsed and we rushed him to the hospital. I think he collapsed from facing the facts. But maybe you should talk to the doctor yourself." Nope, not having that conversation with Annabelle. Maybe we could talk about the wedding instead?

The seizures stopped, thank goodness. "Doc, as usual, yer over thinkin' things. Yer on step seventeen, an' the rest uh us are on step two. So, jus' go back tuh yore corner, an' calm yoreself down. Oh, an' by the way, ya' owe me three dollars an' forty cents. Ya' know, for yore half o' Luci's drink. Yer lucky she ordered a small. Mighta been cuz she was tryin' tuh impress me with her tiny portions." Cue the horse snort.

Someone remind me...why was Shorty one of my dearest friends?

CHAPTER 18

"Dr. Delafose, this is Holliman Fisher. If you recall, my firm represents the Hebert family in all their legal matters. More specifically, I managed Sidney Hebert's case last month. You and your, ahem, colleague, performed a few duties for us."

A few duties? We solved the murder and proved Sid's innocence. My voice caught in my throat as my mother's voice rattled through my brain. *"Evangeline, a respectable Southern lady doesn't correct a gentleman. Rather, she nods and smiles in agreement."*

How did one nod and smile across cell towers? "Yes, sir, I remember that case. As I remember, my colleague and I proved Mr. Hebert's innocence. The district attorney dropped all charges and the judge released him the next day, in time to celebrate Christmas with his family."

Sorry, Mother—you did your best. But sometimes my tongue chose to ignore my respectable Southern upbringing.

"Uh, well, that's another way to look at the situation. Anyway, the reason I'm calling is that I've been reviewing your agreement with Cletus Cormier, the owner of Brown Dog Bakery. I've spoken with Mr. Cormier and I've negotiated an offer for," Holliman paused. "Uh, an offer for Zydeco Delafose. Mr. Cormier has agreed to eight percent of gross sales on all items featuring Mr. Delafose's likeness. Is that an acceptable percentage?"

My brain shifted gears, turning its back on the case to rummage through the dusty nooks and crannies of my memories. When had I hired a lawyer for my dog?

"Mr. Fisher, I'm a little confused. Zy only receives a monthly box of treats for his compensation. Are you saying he'll actually get some money?"

A slight cough from my dog's lawyer, confirming his uneasiness at representing a non-human. "Yes, if you accept the offer. I researched Mr. Cormier's company, and he's doing quite well. His new packaging features Mr. Delafose's face on every item produced. Furthermore, the company's YouTube channel shows the monthly videos of the subscription unboxing are going, uh, viral, with over a million subscribers. Your, uh, dog should benefit from his popularity, and so should you. Are you willing to accept Mr. Cormier's offer, eight percent of all gross sales?"

"You bet! How much do you think that might be?" If Cletus' company brought in fifty thousand dollars a year, Zy would get...my brain struggled to calculate eight percent.

"Brown Dog Bakery grossed $975,728 last year. Assuming the company performs just as well this year, then your dog's share would be approximately $78,000. Do you want me to compute the exact number?"

My stunned silence conveyed a *no thank you*. "But remember, this figure is based on prior year sales. No one can predict for certain the success of any company. I do know Mr. Cormier has purchased a manufacturing facility, and will begin producing his own products for wholesale and retail markets. It wouldn't surprise me if the company exceeds last year's numbers."

My brain struggled to process my new revenue stream. If I wanted, I could quit working and focus on solving cases. I wouldn't have to pick up loose change in the parking lot, or turn off my lights by nine o'clock, or duct tape the bottoms of my shoes to stretch them another season. I could buy name brand shampoo and conditioner, and I wouldn't have to add water to the bottles. My cup overflowed!

"Did you hear me, Dr. Delafose? It's an excellent offer and I recommend taking it. Mr. Cormier has asked that Mr. Delafose be available for commercials and some public appearances. He wants your, uh dog, at the grand opening of his manufacturing facility, and he'll be the star of a series of national commercials. But we can discuss that later. I'll courier over the contract for you to sign, as Mr. Delafose's representative. Please send my assistant the information and I'll get that right to you."

"Mr. Fisher, I'm out of town, but I'll give you my father's address. I should be home in a few days, definitely by the end of the week."

"That's acceptable, and I'll let Mr. Cormier know. Is there anything else I can do for you, Dr. Delafose? Mr. Hebert said to make sure I address all your legal needs, even ones outside this contract negotiation."

"Honestly, Mr. Fisher, I feel a little light-headed from this amazing news. Please thank Sid for asking you to renegotiate Zy's contract. I've been meaning to talk to Cletus myself, and get a better deal. But you've done a much better job than I could have, I'm sure. Do I need to write you a check for your service?" And could Holliman cash it after I'd received some of Zy's earnings?

If I didn't know better, I'd think Shorty was on the other end of my call. Or his horse Festus. Holliman could give Shorty a run for his money in a horse snort contest. "Dr. Delafose, I doubt you could afford my fees for this contract negotiation. Don't worry though, Mr. Hebert took care of the bill."

"Well, please thank Sid for me. I'll be sure and send him a card as well."

"You've misunderstood me. When I said Mr. Hebert, I didn't mean Sid Hebert. I meant Jack. You have a good day now." *Click.*

Hmmm, so Jack kept in touch with the family lawyer. I couldn't help but wonder how he'd spent his Christmas, on his island in the middle of the ocean. With a forty room mansion and servants everywhere, it couldn't have been too bad.

Was Holliman instructed to drop Jack's name? Or did he let it slip? No, with his years of maintaining attorney–client privilege, he revealed nothing by accident. But why? Did Jack want me to have a way to communicate? The phrase *harboring a fugitive* floated in my head. Was I breaking the law? I had no clue about Jack's location. I could talk to the police and tell them...what? Holliman would claim I'd misunderstood our conversation. Sid paid his bills, not Jack.

Since my evening with Jack less than a month ago, I'd struggled to find the justice in arresting him. Yes, he'd killed Ronald Reynolds, but he'd done the world a favor.

"*Ev, my wife dreamed of visiting Paris, but I was too busy. I never made time for the only thing she wanted to do! When the doctor pronounced her terminal, I asked Ronald to return just part of my investment, so I could take Ally on the vacation of her dreams. Of course he didn't, and six months later, she died. Ev, nothing mattered anymore. I'd failed Ally! She never got to sit in a French café, sipping coffee and watching the people go by. And it was all Ronald's fault.*"

I'd taken my thoughts to God many times, agonizing over my worldly emotions. Jack shouldn't have killed Ronald, but part of me envied him. If I had the chance to avenge Doug's death, I just might. Almost four years hadn't softened my heart toward Rocky Ragusa.

From his dirty mop to his scuffed shoes, I'd never forget an inch of that man's body. In the courtroom, I'd bored a hole into my husband's killer. The judge sentenced him to Death Row—the standard for murdering a police officer in Louisiana.

Nate spent the next six months with black circles ringing his eyes, offsetting the bleariness in his features from lack of sleep. My father mirrored Nate, both too shell shocked to offer much comfort. Thank goodness for Elizabeth, with her soothing voice and petitions to Heaven. The woman spent many a morning coaxing me out of bed with a hot cup of tea.

She held my hand during court, planting me firmly in my seat. She knew I was a moment away from leaping on Rocky and tearing out his eyes. He'd ruined my life, and robbed my children. Elizabeth prayed for me every night, that God would show me the way to live my life in peace and not in hate. Four years later, she was still praying.

"Well, Doc, that's pretty good news. Guess ol' Zy's gonna be buyin' the hot dogs from now on." Shorty's eyes grew as large as quarters, marveling that my dog was richer than all of us.

"No hot dogs! Zy jumped to upper middle class but he's still going to eat dog food. Maybe he'll start eating that high priced dog food though. Maybe I can start eating higher priced food too." Be still my heart! Maybe I could add some fresh vegetables to my meals, even some fresh herbs. Oh, and that fancy tea that Doug used to buy me when he worked double shifts.

Curtis interrupted my dream sequence through the grocery store. "Evangeline, I've got a quick minute before the supper crowd arrives at Mercado. I spoke with Jean and I have some news about your mysterious kitchen couple."

Oh, Curtis Delacroix, my favorite club owner! I punched the speaker button. "Go ahead—my team is here with me."

"Hello everyone—Nice to meet you. Jean and I both spoke to the members of our staff who worked at Jacqueline's party. One of Jean's servers, Carrie, recognized the couple lurking by the kitchen all night. They own a new catering company and they snuck in to check out their competition. Jean said at first he didn't remember them from the party. But then Carrie described them, and he realized he'd seen them a few times near the kitchen. Carrie said she's seen those same two people at The Blue Moon. Jean did some checking, and they've scoped out several places in town that cater. Based on this news, we can check them off the suspect list, don't you think?"

"Curtis, this here's Shorty Cormier. I think yer right, sir. That's some mighty good detectin' work. Thank ya'."

Despite Annabelle's icy glare, I grabbed my tumbler of ice water and sloshed the contents down my throat to overcome my laughter. Wouldn't it be interesting if I drowned while solving this case? And what would the headlines say? *Out of Towner Drowns in Sketchy Motel Room. Body Count for Week Increases to Four. Film at Eleven.* Was that too long for a headline? Should I check with Hugh? As the editor of the Graisseville *Gazette*, he would know.

"Evangeline, did you hear me? Jean and I both reviewed Jacqueline's staff and guest lists. Jean saw nothing, but one name stood out to me: Ryker LaPeer. I checked with Marcella, and that's her brother. I pressed her for more information—turns out Ryker's her half brother. Want to guess who the father is?"

What was that bit of gossip about an illegitimate son? "Curtis, is he Beau Romero's son?"

A low chuckle drifted from my phone. "Why Evangeline, you're pretty good at this detecting work too. Rumors floated around for years about Beau's kid wanting his fair share. Truth be told, I never put much stock in them. When I called Marcella about this Ryker fella, I figured she'd say he's a cousin or something. We're pretty good friends, but she's never mentioned a brother—just a bunch of sisters. Marcella came clean pretty quick and told me how this guy's related to her, that they have the same mama but different daddies. But she got real quiet when I started asking how he got invited to Jacqueline's party. Turns out her mother had a fling with Beau shortly after Marcella's father passed away, about twenty years ago. Her mama's black and Beau's white, and even twenty years ago it didn't sit too well with folks around here. Marcella's mama moved them all back to Plaquemine Parish, to be near her family."

"Curtis, this here's Shorty Cormier. Did Beau know about this Ryker fella? Thank ya'."

Dear Lord, please don't let me drown.

"Uh, Marcella says he did. Beau sent money to her mama until the kid turned eighteen. But his last check included a note—that the gravy train had run its course. But if Ryker ever needed a job, he could come to New Orleans and Beau would put him to work. He didn't want a relationship, on account of Chantilly. And that didn't sit too well with Ryker, so he'd moved up here to see about changing his daddy's mind. Just before Beau passed, they'd spent some time together."

Curtis paused and his voice softened. "Ya'll, Marcella doesn't think her brother's involved in Beau's death, or Chantilly's. She believes all he wanted was a relationship with Beau, and he called home crying after Beau passed. Ryker wanted to come home, but his mama convinced him to stay. Now he's working in the distillery, and got promoted to manager last month. He's met a girl and they're pretty serious. Marcella says he wouldn't screw all that up by killing people."

I glanced at Shorty then Annabelle. Their eyes told me volumes. "We agree, Curtis. Ryker likely didn't kill Beau, and it wouldn't do him any good to kill Chantilly. I mean, he might go to court and get something out of Beau's estate. Why risk a good life for a what-if situation? Did Ryker know Jacqueline? Is that how he got into the party?"

"Uh, actually Bea got him on the guest list, and his girl-friend, since Bea's his aunt."

"Curtis, this here's Shorty Cormier. Any idea why Jacque-line got all secret like, wouldn't let anyone near her po'boys? Thank ya.'"

"Actually, I do. According to the staff that night, Jacque-line wouldn't let anyone near the sandwiches, which I found strange. So I confronted her, demanded to know what hap-pened that night. She told me she's got a couple of restaurant developers interested in her po' boy recipe. They're looking to create a chain of po'boy restaurants featuring Jacqueline's sandwiches. She'd invited them to her party to sample her creation, but to also talk to the other guests and find out what they thought. Which explains the other two mysterious names on the guest list: Raphael Radiro and Sebastien Soren-son. Jacqueline confirmed they're the developers interested in her sandwiches."

"Curtis, this here's Shorty Cormier. What about Jean an' Chantilly's love child? Was that kid at the party? Thank ya.'"

Even Annabelle hid her amusement. But Curtis remained the model of courtesy and respect. "No sir, not to my knowl-edge. But I can ask around some more, if you like."

"Curtis, this here's Shorty Cormier. Nah, ya' did good, sir. Thank ya.'"

No, hiding my laughter didn't outweigh the risk of drown-ing. Shorty would have to hear my chuckles.

"Doc, I don't know whatcha think is so funny. I think we got some good stuff here. Now I didn't put much stock into all these babies growin' up an' wantin' t'kill their long-lost mamas and daddies. That sounds like those dumb movies on that channel Annabelle's mama likes t'watch. What's it called? Life Tunes? Life Lines?"

Oh it felt good to laugh! Annabelle saved my skin. "Baby-cakes, I really couldn't say. But I think you're right, as always. Beau's son and the baby Chantilly gave up for adoption aren't important to this case. Actually, if I was reading a mystery novel, I'd say this information is a bunch of red herrings. You know, a lot of extra information thrown into the mystery to keep the reader guessing?"

"Evangeline, this is your Daddy speaking. Honey, you got a strange postcard today. Do you have any strange friends? I think maybe one of your friends is playing a trick on you."

Should I mention for the thousandth time that my phone screen displayed my father's name, indicating he was the one calling me? No, it wouldn't make a difference. He would always announce his name at the beginning of a phone conversation.

"Hi, Dad. I'm fine, thanks for asking." Should I address the question about the strangeness of my friends? No, best to jump straight to the comment. "And I can't imagine any of my friends playing a trick on me. What does the postcard say?"

"Uh, well it's about five inches tall and maybe seven inches long. It has a picture of the Eiffel Tower on it."

Was my father hard of hearing or did he just not listen? Why should I care about the size of the postcard? Wait a minute! "Dad, did you say the *Eiffel Tower*?"

"Uh, huh. You haven't ever been to Paris, have you? If you did, you never told me. Why wouldn't you tell me you went to Paris? And why would someone send you a postcard with the Eiffel Tower on it? They didn't write a single word on the card. That's just strange."

"Dad, I've never been to Paris. And if I ever go to Paris, I will definitely tell you. Could you look at the postmark? Where was the postcard mailed from?"

"That's the strange part. Or maybe it's the even stranger part? There isn't a postmark, because I didn't pick it up from your post office box. When I got to your house, to feed Zydeco, I saw it clipped to the chain on your porch swing, with a clothespin. Child, have you gone and made someone mad, and now they're pulling tricks on you? If your mother and I told you once, we've told you a thousand times, you got to just nod and smile. Don't make people mad, Evangeline. It's a small town and we all got to get along. Why I remember one time, when you were about seven, the neighbor came over and said you'd pushed her daughter into a mud puddle..."

"Dad, could we focus on the here and now? If I made somebody mad, they'd throw eggs at my front porch, not leave a postcard." This wasn't a conversation I wanted to have with my father. If my suspicions were correct, Jack Hebert had left the postcard, and wasn't relaxing on a sunny beach overseas. He'd never left the country, and had probably never even left Louisiana. The less my father knew about Jack and his probable location, the better off we all were.

"I'll have you know I watch all those true crime shows. The criminals out there are more dangerous than a pair of Siamese cats in a kissing booth. Why the other day I watched a show about a man who left his girlfriend's head on her parents' front porch. And he'd have gotten away with it too, if..."

"Dad, I'm sorry to interrupt, but I don't see what your show has to do with my situation."

My father could be a strong contender in a horse snort contest, along with Holliman and Shorty. "Evangeline, you know what your problem is? You don't listen. Child, both criminals left the items on *the front porch*." How did I end up in these conversations?

"You're right, I'm sorry, Dad. If you find a severed head on my front porch, please let me know. I've got to go—love you." Some days I thanked God for my family, some days I thanked Him for giving me enough patience to deal with them.

CHAPTER 19

"Doc, I don't mean t'rain on yore parade, but to-morrow's Tuesday. Don'tcha got t'get back an' start teachin' those ungrateful rich kids?"

As someone whose parents couldn't afford college, or anything else really, Shorty had a low opinion of my students. I couldn't argue—most of them had full rides thanks to their families, with few scholarships or student loans. But if I made one comment about the athletes and their privileges, he shut me down.

Shorty's bulging eyes reminded me of footballs, which was appropriate. "An' before ya' start in on the athletes, that ain't the same thing! Those kids got hours an' hours o' trainin', spendin' their days gettin' all banged up. Then they gotta go an' do all the stuff those rich kids do! Yeah, those men an' women work hard an' deserve everythin' they get from the boosters an' such. Except for those badminton players—they're jus' tennis player wannabes that failed the cut." Someday I'd learn why Shorty nursed a grudge against that sport. Maybe after the case I'd delve into the history of my friend's aversion to badminton.

My PI had worked himself so worked up that he leaped out of the motel chair to pace. The orange plastic cushion squeaked from his exit.

Annabelle jumped forward. "Easy there, Sweetie! You okay?"

But I went further. "Sweetie, be careful. You might damage this high priced furniture in our upscale room." My attempt at humor lightened the mood.

"That's right, ladies! I wouldn't want t'mess up this fancy room. Say, Sugarcakes, do ya' think we could book it for our honeymoon?" Shorty turned to his beloved. "Wouldn't ya' love all this vintage furniture an' stuff?"

We all needed a laugh. After a few minutes of chuckles I started a conversation. "Shorty, to answer your question, I don't need to get back. My boss called me a couple weeks ago, told me he's dropping my class load. He claims parents don't appreciate classes like Crime Fiction and Detective Noir. Even my attempts to beg for mercy fell on deaf ears. Now if I'd teach courses on interpretive dance, or the history of rock and roll, he'd have a full load for me. In the end, he offered me two classes, and I told him it's not worth the drive. So no, I don't have any ungrateful rich kids to teach this semester."

My confession dropped Shorty back into the thrift store reject chair. "Doc, why didn't ya' tell me? Thank the Good Lord ol' Zy's a workin' guy! Now ya' don't need that fancy pants job! Yer rich."

Annabelle moved towards me. Was she going to pat my leg? No, she wrapped both arms around me and squeezed. "Ev,

I'm so sorry. Are you okay?" She released her hug, and I felt like a warm blanket had dropped from my shoulders.

I bent my knees to rest on the bed, then thought better of it. We'd already spotted four cockroaches—who could guess what lay in wait between the covers? "Yes thank you, Annabelle. I'm okay. And thank goodness for Zy—my possibilities weren't looking good. The Gas n' More is hiring, and so is the Dirty Pelican. I talked to both fine establishments and they agreed to give me a chance. Although Shorty, your friend Dino kind of put his head in his hands and muttered something about you owing him a huge favor. I don't think he hires many servers over fifty."

Shorty shook his head—was it because of my rich dog, or the thought of me waiting tables at a dive bar? "Doc, I don't care how bad it ever gets. Yer never workin' at the Pelican! As for the Gas n' More, Chuck's a good boss. An' ya' get free drinks when yer workin'. Come t'think of it, ya' get a discount on yore food, an' they make a real good pepperoni pizza. My buddy Curt says that helps a lot with his meal costs. But thank the good Lord we don't gotta go down that road, do we, Miss *Rock-uh-feller*?"

Did cockroaches climb out of bed sheets to terrorize humans? Maybe, if we sat on their home. No, best to remain standing. "Well, rich enough I don't have to work for Chuck or Dino. God definitely answers prayer."

Annabelle smiled. "He sure does—otherwise I wouldn't have Shorty in my life."

Mr. Blessing leaped from his orange seat of tackiness. "That's right, Sugar Cake, thank the Good Lord above! Now Sugar, Miss *Rock-Uh-Feller*, let's go over our grid."

Annabelle, our voice of soothing and comfort, closed out our conversation regarding my finances. "Ev, this really is such a blessing!" I rated another warm hug, another blessing.

Then I realized something . We hadn't splurged on another white board, so we had to make do with paper napkins from Bubba's Big Burgers. We'd taped them to the wall by the door, covering the holes. Were those bullet holes? Shorty assured us they weren't, but I had my doubts.

God always provides, including makeshift white boards. After our burgers from Bubba, Shorty had spent a half hour at the hardware store to pick up tape for our new elements board, bug spray, a fly swatter, some cleaning rags, and the strongest disinfectant money could buy.

"Guys, what're we thinking? Doug Ray killed Beau, but the suspects don't know that. My money's on Bea—she killed Chantilly as revenge for her brother. Nicotine has a fifteen to thirty-minute window, so Bea could have given it to her sister-in-law before she headed to the bar."

Annabelle shook her head. "Yes, that works. But here's my question: why did Bea invite this Ryker person to the party? Were they conspiring together? Or maybe he did it all on his own. I think we should talk to Bea, maybe we can get a confession."

"Good idea, but where would she be on a Monday night? Her place closes pretty early , for New Orleans that is." The 21 *Jump Street* theme song cut through the air like the bug spray we'd already unleashed.

"Ethan! How are you?"

"Doing really well, Ev. Guess what? I got a job! I'm working in Baton Rouge for Ink and Pixel."

"Oh, I'm putting you on speaker. Here, repeat that for Shorty and Annabelle."

"Hey, Mr. Shorty, Mrs. Almost Shorty! I'm starting my new job the day after graduation this May. It's a graphic design company in Baton Rouge called Ink and Pixel."

Shorty leaned forward, his lips hovering just above my phone. "Ethan, this here's Shorty. That's real good, son, congratulations! Say, are ya' gonna keep helpin' us out? Thank y a.'"

"Uh, well that's what I need to talk about. I have to sign a contract that I won't have any outside jobs. But don't worry! I talked to my friend Duggar, and he's agreed to take my place. Honestly, he's been doing a lot of your research for the last two cases. He really gets off on this kind of stuff, and his programs are more sophisticated. Want to know the best part? He won't take money as payment. Duggar says that's just another way for the government to track you. I told him what a great cook you are, and he says you can pay him in food."

"Ethan, this here's Shorty Cormier. That's great, son. An' he's right about the government trackin' us like that. Now, does this Duggar got a last name? Thank ya.'"

I hit the mute button. "Shorty, I don't think this is a good idea. Who is this person? I'm picturing some guy locked in his parents' house, sitting at his desk in his underwear, squinting at a computer screen and muttering trash talk about the government. He could get us arrested."

A quick glare set me straight. "Well, he's right about people trackin' us through our money. I was jus' readin' about that the other day. I say we give 'im a chance." He jammed his finger into my mute button. The topic was closed to discussion.

"Ya'll, I don't know Duggar's last name, and I doubt that's his first name. I'm telling you, he's your guy. He can dig up dirt on *anybody*. And he's okay with skirting the law. It's either him or nobody."

"Ethan, this here's Shorty Cormier. He sounds like a real good guy. Can ya' send his number tuh Ev? Thank ya'."

"Uh, well he doesn't really work that way. He contacts you. I think he lives somewhere near Baton Rouge, but I have no idea. Anyway, next time I hear from him, I'll let him know you want his services."

"Ethan, this here's Shorty Cormier. How's he gonna know when we need those services? Thank ya'."

"Don't worry, Mr. Shorty, Duggar's going to know when you get your next case. He's pretty resourceful. But if you need anything else on the Romero case, I'll take care of it."

"Thank you, Ethan. I'll miss you, but I'm excited about your new career."

"Me too, Ev. Let me know when you're back in town for classes. We'll have lunch."

We said our goodbyes, and I promised myself to bring my cousin up to speed on my career. Baton Rouge wasn't that far from Graisseville, and with my influx of cash coming soon, I could spare some gas to see my favorite cousin.

"Where were we? Oh yes, Bea Romero. Her store closes at five I think." A quick search on Facebook confirmed my guess. "What'd you think? Shall we stop by, see if she's still there?"

Bea's Bites reminded me of any other trendy bakery in New Orleans. That was the problem. The vanilla exterior with pale blue lettering screamed *nothing special or unique*. Bea didn't share her brother's gift of building great ideas into successful businesses. Or was it Chantilly's gift?

My limited experience as a sleuth taught me that gathering information was less about what people said and more about what they didn't. No one had mentioned Beau's talent for growing successful companies—they'd only mentioned that he owned successful companies.

"Doc, didja hear me? I don't know why we gotta follow all the rules. A man should be able t'protect himself in this den o' iniquity. That's all I'm sayin'"

"Yes, but Bea's store has a sign on it—no guns allowed. We should leave them in the truck. Annabelle can keep an eye on them." I exited the car and stepped toward the storefront, finishing our conversation.

A couple of knocks on the door brought us Bea's wide green eyes peering through the window. A twist of the lock and the door opened. "Hey, ya'll! What a surprise."

"Bea, may we come in? We'd like to ask some questions."

Our hostess swung the door wider and we stepped into the cramped space. Matching vanilla and blue paint greeted us, along with cream doilies on the counter displaying empty plates.

"I'm just closing up, but I could probably scrounge up some cookies or a slice of cake."

Bea locked the front door behind us and pocketed the key. "Let's head to the kitchen. I've brewed some coffee, and I just remembered—I've got some beignets."

Shorty pushed past us and planted himself at the prep table, hands folded together in anticipation. Bea pulled a plate of powdered sugar delights from the pantry and placed them in front of my PI's eager hands. She poured three cups of coffee and I reached for my steaming cup. I took a sip and my taste buds exploded with horror and disgust. Oh my days! Did I pour turpentine into my unsuspecting mouth? How did people drink this bitter liquid?

"Oh, Bea, what a lovely container! Is this sweetener?" I sniffed the white powder, then dumped a spoonful of it into my coffee. It didn't quite look like sugar. Monk Fruit perhaps, or Stevia?

"No! Don't put that in...well, now you've ruined everything."

Once again, an interrogation had taken a right turn and hurled itself off a cliff. *When* would I learn? Shorty sat on the stool beside me, powdered sugar dancing upon his lips. Bea's outburst stopped his fourth bite in midair. I pushed my coffee cup to the middle of the counter.

"This is the part where I confess, right? And then I kill you. Let's discuss the killing part first. I'm going to lock you in the walk-in freezer, which is set at negative ten degrees. I've got a guy, and he'll come in the morning to get rid of your bodies."

She had a guy? Was he in her list of contacts? And what was he listed under? Disposal Services?

Several harsh knocks interrupted our party. I tried to catch Shorty's eye, but his mind worked furiously to get us out of the situation. Bea paused at the doorway. "Don't bother trying to go through the back–it's double bolted and I have the key."

My ears shifted into overdrive as I strained to hear the conversation at the front door. Was that Annabelle's voice? Yes, the look of fear on my PI's face confirmed my guess.

"Please, it's urgent! I saw your lights on, and I've got to use your bathroom! No, I'll never make it to the next rest stop. I've got to go now!"

The door creaked open farther, and Annabelle appeared in the doorframe. "There, through that doorway, first door on the right. And hurry—we're closed."

Before I could process how three of us were getting out of this mess, much less two, our captor continued the conversation.

"Let's be quick, before our interloper returns from the bathroom, Let's begin with the *why* part of the confession."

Seriously? Our killer couldn't wait to brag about her genius. "It's no secret that I hated Chantilly for...for everything! She cheated on my brother, then convinced him the baby was his. Beau wanted to marry her and be a family, but Chantilly panicked. What if Beau figured it out someday, demanded a paternity test? She broke off her romance with the real father, told her parents, and begged to stay with her aunt and give the baby up for adoption."

"Jean's the father, isn't he, Bea?" Could arsenic poison me twelve inches away? I pushed the cup further away while my captor kept watch over the set of chef knives nesting in their wooden block.

"Yes, he's the father. Jean begged Chantilly to give him the baby. But she had a plan, and it didn't include children, especially if they lived here in town. She tried to keep it quiet, but a circle of people knew. Chantilly cried that she was the grieving young mother, it was all her parents' idea. But it was hers. I know that's the truth, because I looked up her aunt right after Beau passed, and got the whole story. Chantilly looked at Jean and she looked at my brother, and she figured out real quick who looked the best on her arm. Everyone loved my brother, but they tolerated Chantilly. Why she killed him I'll never understand."

Shorty opened his mouth, then shut it. One of the top ten rules in an investigation was: never contradict a killer's confession with facts.

"Bea, Shorty and I get it. You wanted revenge for Beau, which makes perfect sense. A man killed my husband in cold blood, and I dream of revenge every day."

We stood ten inches apart, but I felt Shorty tense. We'd never discussed my emotions towards Doug's killer. No doubt we'd be having that conversation soon.

"Oh, I didn't know that about you. I mean, I remember reading about your husband in the paper. But I just assumed, being a Christian, you'd forgiven and forgotten." Bea studied me, her eyes registering a newfound respect.

"Then you understand why I plotted against my sister-in-law. First, I tracked down Chantilly and Jean's child. Thanks to Chantilly's aunt, I found her, living down south in Houma. After a wonderful visit, I came back to blackmail my sister-in-law. She'd pay *dearly* to keep her daughter from turning up. And with Ryker, I could go to court and get him a share of the estate. Beau built this amazing empire, and his cheating wife wasn't going to have it all."

Could I grab my coffee cup, beyond my arms' length, and throw the contents in Bea's face? It worked with Stella Cook.

"But why kill Chantilly, Bea? It sounds like you had a perfect plan to blackmail her and take a piece of Beau's assets for his son."

Bea reached for her largest blade, an exquisite eight-inch serrated bread knife. Was that how I would die? I could hear Bea's confession. "Well, it was either slice a loaf of French bread or kill Ev, and I had to choose..."

Darn New Orleans and their gun laws! There had to be an exception when entering the storefront of a suspected murderer. Ugh! It was too late now. Why hadn't I listened to Shorty?

"Oh, c'mon, Ev! You must understand. Jean explained to me that, according to Louisiana law, Ryker would get a quarter of the estate because he's under twenty-four. That's a really good deal. But all I had was the joy of blackmailing my sister-in-law, and that diminished with time. Then Chantilly started making noises that she'd come clean about her daughter. With her parents dead, she'd pull out her original story: poor young pregnant girl, bullied by her parents to give up her daughter. The girl's sixteen, practically grown, and has her adopted family back in Houma. She's not an inconvenience to Chantilly anymore, more like an opportunity. At our last meeting, my sister-in-law informed me I'd collected my last blackmail payment. She'd already contracted with a publishing company to write her life story and interview her with the long lost daughter. The beginning of her next chapter, she called it, where she embraces her daughter and becomes her role model. The world would have another Chantilly Romero."

Bea rotated the knife in her hand, touching the serrated edges. "You get it, don't you, Ev? Can you imagine a world where Rocky Ragusa trains up a teenager to be just like him? No, I couldn't let it happen. I had to save this poor girl, Maya, who could only see a birth mother wanting a relationship. But I knew better."

Bea placed the knife on the counter. "For the last three months, I've added something special to Chantilly's daily order of hibiscus tea. I've been stirring arsenic into her tacky glitter tumbler, and burying the stir stick deep in the trash can. The first time, she mentioned the extra sweetness, and I bragged about a new plant-based sweetener I'd found. Zero calories, just for her! My sister-in-law never suspected a thing."

She picked up the knife, placing it between us. "I sprinkled in a little more each time, and watched Chantilly's skin thicken and turn dark. I'd sympathize with her stomach pain and diarrhea, suggest a natural remedy or two. Oh how I rejoiced at her discomfort, waiting for the inevitable heart disease, hopefully even cancer."

Shorty slid off his stool and sidled close to me. "Say, Bea. When didja get tired o' waitin' for Chantilly t'die? When didja give her the nicotine?"

Bea's eyes shifted from the knife to Shorty. "What are you talking about? I killed her with arsenic. Everyone knows she died from arsenic poisoning."

"No, ma'am, she didn't. If ya' read the coroner's report, she had arsenic in her body, an' it'd been there a good long while. But she died from *nicotine* poisonin'. So if ya' didn't kill her with nicotine, who did?"

"That would be me."

Oh great! One killer was bad enough—did we have to have two? And let's not forget we officially had three people about to die—Annabelle's guilty face peered into the kitchen from the darkness.

Even Bea registered shock at our visitor. "Uh, well, hello, Jean—welcome to the party. I see you brought a plus one. Let me guess—she didn't come in here to use the bathroom."

Jean crossed the room, hopped actually, his right hand like a vise on Annabelle's shoulder. The pair stood beside Jean's open-mouthed co-conspirator.

Shorty glanced at Annabelle, trying to push the worry from his face. She met his frown lines with a brave smile. "Looks like ya'll didn't work together on this murder situation, didja? Accordin' tuh Bea's face, she ain't got no idea 'bout the nicotine."

Jean ignored Shorty. "Bea, I drove by, to see if you needed any help, and I saw Shorty's truck. My goal was to keep them from learning your secret, but I guess I'm too late."

Jean gave Bea a side hug. "Dr. Lirette's class taught me a lot. I could tell someone was poisoning Chantilly with arsenic, and it was going to take a long time. I couldn't wait, I really couldn't. That woman was infusing her own poison, infecting my daughter's mind with her grand plans. I couldn't allow her to take Maya under her wing."

He nodded toward Bea. "Did you know she'd talked to Maya's adopted parents? Chantilly convinced them to send my daughter here, to live with her and finish out school. No, absolutely not! That wasn't happening."

Jean released the hug and Bea squeezed his hand. "Chantilly sent me to the bar to get her a drink. I stopped by the men's room, drink in hand, and locked myself in a stall. Then I dumped nicotine into her drink, exited the bathroom, and handed it to that hag with a bow and a smile. As she reached for it, I stumbled forward, dousing her hand. Then I took her stupid sandwich back to the kitchen, taking my time to replace it with another one. "

He chuckled, picking up the seven and a half inch vegetable knife. Something told me Jean's plans didn't include slicing produce. "By the time I got back and handed her the po'boy, the nicotine had taken effect."

Shorty smacked his palm on the table, sending us all a good half inch into the air. "Jean, I sure did enjoy yore fancy restaurant the other night. Annabelle made me promise t'bring her back after we're married. Didn't ya', Butter Cookie? I'm mighty upset we ain't gonna get t'do that."

Our captor executed a small bow. "Thank you, Mr. Shorty, for your kind words. I'm sorry about that too, and I hate to kill you, all of you. I really do. But murder isn't for the fainthearted."

"No sir, it ain't But ya' know what my daddy always told me?"

Jean hesitated. Was it a trick? "Uh, no I sure don't. What did he always tell you?"

"Well, sir, he always told me, *son, never bring a knife tuh a gun fight.*"

Well hello, Diane!

Who should I call? Definitely not Doug Ray. I dialed Mitch's cell phone, and he called a trusted friend with the state police. Shorty and Diane escorted our killers into the cooler, and fifteen minutes later our party included twelve officers with the state police and the Louisiana attorney general. I advised everyone to stay away from the coffee, just in case.

After giving statements to the police, Shorty, Annabelle, and I voted to treat ourselves to two rooms at the fanciest hotel in New Orleans. After we called to get the prices, we checked into the Spruce Inn instead. I never spotted a roach, or any holes in the walls, which was good enough for me.

Over coffee and cherry pie at Betty's Diner, we toasted our success. "Sweetie, that was so brave of you! I really thought I was going to die tonight, that we all were. But you kept a level head and saved us all. Baby, I just couldn't be prouder."

My praise was just as strong but lighter on the gush. "Thank goodness you brought your gun, Shorty. But I can't believe the police didn't fuss at you for breaking the law."

My PI took two gulps of coffee and cast a longing glance at his empty plate. Annabelle jumped up and rushed off to find the waitress. "Nah, those guys are state cops—they don't care about my gun. They had their hands full arrestin' that kitchen full o' criminals."

Was this the best cherry pie I'd ever had? Or did our success make it that much sweeter? "We got pretty lucky though, that Jean and Bea didn't search you and find your gun. We're also blessed that neither one of them had a gun themselves."

Annabelle returned with our server. "Doc, the folks livin' in this Sodom an' Gomorrah town think it's jus' cops an' criminals that carry guns. We ain't either o' those, so they didn't think about searchin' us. An' I bet they don't own a single firearm. Nah, they're more comfortable with knives, workin' in kitchens an' all."

Marla waited, pen paused over her pad. "Yes, ma'am, I'd like another one o' yore fine pieces o' cherry pie. Best pie I've ever had, jus' like my mama used t'make, God rest her soul."

A hair flip and a giggle, and Marla sashayed to the kitchen for Shorty's pie. Annabelle snuggled up to her man. *Nope, don't you worry about my quarter cup of coffee, Marla. I'm fine, thanks.*

My PI got all serious, reaching across the table to place his free hand over mine. Of course, as soon as Marla returned with his pie he'd have to reprioritize his appendages.

"Doc, I jus' wanna tell ya' that I understand about yore feelings. Ya' know, yore feelings toward Rocky Ragusa. I'm not surprised ya' think about revenge on that dirtbag. Ya' know what? I'd feel that exact same way, if Annabelle was gone an' I knew her killer was still alive."

Shorty hesitated, taking a gulp of coffee to collect his thoughts. Annabelle patted his arm, suddenly misty eyed. "Ev, I'm probably supposed t'tell ya' the Good Book discourages hatin' others and wantin' to do 'em harm. But I'll tell ya' one thing, iffen I ever see that Rocky Ragusa, that'd be the last time I see 'im. An' I think ya' know what I mean."

My free hand landed with a *smack* on top of Shorty's and I squeezed his fingers. Was that the sound of bones cracking? Shorty's eyes teared up, from pain or emotions I'd never know. *Thank You, Lord for good friends, especially good friends like Shorty and Annabelle.*

"Say, Doc, do ya' think The Blue Moon'll stay open, even though Jean's headed tuh Angola? Annabelle an' me are hopin' t'get s'more o' those crab cakes."

CHAPTER 20

Eight hours of sleep at the Spruce Inn beat any amount of rest at the Welcome Lodge. My face grinned back at me from the mirror. No circles under my eyes, and hardly a wrinkle. My hair fell in waves around my shoulders and my eyes sparkled. Solving the murder of Chantilly Romero had done wonders for my health. And who was knocking on my door?

"Good mornin, Doc. How'd ya' sleep? I brought ya' a *Chay-Tea-Lat-Tay*, an' I told 'em t'make it all skinny, so it's jus' the way ya' like it. Hey, where's Annabelle?"

As my un-caffeinated brain struggled to decipher Shorty's words, my fingers wiggled toward my paper cup of goodness. "She's in the shower. You can put her coffee right there on the table, by the television."

My PI shoved my cup into my hands as he stepped inside. "Didja already have some tea or somethin' this mornin'? Ya' look all fresh an' caffeinated. Dang it, Doc! Ya' shoulda told me ya' were goin' out for a drink." He crossed to the bathroom door, paused to listen and confirm my story, then placed Annabelle's cup as instructed.

He paced back towards the bathroom, then turned and revisited the door. My guess? The cup in his hand was the second one of the morning, possibly the third. The car ride home would be interesting.

"Shorty, how could I go anywhere this morning? How would I even get to a coffee shop? You've got the keys to our only form of transportation. No, I just slept really well. This bed is amazing! When we check out, I'm going to ask what kind of mattress this is. How about you? How did you sleep?" But I already knew the answer.

"Not great, Doc, not great. Look, we're all square with the police an' all, an' we're free t'leave town. Now, I talked tuh yore cousins this mornin'. An' before ya' get yore *un-men-chen-uh-bulls* in a twist, I didn't say a word about us still bein' in this lawless place. Miss Babette's gonna put a package in the mail for ya'll ladies—somethin' about detectives. She said ya'd understand, which is good cuz I sure didn't."

How much caffeine was coursing through Shorty's bloodstream? "She's got a Nancy Drew bookmark for Annabelle. Now that one I get, cuz my sisters used t'read those stories. She's got one for Elizabeth called a *kindred miller*, not really sure what that is. An' there's one for you, an' a bag uh marbles."

"I know what she's talking about. It was a game we played before you showed up, comparing ourselves to famous fictional detectives. Elizabeth is Kinsey Milhouse, Marcel and Babette are Nick and Nora Charles, and I'm Miss Jane Marple. It's Babette's way of thanking us."

A shrug—or maybe a seizure?—from my PI indicated he'd moved to another subject. "Oh yeah, Miss Babette invited Annabelle t'come back to this den o' thieves, so she can get her weddin' dress. Not sure I'm gonna pass that on—I think we've all had 'bout enough o' this place for a good long while."

Mitch's ringtone filled our cozy space. Size wise, our room was probably just a little smaller than the one at the Welcome Lodge. But the word cozy never touched my lips during that stay.

"Ev, I'm so glad you're okay. When you get back, we need to talk. Is it really true? You knowingly withheld crucial evidence from an investigation, so you could solve the case yourself? Please tell me that's not true. Never mind, we'll talk when you get home. For now, I'm just glad you're safe."

Suddenly, the thought of returning home left a knot in my stomach. I told Mitch goodbye and turned to my PI. "Shorty, I've still got a few questions. Could you help me answer them, or are you too far into your caffeine overdose?"

I bent down to examine the carpet. Was there a path pushed into the carpet fibers from my PI's pacing? Had he stopped moving in the...I glanced at my phone. He'd been on my carpet approximately six minutes, his feet never stopping. Would we get charged for the wear and tear on the carpet? If we did, Shorty would definitely get a bill.

"Oh, sure, sure, I can answer some questions for ya'. But there's one more thing I found out this mornin', while ya'll were gettin' all yore beauty sleep. It's pretty funny, Doc, you'll get a real kick out of it. Bea Romero put up a reward, $10,000, tuh anyone who gave the police enough evidence t'put her brother's killer behind bars. Well, yesterday yore boyfriend called his buddy at the state police, told 'im about the gun yore daddy brought over, an' the files fulla evidence we got from Dugoux an' Miller. Well, Mitch's buddy ran all those fancy cop tests, an' said that gun matches the gun that killed Beau, and it's registered tuh Sheriff Ray. He said he'll give the files a good hard look, and if they all check out then *boom!*"

"Shorty, is that you, Sweetie? What's going on in there?"

"Oh nothin', my little cappucino. I'm jus' tellin' Doc about the reward money." And pretty loudly too.

"Anyway, looks like we got enough facts an' they're gonna arrest Sheriff Ray. Yeah, he's gonna go away for a long time, an you an' I got the reward! Now I don't know what yer gonna do with yore half, but I'm gonna put my money towards my honeymoon. Annabelle's always wanted t'go tuh Hawaii, an' now I can take her." Was the caffeine wearing off, or was Shorty basking in the love he had for Annabelle?

"Shorty, that's wonderful. I'm so happy for you. It sounds like you've made quite a few phone calls this morning. Let me run these questions past you, and hopefully you've already got answers."

Shorty tossed his cup into the trash, his feet never slowing their pace. Should we move outside, where he'd have more room? "Go ahead, Doc. Fire away." He pulled out a moon pie. Yes, pile an overload of sugar on top of the overdose of caffeine. How fast would the ambulance arrive when Shorty's heart exploded? Scratch that—it wouldn't even matter.

"First question is, Jean let himself in Bea's shop last night, right? Did he have a key?"

Moon pie a quarter gone—what was that called, when the moon in the sky looked like Shorty's moon pie? There was new moon, crescent...

"...an' he'd stop by most every evenin' an' help Bea close up. So she gave 'im a key."

"Has anyone told Bea that Sheriff Doug Ray killed her brother? She's going to be pretty mad." Half the moon pie was gone, or was half of it left? Which was it?

"Yeah, she was pretty hot. Yore buddy Brad said she pitched a full-on hissy fit, like his young 'un used t'do."

"Brad? You mean Doug's partner? I thought he warned us off the case."

Less than a quarter of the moon pie left—that was definitely a crescent moon...maybe?

"Now don't be too hard on 'im, Doc. Brad's a good guy. See, he was gettin' a lotta pushback from his boss, an' he was worried about ya' too. He had to get his boss t'think he'd scared us off the trail, but he had a feelin' we'd be the best ones t'solve it. So he baited ya'! Yeah, 'member his little comment, *those little cases ya' played aroun' with in ol' hick town?* He did that on purpose, t'keep ya' goin'. He said ol' Bulldog'd be mighty proud o' ya'."

"Brad *wanted* me to solve the case? Well, I definitely didn't get that impression. But I'm glad that our friendship's still intact." I'd call Brad when I got back home.

"Next question, any idea who tried to run Chantilly off the road? Remember Clifford told us the night she died, someone tried to run her off the road."

What's that called when there isn't a moon? Eclipse? Oh wait, never mind—Shorty had another moon pie in his pocket.

"We ain't real sure, but Brad an' I have a theory. Seems like everybody was at the party, so we think one o' her buncha enemies did it. Cuz she had a lot o' 'em. Or maybe jus' some-one with some o' that parkin' lot passion."

What the heck? What did kissing in a parked car have to do with... "Shorty, do you mean *road rage*?"

My PI shifted his shoulders, intent on his creamy goodness. "That's what I said, *road rage*. Doc, I think ya'd better get yore ears checked."

"Of course. I'll be sure and do that when we get home. Anything else?"

"Yeah, Miss Babette said to tell ya' she's changed her mind. She an' Marcel ain't gonna take on any murder cases for their date nights."

"I think that's an excellent decision. I'll text her a couple other suggestions. They might like a murder mystery dinner, or even an escape room."

Shorty licked his fingers. "Well, I don't know about that 'scape room idea. Annabelle tried t'get me into one o' those, but I gotta wonder—why would I wanna lock myself up in some room, on purpose, then try t'get outta it? It jus' don't make sense."

"Well, different strokes for different folks, I guess." Were Shorty and I the only people who solved real life murders for fun? Dead bodies? Yes, please!

"Uh, one more thing. Annabelle an' I had a little talk last night, after ya'd gone tuh bed. She's hangin' up her detective cap. She says we bicker and fuss at each other so much, we take all the fun outta solvin' crime. Now I told 'er that's jus' how we operate, me an' you, but she says she don't want no part of it. 'Tween you an' me, Doc, that suits me jus' fine. I'm happy with date night at the junkyard. Oh, hey! When ya' text Miss Babette yore list uh date ideas, put that one on there too. Speakin' o' that, Doc, we gotta get on the road. It's Tuesday, an' I gotta get Annabelle home so she can get all ready in time t'get tuh the junkyard."

"Shorty, I must have misunderstood you. What did you say?"

Ah, Festus, old friend, good to hear your familiar snort. "Do ya' got wax in yore ears? I said it's date night at the junkyard. Ol' Fred always saves me an' Annabelle a spot right at the front."

Should I ask? Oh, who was I kidding? I couldn't remain in the dark. "No one has ever told me about this trendy adventure! Please tell me everything that goes on during date night at the junkyard. And don't leave out a single detail."

Shorty cast an eyeball in my direction, pondering whether I was making fun of him or sincerely interested. He settled on the second option. "It's a lotta fun, Doc. Ya' should bring the sheriff along some time. It starts at seven o'clock, but ya' gotta get there a good half hour early. Yeah, people start linin' up about six thirty. If ya' wanna dress up, that's okay, but don't wear no high heels or open toed shoes. Ya' better wear those pink leopard print boots that ya' wore tuh the mud wrestlin' at The Dirty Pelican last fall. Yeah, those'd cover yore feet an' legs real good. Oh, an' be sure an' bring a wagon, t'carry all yore treasures home. Iffen ya' don't got a wagon, one o' those big ol' tote bags would do all right. Oh, an' make sure the sheriff brings his truck, in case ya' find somethin' big, like a genuine Chevy truck door from the 1970's, or some halogen he adlights."

In what universe did a truck door and headlights qualify as rare finds? Only in my PI's universe. Oh, and probably the loads of people lining up a half hour early to get a head start on the treasure hunting.

"Ya' gotta bring cash—ol' Fred don't take credit cards or checks. Annabelle an' I bring a couple hundred, jus' in case. Last month we didn't have much luck, but a couple months ago we got a real nice car jack, an' a whole case o' motor oil. An' I wrestled yore daddy for a fishing reel. I beat 'im fair an' square, but Annabelle made me give up muh reel. She said it's bad manners tuh arm wrestle an old man. But, for the record, I won fair an' square."

"Good for you—you bested an eighty-one-year-old man in arm wrestling. You should be proud of yourself. Should I call Hugh and ask him to run an article about your physical prowess?"

And one more snort for the road. "No, Miss Smarty Pants, ya' don't need t'do that. I'm jus' sayin' it was real nice o' me t'let your daddy have that reel. An' I know he's gonna go all over the village tellin' everybody he wrestled me for it. Then everyone's gonna think he beat me cuz he has the reel an' I don't."

My friend shook his head, weary with his impending task. "Yeah, I'm gonna hafta go all over the village, correctin' his story. I can't have people thinkin' an ol' man beat me arm wrestlin'!"

"Shorty, I promise you right now, if anyone asks how my father beat you in a contest of arm wrestling, I will set the record straight. Now could we get back to date night at the junkyard? This subject fascinates me."

"Oh yeah, sure. See, ya' get t'pop the trunks on the cars, that's where the real treasure is..." The creak of a door interrupted my education of Graisseville's newest dating fad.

"Shorty, honey, I hate to interrupt ya'll, but we need to get on the road. I'm all packed and ready to go. Ev, why don't you finish up, while Shorty and I load my bags?"

The tone of Annabelle's voice told me she had something on her mind other than loading the truck.

My bags stacked by the door, resembling a miniature log-jam. Without the water of course. Had I given the lovebirds enough privacy?

"Ev, are you ready?" Annabelle's voice through the door answered my question.

"I'm all packed—here, let me bring out a load."

The three of us loaded the truck in record time and I climbed into the back seat with Agatha Christie's *The Pale Horse* tucked into my bag. My plan was to tune out all comparisons of food the front seat threw into the conversations.

"Ev, I wanted to let you know that Shorty and I had a talk, and we're going to cut down on the cutesy nicknames. He chose Honeybun for me, and I picked Sweetie for him. We're going to tone down the sweetness, especially in front of our friends. Also, Shorty explained to me how your bickering actually relieves tension and stimulates your cognitive reasoning skills." Huh? Shorty said that?

"I sure had a lot of fun this weekend joining in on the fun. And surprisingly, almost being killed was the highlight of it all. In my opinion, anyway. All that to say, I'm not sure I'll join in on every case—I don't have the flexible work schedule, or lack of work schedule that you both have. And I know I named Nancy Drew as my childhood hero. But I've been looking at deerstalker style caps, and I think I'd look really good in one."

Shorty put in his two cents. "What's that, Honeybun? Ya' never told me ya' like t'hunt. Deer season's still goin' on, I could take ya' out next weekend. Whatcha think about that?"

The traditional pat to Shorty's leg—maybe I could live with that. "Sweetie, remember those pictures I showed you of the detective Sherlock Holmes? A deerstalker cap is the style of cap he wore."

My PI nodded. "Oh, yeah, yeah, I 'member that. Yeah, that'd look real cute on ya."

Annabelle turned back towards me. "I will tell you one thing though—I'm going to start reading more mysteries, especially the murdering kinds. Dead bodies are a lot of fun!"

One good thing about the weekend, other than solving two homicides, was that I'd created a kindred spirit. It sounded like Annabelle enjoyed dead bodies as much as Shorty and me.

"All right, ladies, let's get this show on the road. Some o' us got plans at the junkyard."

My two comrades in crime began an animated conversation about how much money to bring and what snacks to include. Yes, these two were truly perfect for each other, despite their differences on the outside. As the conversation turned to wedding plans, I slid out my book. Despite reading it at least five times before, Agatha always trumped romance.

LAGNIAPPE CHAPTER

H ere in Louisiana, a lagniappe is a little something extra, a bonus. An additional donut at the donut shop, an extra play for a season ticket holder, a little something special tucked into your order at the boutique. My lagniappe to you, my dear reader, is this short story about one of my characters. It has nothing to do with the story you just read. Instead, it gives more insight into the character.

Shorty

Yeah, I got kicked outta the Scouts, but it ain't no big deal. Heck, I was only eight, an' it wasn't even my fault. Now, it sounds bad, settin' fire tuh my leader's tent. But it was an accident, an' that's the honest truth! My leader, Mr. Guilbeau, he was real nice about it, told me no hard feelin's or nothin'. "Son," he said, "not everyone's cut out for this sorta thing. An' that's okay."

He even let me keep my pocket knife, an' I still got it. Yeah, that was real nice o' Mr. Guilbeau an' all, 'specially since his hair caught on fire, cuz he was sleepin' in the tent an' all. But it jus' caught fire a little, so he wasn't real mad. Lemme start at the beginnin' though, an' it'll all make sense. You'll see.

When my brothers turned seven, they started helpin' out Daddy on the farm. When it came my turn, well...he had his hands full.

"Madie, I've been prayin' tuh the good Lord for more patience, but I'm plumb tuckered out right now with that boy. Honey, I'm gonna hafta duct tape Shorty's hands tuh the pitchfork, else he's not gonna get those stalls cleaned out. Do ya got any ideas? I'm fresh out."

Mama signed me up for Cub Scouts, tellin' Daddy they'd teach me some good values an' life skills. It was a lot of fun too, 'specially our spring camp out, jus' after I turned eight.

Mr. Guilbeau said one parent had t'be on the camping trip, but Daddy was busy with the farm, an' Mama doesn't sleep anywhere that don't have a bed. Mr. Skeeter volunteered t'go with me. He only had daughters, Evangeline an' Madeline, an' he was real excited t'do some guy stuff. He even bought a tent an' a coupla sleepin' bags. Mama took some o' her egg money and got me a canteen. I think I still got that too.

We left on a Friday for Tickfaw State Park, singin' "When Johnny Comes Marchin' Home Again," "Camptown Races," an' all those other great kid songs durin' the entire trip. When we got tuh Tickfaw, we pitched our tents an' roasted marshmallows. Mr. Guilbeau gave everybody in my den a genuine scout pocketknife! It was a Buck BSA 722 Spitfire, with a 3 ¼ inch blade that locked in place. It even had a clip, so we could put 'em on our belts. All o' us boys, we were sittin' in tall cotton. Yep, I still got that ol' Spitfire. I hear nowadays scouts don't get a knife until they're ten, an' then they gotta take some sorta class or somethin'. I tell ya, that's jus' too bad

.

Anyways, the men all got t'talkin'—there weren't no women, I guess they all felt like my mama. An' us boys scattered t'look for wood so we could whittle with our new knives. My buddy, Lee Guilbeau, an' I got our sticks and took t'whittlin'. We started discussin' our sticks, an' wondered if we could start a fire by rubbin' 'em together.

In case yer wonderin', two eight year old boys can't start a fire with jus' two sticks. But Lee said his daddy brought some matches, since he was the leader an' all, so Lee snuck in the tent an' got 'em. We tried an' tried, but we couldn't get our sticks t'set fire. 'Fore we knew it, Mr. Guilbeau yelled that it was bedtime, so I crawled in my sleepin' bag next tuh Mr. Skeeter an' I was out like a light.

Suddenly, I hear Mr. Guilbeau an' Lee yellin' 'Our tent's on fire! Our tent's on fire!' Mr. Skeeter an' me, an' all the other scouts an' their daddies crawled outta our tents an' headed over tuh the Guilbeau's tent. It was pretty easy t'spot, since it was the only one covered in flames an' all.

Mr. Guilbeau was smackin' his head, an' Lee kept sayin', "Over there, Daddy! No, closer tuh yore ear, Daddy!" An' Mr. Guilbeau jus' kept smackin' his head an' hoppin' around. Some o' the men grabbed a couple buckets an' got some water outta the faucets in our camp so they could put out the fire. Oh, an' somebody must've gone t'get the park ranger, or else he heard all the yellin' an' saw the fire. But he showed up t'help. Finally, all the fires were out, but I think Mr. Guilbeau mighta had a concussion, or somethin'. He never seemed the same after that night.

Anyway, Lee an' I told the truth, that we'd been tryin' t'start a fire, but we didn't mean t'set the tent a blazin'. The men guessed that we must've started a fire anyway, an' didn't realize it. It spread tuh the tent, an' from there it moved pretty fast. The ranger said we were all pretty lucky no one got really hurt. Mr. Guilbeau couldn't get too mad, cuz his son helped start the fire, so he jus' told us all t'go back tuh bed, an' he an' his boy slept in their truck.

The rest o' the camp out was great—we went fishin' an' hikin', an' I even saw some coyote tracks. We left Sunday mornin' tired but with a lotta good memories. Mr. Skeeter said, except for Mr. Guilbeau catchin' on fire an' almost dyin', that was the most fun he'd had in a good long while.

Monday night Mr. Guilbeau came tuh the house t'see my mama an' daddy. "Now, Mack, Madie, I'm not angry or anything. Shorty's a good boy, and I think you're raising him to be a fine young man. But our kids did set a fire, and Lee's serving out his punishment right now. However, the other parents think it'd be best if our kids weren't in the same scout pack."

Mr. Guilbeau scratched his head, which probably itched somethin' awful, what with mosta his hair missin'. "Lee and I are willing to move to another pack, but none of the parents want to step up and lead our boys. I'm afraid Shorty's got to be the one to go." He leaned down and looked me in the eye. "Son, not everyone's cut out for this sort of thing. Camping and such. And that's okay." He patted me on the head as he sat back up. Then he stared at my parents. "No hard feelings, okay? Mack, you're always welcome at the dominos game on

Tuesdays. And, Madie, my wife still hopes you'll come to her Bible study every Thursday morning."

He stood up to leave, and my father followed him to the door. Then Mr. Guilbeau turned. "Oh, and Shorty? Please keep that knife, okay? Son, I know someday you're going to do great things. And I'll keep praying for you. Ya'll take care now."

Daddy came back after walkin' Mr. Gilbeau out, an' I was sure I was gonna get a whippin'. But he jus' sat down an' stared at me. "Well, son, I reckon if ya can start a fire, an' burn down a tent, not t'mention mosta Mr. Guilbeau's hair, then you can do some chores aroun' the farm. I guess I didn't try hard enough t'find somethin' for ya t'do. Tomorrow after school, let's you an' me walk aroun' the farm, an' find some chores for ya'. Okay?"

Guess who showed up at my swearin'-in ceremony when I joined the Army? Other than my mama an' daddy, brothers an' sisters, an' the Bergerons? Mr. Guilbeau was there, right in the front. He asked Mama t'take a picture, jus' the two of us. "Shorty," he said, "I'm going to hang this picture on my refrigerator, right in front. Want to know why? Because I want a daily reminder of First Corinthians 2:9. 'No eye has seen, no ear heard, no mind conceived what God has prepared for those who love him.'"

JOIN MY TRIBE!

I'm looking for readers to join my twisty Southern mystery tribe! Would you like to apply and potentially receive free copies of my eBooks in exchange for an honest review? Scan the QR code below and submit your application, or click here and note you want to become a Twisty Tribe member.

Scan me

Ev's Fifth Adventure

"Hey, Doc! Did ya' file the Augie Fontenot case like I told ya' to?" Shorty's voice echoed against the walls of our new office.

"Yes, Shorty I did. And for the hundredth time, we really should go paperless. We'd save a lot of money on file cabinets and pens and, well, paper."

My supervisor wadded up an 8 ½ x 11 inch, white as snow piece of printer paper and dunked it into our twelve dollar wire trash basket. "Now, Doc, we've gone over this already. I've got pine timber on my land, an' so do a bunch uh other people in this community. With all these newspapers an' magazines goin' outta business, the price uh timber's in the toilet. We've gotta do our part, an' use as much paper as we can. The economy's countin' on us." He crumpled another perfectly good piece of paper, squinting as he aimed for a second shot. But all I saw were dollar signs hitting the rim.

We'd been in our space exactly three weeks, and I'd spent a quarter of that time regretting my decision. Which had been my worst idea? Was it passing my private investigator's test? No, that was a good one—and a free one too. Dad had lent me his credit card and I'd signed up for my courses, blowing through them and passing my exam with a ninety-seven. Actually, that had been my first poor decision, scoring higher than Shorty. My grade had sucker punched his eighty-two percent, leaving him gasping.

The second not so brilliant decision had to be apprenticing under Shorty. In Louisiana, an investigator must complete the forty hours of training courses, pass the exam, and work for a private investigation agency as an apprentice for two years. Shorty had worked for Howie Robichaud out of Baton Rouge, with little supervision. Everyone insisted I apprentice with Shorty. After all, we worked well together, so he'd continue to solve cases with me side by side. In the beginning it made sense, until his bruised ego took over my training.

"Doc, yer two minutes late! Did ya' stop by the coffee shop an' chat it up with Maggie? We don't got time for sharin' recipes or catchin' up on all the soap operas. This is a business, an' ya' gotta act as such."

"Hey, I asked ya' t'call the sheriff an' see if he's got any cases for us. Have ya' done that yet? We don't got time for ya' t'file yore nails or order off the inner net. This is a business, an' ya' gotta act as such."

If I heard the words *as such* one more time, blank pieces of paper wouldn't be the only items flying towards the trash can.

"Did ya' start the Bubba Reeves file? I told ya' t'do that yesterday. Did ya' do it? We don't got time for sailin' on the inner net or textin' yore friends. This is a business, an' ya' gotta act as such." More echoes, reminding me that we still needed furniture. "That's surfing the internet, not sailing. And yes, I did. Oh, before I forget...how much do you weigh?"

□*Pop!* Or was it a *piff?* I'd calculated our cost of paper at one cent per sheet, which meant three cents rested at the bottom of Shorty's trash can. "What uh I weigh? Oh, about one eighty-five. Annabelle's too good uh cook, or I'd weigh one seventy-seven. Why do ya' ask?"

□"Oh, no reason." No, I couldn't lift a hundred and eighty-five pounds, much less heave it into the trash can. I'd have to find another way to channel my irritation.

□*Zip!* Shorty had thrown four cents worth of paper into our trash can, and it was only eight-thirty. We needed a distraction, preferably the felonious kind. And hopefully one not involving either my supervisor or myself.

□"Say, Doc, did ya' hear about the sheriff's Wheel uh Fugitives show on You Toot?"

□Hello randomness—it was about time you entered the conversation. "Uh, I think you mean YouTube. And, well, I guess not. But then, Mitch and I try to keep our careers out of our conversations. We focus mainly on sharing recipes, catching up on all the soap operas, and ordering stuff off the internet."

□Shorty squinted one eye in my direction, gauging whether I'd doled out sarcasm or secrets about the sheriff. His other eye set up the next shot. "Uh, well, it ain't none uh my business what ya'll do in yore free time."

□Since when? "Tell me about this Wheel of Fugitives. I'm intrigued." Was *intrigued* the right word? Maybe *ready to change the subject* was the better choice.

□"I can't believe yore boyfriend never told ya'! It jus' started last week, an' they already caught one. There's a sheriff down in Florida that started it, an' ol' Mitch called him up t'get the details. He got permission t'do the same thing here, an' it's a big success!"

◻Our first week in the office I'd perched my feet on top of my desk, then crossed my ankles and leaned back. I popped up pretty fast when the back of my chair continued its journey towards the floor. From then on, I tipped my chair back just an inch or two and planted the soles of my feet firmly on our blue gray rug. It was an almost new, professional looking rug, courtesy of Shorty's sister, Dottie.

◻I was in that position during our wheel discussion. "Start from the beginning, please. Assume I know nothing, which will be extremely helpful. Because I don't."

◻My supervisor, on the other hand, had perfected the feet perching and ankle crossing combo, and demonstrated his trick as often as he could. "Okay, so there's a spinnin' wheel, kinda like a roulette wheel only it's mounted on a pole or somethin'. My buddy Monty films the sheriff, who starts out by tellin' the audience there's a jail cell waitin' for everybody on that wheel. Then he gives it a good spin, and waits for it t'land on a picture. That guy's the fugitive uh the week, an' the sheriff tells 'im he'd better jus' go ahead an' do the right thing. Cuz if he don't turn himself in, somebody watchin' the show's gonna tip off the deputies. An' the fugitive unit's gonna come kick down their door an' haul 'im away tuh jail."

◻I grabbed my phone and texted Mitch. *Why have you never told me about this wonderful Wheel of Fugitives? And can I spin the wheel next time?*

◻"Hey, Doc, iffen yer textin' the sheriff, ask 'im if I can spin the wheel next time. I already asked Monty, but he said I gotta get permission from Sheriff Dupre."

◻I could see my big city friends scrolling through Facebook, coming upon my tag in the East Baton Rouge Parish sheriff's department post. Their curious fingers would click the link, and there I would be, spinning the wondrous Wheel of Fugitives. Then they'd finally understand. They'd realize that small towns have just as much fun going on as those bustling mega cities. Hmmm, or maybe they'd laugh so hard they'd choke on their fancy coffee drinks. Then they'd thank their lucky stars they didn't live in Hicksville. No, best to stay off YouTube.

◻"No problem, Shorty. I'll ask the sheriff for you." My eleven-year-old nephew Jack had taught me how to edit my text messages. I changed my message to read *Why have you never told me about this wonderful Wheel of Fugitives? And can Shorty spin the wheel next time?*

◻"Anyway, Doc, it comes out every Friday, an' they caught the guy from the first show last week. Today they're filmin' aroun' two o'clock. Iffen we finish up early, how about we head over an' watch the show? Hey, does my shirt look alright? Do I need a haircut?" I edited my message again. *And can Shorty PLEASE spin the wheel on today's show?*

◻"The next item we gotta discuss at our staff meetin' is gettin' a secretary. We need someone tuh answer the phones, do the filin', an' make the coffee. I talked tuh my cousin at the paper, an' Hugh says we can get an ad for fifty dollars a week."

◻"Gosh, Shorty, I don't know what to say first. How about...is your cousin crazy? Fifty dollars for an ad? And next, I think I'll say...if we hire a secretary to do all those things, then what am I going to do? Because you've already ruled out catching up on soap operas, filing my nails, and ordering off the internet."

Shorty was like a dog with a bone, and his bone was hiring a warm body. "Doc, we ain't no shoddy outfit! We're experienced investigators. Well, I am anyway. You're still *prent-issin*. This is a business, an' ya' gotta act as such."

"Maybe I should just record you for a couple hours. Then, instead of repeating yourself, you could refer me to the specific words of wisdom you've already spouted. For instance, you wouldn't have to waste your breath telling me for the thousandth time that this is a business, and I've got to act as such. You could just say *first words of wisdom*. Or *first rule of the PI business*. Or something like that. You would save us both a lot of time."

Fortunately for me, the phone rang. But why had Shorty insisted on a land line for the office, tying us to the same four walls all day? Why couldn't we have a separate cell phone number for our company? "Doc, only drug dealers an' spies carry aroun' a buncha cell phones. An' we ain't either. Respectable businesses like Cormier Investigations *Elle Elle See* have a land line. End uh the discussion."

Being the *prent-iss*, I answered the phone. "Cormier Investigations LLC. How may I direct your call?" Don't get me started on the fact that Shorty made me say *LLC* and ask how to direct the call. Where else could I direct it, but to Shorty's extension? A *prent-iss* wasn't experienced enough to talk to a client, at least not at Cormier Investigations LLC.

"Evangeline, this is your daddy speaking. I need you to call your boyfriend and ask him if I can spin the wheel today. Do it now, child, before someone gets ahead of me."

How did everyone know about Mitch's new show except me? I glanced at my cell phone, which told me that Mitch had read my text. Should I edit it for the third time, and ask if my father could spin the wheel? No, too late—Mitch was texting back.

◻*I already promised my mother she could spin the wheel. But Shorty can do it next week. Or should I ask your father to do it? I can always use brownie points.* He added a couple of winking emojis.

◻"Who's tyin' up our business phone? That better not be Elizabeth, tryin' t'stir up lunch plans. This is a business..." I tuned out my supervisor, focusing instead on my father.

◻"Dad, Mitch's mom, Daphne, is spinning the wheel today. But you can spin it next week." I covered the mouthpiece. "Shorty, Mitch texted that you can spin the wheel after my father. And he's going to put up the meanest, nastiest fugitives on the wheel, just for you." Mitch wasn't the only one needing brownie points.

◻I paused to hear my father's response. "Well, that's fine, I guess, putting his mama over his girlfriend's daddy. I know I wouldn't do that, but to each his own." My cell phone read 8:45 a.m. Would this Friday never end?

◻"Okay, Dad, we've got that all settled. I can't tie up the business line, so I'll let you go. Love you."

◻"Wait! Tell Shorty that Amy Meloncon's cousin's daughter's looking for a job. She took typing in high school, and she's taking some of those over the line classes. Business classes I think."

◻"Dad, they're called online classes. Is this for the secretary position? How much does she want to be paid?"

◻Bang! Shorty's feet hit the rug and he leaped from his chair. "Gimme that phone. Skeeter! Don't ya' be tyin' up this business line chit-chattin' with yore daughter. This here's a business..."

I glanced at the quarter inch stack of files on my desk. What was less taxing on my soul: filing two files or listening to Shorty argue with my father? My cell phone rang, saving me from both tasks.

"Ev, did you hear? There's been a murder at the community theater, and Jen Guidry's been arrested!"

My right arm transformed into a wild pendulum, swinging back and forth across my body. Unfortunately, Shorty and I hadn't worked on our hand signals—he'd been too busy teaching me how to file.

"Elizabeth, that can't be true! The entire Guidry family goes to our church. Jen volunteers in the nursery, and she's in our Bible study. I'd peg my Aunt Ruby as a murderer before Jen."

Shorty stopped mid-sentence at the word *murderer*. Who says men aren't good listeners?

"Skeeter, I gotta get off the phone. Tell this Tracy lady t'send over her resume." He twisted round to face my desk, punching his index finger towards the floor. I recognized the international sign for *put the call on speaker*.

"El, I'm putting you on speaker, so Shorty can hear too. Start from the beginning."

My sweet bestie had never been on this side of a murder case. She'd come in alongside me, interviewing suspects and talking to witnesses. But this was a whole new adventure.

"I talked with Jen's mother-in-law, Ava this morning and she gave me the story. Last night was the dress rehearsal for the play. Everybody left the building right after rehearsal, except Daniel Sullivan. He's the lead, or was the lead. Someone must have come into the building after everyone else left and killed him! But not Jen—there's no way she did this."

□Elizabeth stopped to catch her breath. "Anyway, this morning, a deputy drove by and noticed the back door was ajar. He came inside to investigate, and he found Jen hunched over Daniel's body. Oh, Ev, this is terrible!" Elizabeth's voice caught as she stuffed the sobs back into her throat.

□My poor bestie! "It's okay, El, take a breath. But why is Jen a suspect? It sounds like she was just trying to help the victim."

□A rattling breath and my bestie regained her composure. "She's the stage manager, you see, and it's her very first time. She wanted to make sure everything was ready for tonight's show. Jen has been trying so hard to get everything right, and she wanted everything to be perfect."

□"Elizabeth, this here's Shorty Cormier. Why was Miss Jen at the theater? Thank ya."

□I bit my lower lip and made a mental note to explain once again how the speaker option worked.

□"Oh, hi, Shorty. Uh, well, Ava said Jen came to the theater early this morning, to make sure everything was ready. She went in the back door and was straightening up the props backstage. Then she stepped on to the stage to double check everything, and spotted the body. She kneeled on the floor to examine Daniel more closely and see if he was still alive. That's when the deputy walked in. He didn't believe her story, because she was all flustered and out of sorts. Who wouldn't be? I'd be hysterical if I'd found a dead body!"

□More jagged breaths. "This so-called deputy put Jen in handcuffs–handcuffs, Ev! He threw her in the back of the squad car and took her down for questioning. Poor Jen was so upset that she couldn't remember all the details. The deputy said that's how guilty people act. Can you believe that? The district attorney's convinced she's guilty, and he's going to charge her. Oh, Ev, this is terrible! Her husband Mike's just shattered-Ava picked up their boys from school, before anyone could tell them that their mother's in jail. Oh, this is awful!"

◻"Elizabeth, this here's Shorty Cormier. Is Mike gonna close up Big Ed's while his wife's in jail?"

◻I glared at my supervisor. "You've got to be kidding me! What does that have to do with poor Mike and Jen?"

◻Shorty's shoulders lifted a couple of inches. "I need some hog feed, an' Mike's got the best prices in twenty miles. If he shuts down Big Ed's, I'm gonna hafta drive a good long ways to get some."

◻Elizabeth had the scoop on everything. "Don't worry, Shorty-Mike's got Amy and Jimmy Meloncon keeping the doors open. And I think Ken's going to step in too. The whole Melancon family's going to manage the store until this mess gets straightened out. But ya'll have got to get down to the jail and start clearing Jen's name. That's why I'm calling. Ava wants you two on the case. She said there's some sort of fund to pay legal costs for founding family members. I asked Cal about it-turns out he's in charge of it, since he works at the bank. He's working on a lawyer for Jen, and he said your expenses are covered. My son said to spare no expense, and clear the poor girl's name!"

◻ "We're on our way, Elizabeth. Uh, unless we need to stop at Big Ed's and pick up some hog feed. Then we'll be on our way. Love you, friend-I'll keep you posted."

◻

***

◻Shorty didn't mention hog feed during our trip to the East Baton Rouge Parish detention center. He resurrected the secretary discussion. Honestly, I'd rather talk about hog feed.

◻"See, Doc? If we'd gone ahead and hired that secretary like I said, we wouldn't be in this situation."

◻I closed my eyes as I contemplated our situation. "Uh, I'm not following. We need to pay someone to sit at the office and file the two files on my desk? Oh, and make a new file, I guess. One that says Guidry, Jennifer. But other than those two tasks, I still don't see the need for a secretary."

◻"Ya' gotta spend money t'make money. An' we're not some shoddy outfit, we're a professional business. We need a friendly face t'greet our visitors an' serve 'em a cup uh coffee."

◻"Okay, I'm going to skip the part where we debate my friendly face and the quality of my coffee. And I'm going to jump past the old discussion about paying someone to do the job I'm already doing. Let's flash forward to the end of our conversation, just to keep things fast paced and interesting. I'll throw a crazy idea out here, just bear with me. How about we hire an intern instead? A college student getting a degree in criminal justice, or psychology, or something similar. Someone you can mentor and influence and guide." I finished the conversation in my head by adding *someone who costs a lot less than a secretary but can still file and make coffee.* I also pondered what I would do if the intern did my job. Maybe I could supervise the intern, and Shorty could supervise me. Our infrastructure was starting to look like a mid-level corporation, minus the profits.

◻If I didn't know Shorty so well, I'd think he was ignoring me. But there it was, the almost hidden crease along his forehead. The man was mulling over my idea, allowing it to simmer like a pot of gumbo on low heat. At last, the gumbo was ready.

□"Now ya' might be on t'something there, Doc. Yeah, a young mind I could take under my wing, guide and direct, even teach. Yeah, that's a good idea." Shorty sunk his shoulders into his seat and dropped his left hand to his knee. My supervisor had embraced my idea, which was good. But it sounded like he would supervise the intern, which left me with time to fill each day. Maybe I could take up knitting? Hmmm, the knitting PI. Maybe the intern could create a logo, with a cute ball of yarn...

□"Yeah, Doc, that's a real good idea. I mean, I thought I was gonna do that with you. But yore problem's that yer too hard-headed. Yeah, yer too stuck in yore ways." There it was, the other shoe had dropped.

□"Yeah, I was jus' tellin' yore daddy the other day that I've taught ya' all I can. Yer jus' too stubborn t'listen tuh my wisdom an' experience. But someone who's young an' eager, someone who's ready t'lap up all the advice an' experience I've got. Yeah, that's the kinda person we need aroun' the office!"

□The average person didn't rejoice at the parish detention center on the horizon. Then again, the average person didn't spend every blessed day with Shorty Cormier.

***

□

□Jen Guidry sat across the metal table, her fingers resting on its scarred top. Her shoulder length brown hair normally resided in a ponytail, but rubber bands weren't allowed in the slammer. Neither was makeup, but she didn't wear much, anyway. Dark circles sat under her eyes, the despair spilling out of her soul. How could anyone believe this early thirty-something mother of two and nursery volunteer would kill anyone? Of course, true crime shows told us these kinds of people killed all the time.

□I didn't know Jen well, but she'd always given off a bubbly vibe. She over shared and overstepped, but in the nicest way. I'd heard a story that she'd talked to someone at a party for fifteen minutes before the hostess intervened. Jen's fellow conversationalist didn't speak English, the hostess explained, and she had no idea what Jen was saying. This young lady wasn't the most observant person in the room, but she didn't strike me as a killer.

□"Ev, Shorty, thank you for coming. I was praying earlier, and I asked God to put you on this case. I just know you'll bring me home ." Jen's brown eyes flooded with tears and her shoulders shook. I couldn't keep my tears locked up either, and we cried together. Shorty paced the room.

□"Ladies, I hate to break up this sob fest, but we ain't doin' anyone any good. Miss Jen, I'm real sorry yer in this situation, I truly am." He looked toward the guard. "Could ya' do us a favor, an' get these ladies some tissues? Unless ya' wanna clean up a buncha tears an' other stuff, I think ya' better get us a big ol' box."

□The guard made a motion to the window and Shorty joined us at the table. "Miss Jen, take us through this mornin'."

A Little About Me

I'm a faith-based cozy mystery writer entertaining readers who enjoy twisty Southern mysteries with a touch of romance and a dose of humor.

My books offer mysteries in Louisiana with curious clues and characters who exasperate as much as they endear.

My quirky yet charming residents are just like family—sometimes you want to hug them, and sometimes you want to disown them. You'll immerse yourself in small town culture as you exercise your sleuthing skills and your funny bone. I promise!□

I live in the small town of Grand Cane, Louisiana. Less than three hundred other people also live in Grand Cane, and many of my chapters came from my weekly visits to the downtown coffee shop.

My husband, John and I enjoy Sundays at Grand Cane Baptist Church, dinner with family and friends, and watching the lightning bugs in our backyard. Our kids come to visit, when they aren't too busy living their big-city lives. Visit me a t jannfranklin.com

Want more of me? You can enjoy stories of my goofy dogs, my lovely kids, and my small town life in a couple of ways:

1-Sign up for my twice a month newsletter at jannfranklin .com— you'll be the first to hear about my upcoming books, contests, and any other fun things going on in my life.

2-Follow me on social media! I'm Jann Franklin Author on Facebook and @jannfranklinauthor on Instagram

www.ingramcontent.com/pod-product-compliance
Lightning Source LLC
Chambersburg PA
CBHW050740230626
47052CB00004BA/719